Fiction
Hewett, Lorri.
Coming of age

"_____, bitch!"

"And what good would that do?" I exclaimed.

She laughed harshly. "Mess you up real bad!"

She began circling me, fists clenched. I kept my eyes on her, careful to stay out of her range, careful not to make any sudden movements that would send her flying over to knock the sense out of me. My mind raced as I attempted to think of a way to get out of this fight. I attempted diplomacy. "I know you came out here for a fight, but you won't be getting one out of me."

"No, cuz I'm gonna kill you!" Erika took a swing at me but I jumped out of her way, keeping my eyes on her. Again, she circled me and I danced in and out of her path.

Finally, she stopped and laughed. "What kinda chickenshit are you?"

# Coming Of Age

## LORRI HEWETT

An Original Holloway House Edition

**HOLLOWAY HOUSE PUBLISHING COMPANY**
**LOS ANGELES, CA**

Published by
HOLLOWAY HOUSE PUBLISHING COMPANY
8060 Melrose Avenue, Los Angeles, California 90046

This is a work of fiction. Names, characters, places, and incidents
are either the product of the author's imagination or are used fic-
titiously. Any resemblance to actual events or locales or persons,
living or dead, is entirely coincidental.

International Standard Book Number 0-87067-928-7
Printed in the United States of America

Cover photograph by Jeffrey.
Cover design by Greg Salman.
Cover posed by professional model Gabrielle Haughton.

*Dedicated to*
*Lyda Acker,*
*as I always said*
*it would be.*

# PART I

# AJ

I come to school this morning feeling like shit cuz I'm a little hung over and my girlfriend Erika starts yelling at me and clawing me with them blood-red nails of hers cuz I didn't come see her last night. I should have just told her the truth, that I didn't wanna see her cuz she's been getting on my nerves, but that would've made her even madder and man, could she get mad! So I just told her I had stuff to do to keep her mouth shut. I didn't tell her me and the fellas went to watch our basketball team lose to Glendale, then went over to Jamil's to drink Mad Dog 20-20 till Doug got sick and puked all over Jamil's floor. I stayed at Jamil's to help him clean it up, but I'm gonna kick Doug's ass after school today!

Besides that and my hangover, I was in a pissed off mood this morning and didn't want to be putting up with Erika's shit. Erika's got a temper but you wouldn't know it by looking at her. She's really little and mixed, with light skin, long hair, and blue eyes. I like light-skinned girls. But other than her looks I don't know why I put up with her. She can be a real bitch.

"Hey, are you going to help me with this?"

I looked up, suddenly remembering I was in second hour chemistry class. I turned to look at my lab partner, this studious chick named Ruthie something or other.

"Daydreaming?" She didn't really sound mad, even though she'd done most of the lab *we* was supposed to be doing by herself. "Yeah," I said and tried to keep my mind on chemistry. But shoot, why should I? One more semester and I'll be graduating. And I got five schools waiting for me to sign whenever I get around to making up my mind; Florida State, Colorado, Michigan, Southern Cal, and Auburn. I've played varsity football since sophomore year; I'm a cornerback and kickoff returner. I was even named defensive MVP by the Colorado High School Sports Association. I made first team All-State for the second year in a row and this year I was named a second team All-America. All those schools was treating me like a king, telling me what they'll buy me and what they'll do for me if I come to their school. It's kinda fun. And after I sign with whoever I sign with, my grades won't mean a thing. So I'm blowing off this semester. I'm lucky I got Ruthie for a science partner so she can do all the work. "There you go again!" she said to me.

I shook my head. "Sorry. It's kinda hard for me to concentrate, y'know?"

She looked me in the eye for a second, something I hate people to do. "No, I don't know."

I rolled my eyes. She's okay, but man, she's so proper! She talks proper, dresses like some businesswoman or something. I don't know her that well. I never see her at parties so I guess she don't drink. She hangs out with all the smart white kids, the ones that go to Harvard and all that.

10

"What you want me to do?"

"Pour the TTE over the carbon sample."

I really didn't know what she was talking about so I picked up a container of purple stuff and poured it in a test tube. She was busy writing down stuff. I figured this was pretty stupid. Nothing was happening. So I put the stuff on a bunsen burner to see what would happen. After a while I started to smell something burning.

Now Ruthie looked up and her eyes widened when she saw what I did. "What are you doing? You're not supposed to heat that!"

I shrugged. The stuff was sizzling and popping. "Why not?"

"AJ!" She leaned over to take the stuff off the burner. Then I heard this loud popping noise and saw all this black smoke. Then Ruthie flew backward, her hands covering her face.

"Hey Ruthie!" I said. She wasn't saying nothing. Now Mrs. Fleener came running. So'd half the class.

"You okay Ruthie?" I asked, but I knew she wasn't. She was shaking pretty badly.

"What's happened here?" screamed Mrs. Fleener, coughing from the smoke. Somebody came running with a fire extinguisher and it seemed like everyone in the room was going crazy. "Who told you to heat the solution, it's explosive!"

I felt stupid. How the hell was I supposed to know the crap would explode? I turned back to Ruthie, who was still covering her face and shaking. "What is it? What's wrong?" I tried to move one of her hands but she wouldn't let me.

"It's her eye! Take her to the clinic! Hurry!" said Mrs. Fleener.

I helped Ruthie stand up. "C'mon, let's go!" She stood up, still shaking. "We going to the clinic," I told her. My

11

voice sounded funny. I sounded scared. Well, she wasn't screaming or nothing but what if she was really hurt bad? I got her down to the clinic as fast as I could, leading her inside and sitting her down on one of the beds. I looked for a nurse but I didn't see one so I went to the office next door to get a secretary.

"This girl was in an accident!" I said to the first secretary I saw, a big black woman who looked more like a wrestler than a secretary.

The lady looked bored. "Who is it?"

"Ruthie somebody. She a senior. We was in chemistry and—"

"Ruthie Bates!" Now the secretary jumped up and went running to the clinic. I guess all the administration people like Ruthie. She looks like the teacher's pet type.

Ruthie was still holding her eye, not saying nothing. She still looked like she was in pain.

"What happened?" yelled the secretary.

"Something exploded in her face," I said.

The secretary scooped her up in her big arms and carried her to the sink. "Now move your hands!" she ordered. "Come help me, boy!"

I ran over to the sink and grabbed Ruthie's hands. She resisted but I managed to pull her hands away.

"Ow, it hurts—" she cried. The secretary turned on the water and rinsed her eyes. Then the principal came running in, this big guy named Mr. Ferris. "What's the matter!" he yelled in that loud voice of his.

"Ruthie Bates was in a chemistry accident," the secretary mumbled.

He turned to glare at me like he knew it was my fault. He don't like me too much. We had a lot of run-ins when I was an underclassman. "Where's the nurse?" he yelled. "No nurse scheduled now," said the secretary.

Mr. Ferris started mumbling under his breath about shortages and budgets and stuff. Then he glared at me again. "What happened?"

"I accidentally put something on a burner and it blew up," I muttered.

"You should have been more careful! Don't you know how dangerous that stuff can be?"

I rolled my eyes. I wasn't in no mood for a lecture.

"You better hope she's not seriously hurt!" he said with frown lines all over his face. "Lord, lord you kids—"

I wanted to tell him to shut his black ass up but I didn't cuz he'd throw me out in a minute.

He turned to look at the poor girl, who was still under the sink. "That's one of our top students there, you know that? That girl right there is America's future, Black America's future! You wanna know why? Because she's smart! She's gonna make it no matter how high she can jump or how fast she can run!"

I just looked at him. "So what you trying to say?"

"I'm trying to say that you could learn a lot from that girl right there!" said Mr. Ferris, staring me up and down. "I don't care how well you play ball!"

I rolled my eyes again. He went into that pity-the-poor-black-man shit every opportunity he got and tried to feed it to anyone who'd listen. Well, I wasn't gonna listen to it!

The secretary got done rinsing the girl's eye and gave her a piece of cloth to put over it. Then she led Ruthie to one of the beds and Ruthie lay down. Mr. Ferris went to her side, looking all concerned. "Are you going to be okay, Ruthie?" he asked, sounding like a different person than when he was preaching to me. "Yeah, I'll be fine." She sounded like a weak kitten.

"Make sure your parents take you to the doctor when you get home," he said all gently. "I'll excuse you to go home now. AJ will take you home."

I rolled my eyes. "Yeah, I'll take you home."

"Be careful next time!" Mr. Ferris yelled at me as he and the secretary left.

"Shut up," I mumbled. Then I turned to look at Ruthie, who was holding the cloth over her eye. I didn't know what to say to her. The room was dead quiet, making me even more uncomfortable.

I cleared my throat. "Uh, sorry—"

"It's okay," she said softly. "Just watch it next time."

"Yeah...you not gonna go blind or nothin, are you?"

She grinned, still looking like she was in pain. "I hope not."

I sat down next to her. "I don't know how I'm gettin you home. I don't got a car—"

"You can drive mine, that is, if you have a license—"

I rolled my eyes. "Yeah, I got a license! C'mon!"

"I need my purse—"

"Oh yeah. Wait here, I'll get it." I left the clinic and ran to the chemistry room to get her purse and stuff.

Well, everything looked like it'd went back to normal. Kids was putting their stuff away and getting ready for the bell to ring. But everyone looked at me when I walked in.

"How is she?" Mrs. Fleener asked me.

"I'm taking her home," I mumbled, then went to get her stuff and get out of there before Mrs. Fleener could yell at me some more.

Ruthie had a plain white leather purse. I opened it and saw everything nice and neat inside. I wanted to open her wallet but I decided not to. My days as a thug was over. I found her keys on a bunch of cute keychains.

I went back to the clinic and saw Ruthie sitting up and waiting for me. I helped her stand up. "My car's in the student lot," she said, still holding the cloth over her eye.

14

"It's a blue Ford Escort. I take it you found my keys."

"Yeah—" I walked her outside and saw two of Erika's friends sitting on the lawn smoking. I hoped they didn't see me.

"Which car is it?" I asked again once we got to the parking lot.

"It's in the corner space."

I walked her over to a blue Ford Escort LX. 1990. It was nice. "Who got you this?"

"My parents—"

I opened the door for her, then got in the driver's seat. I moved the seat back and adjusted the mirror. The inside was nice, too. I'll bet the car drove real good, even if it was an automatic. But the stereo could've been better.

"Now where do you live?" I asked her.

"In Northridge. Take York Street north—"

"Yeah, I know where it's at." So she lived in one of them quiet neighborhoods with nice houses and friendly neighbors and stuff. Figures.

Northridge is where all the Buppies (you know, black urban professionals) and middle-class white people live. She directed me to her house and I helped her out of the car and up to the front door. "Is anybody home?"

She shook her head. "Can you open the door?"

I found her house key and let us both inside. The inside of her house was spotless, like one of them show homes. I led her to a living room and sat her down in a chair. I sat on a couch and looked around. "Your house is nice—"

"Thanks."

Then I remembered I had no way to get back to school. I looked at Ruthie. She didn't look like she'd be able to drive me back or nothing. I cleared my throat again. "Uh...how'm I gonna get back to school?"

"Oh yeah. What time is it?"

I looked at a large mantle clock. "Ten thirty."

"My mom usually comes home for lunch around eleven thirty. I'll have her take you back."

I nodded, feeling kinda stupid cuz I didn't have nothing to say. "Uh, sorry—"

"Hey, it's over. You must be feeling pretty stupid."

"Yeah—"

She laughed a little. "It's kind of funny. You're usually so conceited—"

I didn't say nothing.

"Because of football and all—"

"Hey, why you talk so proper?" I asked suddenly.

She grinned. "What's wrong with the way I speak?"

"Listen to you! You don't even sound black!"

"I used to live in Littleton. That's southwest of here. In the suburbs."

"Yeah, I know where it's at. We played one of them white schools. Kicked their ass, too!"

"This is only my second year at Centennial."

"Why'd you move?"

"My dad works downtown. He thought it'd be nice to live closer to his work. And . . . he thought I needed more black influence."

"You don't look too happy when you say that."

"There were only about six black kids at my old school."

I shook my head. "Man—" I don't think I could handle that!

"But I grew up like that," she said. "Then I came to Centennial and I don't fit in here at all."

"Why not?"

"I just can't . . . relate."

I didn't know what she was talking about so I changed the subject. "So what do your folks do?"

"My dad's an engineer and my mom's a secretary."

16

I shook my head and chuckled. "You must be pretty well off then!"

She shrugged. "I'm comfortable. So what's it like, being a big football star?"

I was caught off guard. "What's it like? I dunno—"

"I mean, everybody likes you, you get a lot of female attention—"

I laughed. "Oh yeah. It's all right."

"It seems pretty artificial, though—"

Artificial? She was going into that proper talk again. Man, if I was blind I woulda swore she was white! And it wasn't just the way she talked. It was the way she...acted.

I took a good look at her for the first time, really. She was about my skin tone, medium, with shoulder-length hair. I wondered if it was a weave. It was pulled up nice and conservatively. She was kinda pretty but in a...calm way. I don't think I could ever be attracted to her. She'd make me too uncomfortable. She was already making me feel stupid.

I heard a garage door opening and in walked this lady who looked just like her. I figured it was her mom. She looked surprised to see me and Ruthie sitting there and came running to us. "Ruthie! What are you doing home?" she said, sounding all worried.

"I was in an accident in chemistry," Ruthie said. "AJ brought me home."

"Are you all right? Why didn't you call me?"

"I'm fine, but I should probably go to the doctor later on. Mom, this is AJ Johnson, my chemistry partner."

Her mom grinned at me. "Hi AJ." She talked proper too, but not as proper as Ruthie.

I grinned back. "Hi—"

"Can you drive him back to school?" Ruthie asked. "He drove my car here."

"Sure," her mom said. "Let me go get my purse and we'll be ready to go."

I stood up. "I hope you feel better, Ruthie."

She grinned, still looking like she was in pain. "Thanks for driving me home."

"My car's in the garage, AJ," her mom said and I followed her to the garage to this real nice red Audi.

It was sorta weird riding back to school with someone I didn't know but her mom was nice. She talked the whole time about nothing, really. The weather and stuff like that. I could tell she wasn't as smart as Ruthie so I relaxed a little.

She let me out in front of the school. "Thanks for bringing Ruthie home."

"Yeah, thanks for the ride," I said, then walked toward the school. Lunch hour was just ending and I wondered if I should go to my fourth hour class. I really didn't feel like it but I didn't have nothing else to do. So I headed for my locker and on the way ran right smack into Erika.

# ERIKA

I just look at him for a second. He sighin and rollin his eyes and lookin like he don't wanna talk to me. Well, I got a few things to say to him! "Imani say she saw you leavin the school with your arm around some girl!"

He roll his eyes.

"No don't be rollin your eyes at me, I want an answer AJ! And why didn't you come see me last night like you said you would? Y'know, I don't appreciate sittin by a damn door waitin for you to show your ass up!"

"Can you shut that big mouth of yours for just one second!" AJ say.

So I cross my arms and look at him. And man, do he look fine! He about six foot, with a body like you wouldn't believe. But I can't think about that cuz I'm mad at him.

"I had to take Ruthie home cuz—"

"Ruthie! Who's Ruthie? I don't know no girl name Ruthie! Hey, you better not be cheatin on me again—"

"If you just shut up I'll tell you who she is!" he say all huffed up. "She in my chemistry class and somethin blew up in her face so Ferris made me take her home!"

"Yeah?" I say, but I'm not really believin him.

He smile and come up next to me. "I got conditionin and stuff after school, but I'll come over after that."

I smile back and put my arms around his neck. "You better, or I'll be comin after ya!"

He shake his head. "Man, I got me one vicious girl!"

I laugh. "You know it!" He kiss me, then I back away. "I gotta be meetin the girls. I'll be waitin for you tonight."

"Yeah," he say and walk away. Now I open my locker and fix up my face. I got a reputation to keep up so I gotta look good. I put on more lipstick and brush my hair. One good thing about being mixed is I don't gotta worry about that nappy hair other black folks got.

I look at the picture of me and AJ at Homecoming hanging on my locker door and smile. He look good. And I look good standin with him. We look good together. Then I shut my locker and go down to the cafeteria to meet the girls.

They all sittin by a window, Kelli, Monica, Imani and Michella. "Whassup Erika?" say Imani, my best friend.

"Just got done talkin to AJ."

"I saw that chick he left with today," say Kelli. "She's okay, but she's dark!"

That's somethin about all us girls. We all light-skinned, except Kelli and Monica, who's white. All the dark-skinned chicks start up shit with us all the time. They probably jealous.

"He had his arm around her and he was takin her out to her car," say Imani. "They was lookin pretty close!"

I roll my eyes and take off AJ's jacket. "Shut up girl, you full of shit! He told me something blew up in her face and he had to take her home."

20

Now Monica roll her eyes. "If she was hurt so bad, why'd he have to take her home?"

"I think he was lyin to you, girl," Imani say. "Cuz I saw them together and like I said, they was lookin pretty close!"

"Better keep an eye on your man, girl!" say Michella. "Cuz it wouldn't look too good if you lost The Dream to a dark!"

Now I get mad. They right, AJ's my man and I got to keep an eye on him.

Kelli giggle. "Oh...Erika's gettin mad!"

"Ruthie, that's her name," I say. "Do any of y'all know a Ruthie?"

"Ruthie?" they all repeat, wrinklin their noses. "What kinda name's that? I ain't never heard of no Ruthie!"

"Then I'll make sure I find out who she is!" I say.

Monica ask, "What're you gonna do?"

I just smile. "I dunno. I'll see how much trouble she give me."

# RUTHIE

Mom took me to the doctor, who prescribed for me special eyedrops that made my eyes sting even worse than they did when I had the accident. So I stayed at home for two days, lounging around the house, worrying about the schoolwork I'd missed, but not really wanting to go back.

I went back to school Friday morning, and the same dread I'd felt during my little vacation burgeoned in me as I drove into the student parking lot of Centennial High School. It'd been a year and six months since I'd transferred and I was still having mixed feelings about the school. Up until my junior year, my entire school career was spent in the comfortable suburban schools of Littleton, twenty miles southwest of Denver. It didn't occur to me until mid-sophomore year that I was one of only six black kids at my high school. I'd never before given it any thought. I'd always lived in semi-affluent neighborhoods, had white playmates, white teachers and white school friends. But one March afternoon I was sitting in my Honors English class listening to my teacher drone about major twentieth-century American poets and I noticed she'd made no mention of Langston Hughes. At the time I didn't know much about Langston Hughes except that my father kept a book of his poetry on the living room table. I did know that he was a major poet from all the casual allusions my father had made to him over the years at the dinner table and in conversations. When I pointed this out to my teacher, she looked at me in a surprised way, then swallowed and said "Yes...I read one of his poems. He's very good." She then changed the subject back to EE Cummings. I'd sat there bewildered, the hollowness of her answer hitting me as if it had been filled with lead. For the first time, I felt a strange sense of cultural isolation and after that I realized my whole identity was somehow...missing. Several months later, my father decided my brother and I needed more access to the black community, and that it would be more convenient for him to live closer to his work.

That's how I ended up attending Centennial.

I found myself admiring its beauty as I parked my car. The building itself is an anachronism; a red brick Gothic colossus with high vaulted ceilings and arched windows. It's really an eyesore because it sits right in the heart of Denver.

Though the school is in the inner city, the area where I live is just as serene and quiet as where I'd lived before. My neighborhood, Northridge, is predominantly white with a nice splash of professional black families. Yet a short distance away are several distinct worlds. Directly south lies Capitol Hill, where Denver's rich establishment live in stately mansions on tree-lined streets. To the east and the west are the lower-class neighborhoods, home to many of Denver's blacks to the east and hispanics and Vietnamese to the west. Centennial High School sits right in the middle of these four worlds, drawing its students from all directions.

The diversity is probably Centennial's most interesting feature. The school's about forty percent white, twenty-five percent black, twenty-five percent hispanic and about ten percent oriental. Just as all the races are present, so are all socio-economic backrounds. You'd expect a lot of racial and class conflicts in a place like this, but those are practically nonexistent because all of the various groups tend to keep to themselves. I'm not sure if that's good or bad, but that's the way it was.

That's where my problems lay. During my first few days of school the black students eyed me suspiciously, especially when they heard me speak. That made me feel self-conscious, as I learned that exposure to black people did not mean automatic kinship, as I had previously thought. I felt even more isolated than I did during my last few months in Littleton. So I ended up making friends with people who shared my interests; school, student council, things run primarily by the white kids. Ironically, even in this diverse environment, most of my friends were still white and I was more confused than ever about my black identity. This never-ending confusion combined with the normal second-semester senior burnout had put me in a pretty sour mood. I was practically counting the days until graduation and it was only January.

My best friend Andrea McCormick was waiting for me at our locker. Her large eyes grew even larger as I approached. "Ruthie! Omigod how are you?"

"Fine," I told her, gathering my books for first hour.

Andrea still looked worried. "We heard about the accident in student council Wednesday, Kevin told us all. I was afraid you'd go blind or something—"

"I'm alive and well. What's been going on?"

She shrugged, tossing her auburn hair. "Nothing, really.

24

I guess Kevin and Monica are in a fight, and—"

I rolled my eyes. "I don't mean gossip!"

"No, but listen to this! You'll die! Do you know Erika Whitman?"

"No...am I supposed to?"

"She's the light-skinned black girl who hangs out with that one group of light-skinned black girls, the ones who fight and—"

"Oh yeah, the ones who hang around all of the athletes and think they're God's gift because they're light-skinned—"

Andrea nodded. "Yeah, them. I guess Erika's AJ's girlfriend and she saw you and AJ leaving school together Tuesday."

"And?"

"She got mad at him, thinking you and AJ have something going!" Andrea finished, out of breath.

I laughed. "That's ridiculous! AJ and me? That'd be the day!"

Andrea looked thoughtful. "I don't know. He's pretty cute—"

"And stuck-up!"

"I'd watch out for Erika if I was you. She's probably going to have an eye out for you."

I shrugged. "Big deal, I don't even know the girl. We should get going, we're going to be late." The student council officers meet first hour every morning. Both Andrea and I are officers; I'm student body vice president and she's senior class secretary.

I was surrounded the second I walked into the classroom. "Omigod Ruthie, are you okay?"

"I heard you might go blind!"

"Does your eye still hurt?"

I broke away from the crowd, assuring them, "Yes, I'm okay, no, I'm not blind and yes, my eyes feel fine." Then

I took my usual seat at the front of the room.

Student body president Christian Weisburg was sitting in the teachers desk with his feet propped up. He winked at me. "I take it you're feeling better?"

I smiled. "You heard right!" Christian's one of my best friends, much to the envy of the majority of the girls at Centennial. Not only is he extremely good-looking and well-dressed, he's one of the Capitol Hill wealthy set, complete with his own BMW. He has a teen-dream type of handsomeness, resembling a modern-day James Dean with ruffled brown hair and blue-green eyes, plus a tennis player's physique.

As I opened my notebook, Kevin Blane, one of AJ Johnson's good friends, came to sit in the desk next to mine. "Y'know, AJ feels really stupid about all this—"

"You can tell him I'm fine."

Kevin's eyes widened. "I heard he accidentally put this chemical crap on a stove and it blew up in your face!"

I laughed. "That's a little overdramatic, but that's basically what happened."

Kevin laughed too. "Man, I always knew AJ was a dumb-ass. I mean, only a dumb-ass would put chemicals over a fire!"

I smiled. "I guess dumb-asses flock together, don't they."

He rolled his eyes. "Yeah, real funny!"

Somehow or another he was voted senior class vice president. Don't ask me how; he possesses as much intelligence as your average doornob. But Kevin's very popular because one, he's an all-state quarterback and two, he's very good-looking, striking really, with coal-black hair, light blue eyes and a great body. But he's a moderately nice guy, that is, when he wants to be.

I scanned the room as we went over old business, observing one other black student, sophomore class president Eddie

Howser. Two blacks and one hispanic representing a school sixty percent minority. I shook my head.

I then thought about AJ Johnson. I guess this whole ordeal had made him Asshole of the Week. It'd be interesting to see what he'd have to say to me next hour in chemistry. When the bell rang, I gathered my books and met up with Andrea and Christian.

"You didn't look like you were paying much attention today," Christian said to me as we left the room.

"I wasn't. I'm sick of school."

Andrea groaned. "Aren't we all!" Then her eyes widened and she pointed straight ahead. "Isn't that Erika Whitman and her friends?"

Christian smiled. "Oh yeah, she and AJ got in a fight over you Tuesday."

I rolled my eyes and looked to see a very pretty girl with light skin, long brown hair, and blue eyes standing amid a group of pretty girls, white and light-skinned black, all wearing too much make-up and tight clothes. Erika must've known who I was because she glared at me. "That's ridiculous! I don't even know the girl!"

"I hear she's pretty vicious," Christian told me.

"I haven't done anything to her. I'll see you guys at lunch," I said, then headed upstairs to my chemistry class. Again, I was surrounded the moment I walked into the room. Again, I assured everyone I was fine, then took my seat.

AJ walked in right as the tardy bell rang, taking his seat behind me. "I'm sorry about—"

"I don't want to hear it anymore, I know!" I interrupted him and smiled. He smiled back somewhat nervously and I could see why he got so much female attention here, white and black. He's six feet tall and well-muscled, with wide-spaced brown eyes and masculine, square-jawed good looks. His only flaw was his arrogance, but I suppose that was to

27

be expected.

"What'd I miss in here?" I asked.

He shrugged. "I dunno...I missed the last coupla days—"

I nodded. So I'd have to ask someone else.

Mrs. Fleener was lecturing and I usually listen, but today I didn't feel like it. I turned around to look at AJ, who was doodling on his notebook. "I heard your girlfriend saw us leaving together Tuesday and thought you and I had something going."

He looked up at me, his eyes wide with surprise. Maybe he hadn't expected me to mention it. "Yeah, well, she kinda jealous—"

"Must be. I'm sorry to have caused your girlfriend troubles."

AJ chuckled. "Don't worry about it."

Mrs. Fleener turned to give us a dirty look. I turned to face forward but turned back to AJ a few minutes later. "I guess she's already taken a disliking to me," I whispered. "She gave me a dirty look in the hall today."

AJ was still chuckling. "Yeah? I'll talk to her about it."

"No, it's okay. I don't need a bodyguard. I just think it's funny how some girls can be so...petty."

"Huh?"

"You know, jumping to conclusions, holding grudges, stuff like that. It's all so...juvenile."

He looked at me strangely.

"Is she a senior?"

"Yeah."

Mrs. Fleener spun around to face us. "Ruthie and AJ, will you be quiet!"

AJ rolled his eyes. "Old bat," he said under his breath. I chuckled, then turned to listen to what she had to say for the rest of the hour.

AJ met up with me after class. "Man, that lady gets on

my nerves!''

"Mine, too," I said. We fell silent as we walked down the hall.

"Hey, how come you always hang with the white kids?" he asked suddenly.

I took a deep breath. "Well...it doesn't seem like many of the black kids like me too much."

"They think you a snob."

I turned to him. "Do you think I'm a snob?"

His face wore a confused expression. "I dunno—"

"What do you mean, you don't know?"

"I mean, the way you talk and act and dress and all—"

I said nothing else. What was new? "See you, AJ," I said and went to my locker. I passed Erika standing with some of her friends. I could feel her eyes on my back as I made my way down the hall. I shook my head, disgusted. Some people could be so petty!

# ERIKA

"There that girl Ruthie!" Imani say, pointin to her.

I frown, watchin her walk away from AJ. She turn and look at me and I give her the glare. The glare that say, "stay-away-from-my-man!" I'm about to go yell at AJ again cuz obviously, one yellin wasn't enough! But he turn and go off in another direction.

"So what you gonna do about that girl?" ask Imani. "It look like she and AJ gettin close!"

"Shut up!" I say cuz she startin to get on my nerves. She shut up.

We head toward the choir room, meetin up with Kelli and Michella on the way. I tell them I saw that Ruthie chick and they both laugh.

"That girl's lookin for trou-ble!" say Kelli.

"Hey, I seen her around!" Michella say suddenly.

I turn to her. "Yeah?"

"She the girl who hang with all the white kids! Them

snobby ones!''

I smile. Figures. "Well she better keep away from AJ! I gotta find some way of givin her the message—'' Before I finish what I'm sayin I feel someone's arm around my waist and a hand on my neck.

"What the—'' I shout and knock my head into someone's jaw.

"Ow, shit!'' I hear Ronell Wood's loud voice and turn around.

"I told you not to do that to me!'' I yell.

He rub his jaw. "Damn girl, you got a hard head!'' Kelli and Imani and Michella laugh at him.

"So what you doing?'' he ask.

"Going to class like good students. What you should be doing!''

Ronell just shrug. "Whassup? All of y'all look like someone dissed you!''

I sigh. "Just AJ—''

Ronell laugh. "He out chasin skirts again?''

"Not just skirts!'' say Kelli. "Some ole Miss Proper named Ruthie!''

"Ruthie,'' Ronell repeat. "Ain't she the one who got the chemicals blown up in her face? Yeah, I seen her around! She fresh!''

"She dark!'' say Imani.

Ronell laugh. "She ain't much darker'n you! This girl just think she light!''

"I am too light you midnight-black crusty son of a bitch!'' Imani holler.

"C'mon, you got hair nappy as mine, you ain't light!''

Now Imani grab him by the hair. "I'm gonna knock your head into that wall if you don't shut up!'' she hiss like a snake.

Now I laugh. "C'mon, he just messin with you, girl!''

31

"He gotta learn when to shut up!" Imani grumble.

Ronell rub his head. "Damn, you got some nails, girl!"

"What're you doing here anyway, Ronell?" ask Kelli. "I thought you dropped out!"

Ronell shrug. "Yeah I did you see, but I came back."

"Why? Ain't you got your roguish self in enough trouble?" I say. Ronell down with the Compton Posse, one of the gangs around here.

"Nah, not lately—" Ronell try to get up close to me. He always tryin to get up close to me.

"AJ gonna kick your ass if you don't leave me alone!" I say.

He smile. "Not if you don't tell him!"

"I will!"

He shrug and go flirt with Michella.

"Oh man!" Kelli say out of the blue.

"What?" I say.

Kelli's eyes go narrow. "Look who's comin!"

Coming down the next hall is the Black Cows, Shanice, Yvette, Alisha and Patrice, four dark as shit girls who always startin up shit with us light girls. We call em cows cuz they fat and ugly.

"Somebody got a weave!" Imani squeal, lookin at Shanice. I look at the girl and laugh out loud. Yesterday her hair was short but today it hang past her shoulders. The weave look terrible. The hair two different textures and real short on top. You can tell it's a weave a mile away.

I laugh as they walk by. "Man, someone messed up her hair!"

Now Shanice and the cows stop in front of us and look at us with mean looks on their ugly faces. "What was that, bitch?" Shanice say, glarin at me.

I keep laughing. "That's some messed-up hair!"

"Bitch—" Now them big nostrils of hers flare and her fists

32

clench. I laugh some more. I'm up for a fight.

"Shut up, ya stinkin cow!" say Kelli.

Now she spin around to Kelli. "I'm gonna rip that blond hair from your head!"

"And I'm gonna rip that nappy-ass cat hair ugly weave from your head!" Kelli drop her books and shove Shanice. Now her friends jump in and start yellin. So do my girls.

"White slut bitch!"

"Who you callin a slut?"

"Ugly black-ass can't get a date—"

A bunch of people gather around us, watchin us yell back and forth. The bell ring for class but nobody move.

Finally, I decide I had enough and start walkin away.

"I'm gonna get you, light-skin bitch!" Shanice yell as I leave.

I turn around. "Right, you black-ass jig!" Then I leave before the principal come runnin. I ain't up to gettin suspended again. Mom throw a fit every time I get suspended for fightin.

The girls stop yellin and come join me. "It don't look like we gonna make it to choir!" Imani giggle.

I shrug, my mind turnin to AJ. "I think I'm gonna go home."

"So we're all going to your house?" ask Kelli.

"Nah...I got a headache," I mumble. "Come by at seven and tell me what's up for tonight."

"Yeah, all right—"

I walk out of the school and head home. I don't live too far from school so I walk home a lot. I don't pay no attention to all the cars honkin at me on Colfax Street. Colfax is a prostitute strip so it ain't safe for a girl to walk alone, but I do it all the time. I can defend myself. I'm good in a fight.

I start thinkin about AJ. Son of a bitch. Never calls me anymore. Always flirtin with other chicks and now this girl

33

Ruthie. I guess I'll have to knock some sense into him. Either that or flirt with some other guy. Make him jealous. Cuz lord, could he get jealous! I smile. Yeah. That'd teach him!

I live in an apartment with my mom. My dad live in Phoenix. I used to live out there with him but I came here three years ago. Me and Dad don't get along. Well, neither do me and Mom, really. Mom's white and I don't think she too proud of havin a half-breed for a daughter, cuz she got all these white boyfriends now. One time she even made me tell one of them I was her niece cuz I guess she was too ashamed to say I was her daughter. It's cuz of her I don't like white people much. That's why it piss me off whenever AJ flirt with white chicks. And the white chicks'd be hangin on him all the time if it wasn't for me. I mean, I like Kelli and Monica cuz they down with us, but I hate all them snobby white chicks at school who look at me like I'm dirt.

I open my door and see Mom sittin on the couch watchin Donahue. There's a glass of Scotch on the coffee table. "Hi Mom," I say.

She don't look at me but she say, "Hello Erika."

I stand there feelin stupid cuz I don't got nothin to say. So I just ask, "What you doing home so early?"

Mom shrug. "I felt like coming home."

I sit on a chair and stare at the TV. Donahue talkin about men who dump their women.

Mom got pretty blond hair. She always messin with it, flippin it up with her hand, twirlin it. When I was little I wanted to have blond hair like her but she said I couldn't cuz of the black in me. "So I take it you're still seeing that...black boy?"

I shrug. Son of a bitch.

Mom's mouth tighten up and she start twistin her hair. I know she don't think much of black men cuz of Dad. "You watch out for him," she say. "You know how they are—"

34

Mom shake her head and finish her drink. "Take a lesson from me, Erika. Black men are no good."

I stare at her. "Mom, I'm black! You can't be sayin shit like that!"

Mom roll her eyes as she pour herself another drink. "There you go with that...black talk! Thanks to your good-for-nothing father I have a daughter who can't speak decently."

"Speak decently!" I exclaim. "First you get mad at who I go out with, then with the way I talk, what the hell can I do right?"

"I don't know what you're talking about," Mom say, starin at the TV.

"It's just that you ain't even proud of me! It's cuz I'm half a nigger, right?"

Mom narrow her eyes and hiss. "It wouldn't be so bad if you didn't act like one!"

That piss me off so bad I yell "You bitch!"

Mom slam her glass on the table. "I should slap you for speaking to me like that!"

I glare back. "Go ahead and try it!"

Mom shut her eyes and shake her head. "I'm not going to put up with this..."

I stand up, still glarin at her. "Why, you got someone comin over, is that it? You want me to pretend I'm not your daughter, that I'm the fucking maid?"

"Do what you want, just get out of my sight!"

I stare at her, hatin her cuz I know tomorrow she'll come cryin her sob story to me, sayin how she didn't mean what she said. And I'm hatin myself cuz I know I'll forgive her, like I always do.

But right now I don't wanna be in the house with her so I say to hell with it and leave. Screw Mom. Screw AJ. Screw everybody.

# AJ

"So she's still mad at you?" Doug asked me while he was pressing in weightlifting class, our last class of the day.

I shrugged. "I don't care. I'm sick of her shit."

Doug shook his head. "Man, that is one JEALOUS chick!"

I shrugged again. One of Erika's friends told me last hour Erika wasn't feeling good and went home. I was glad cuz all her crap was really starting to get on my nerves.

"AJ, gimme another twenty pounds!" Doug said, rubbing his arms.

I grinned. "Sure you can handle it?" His face was all red and he was sweating, but he said "yeah," so I brought his weight up to 400 pounds. He could only press it four times. The veins in his head was sticking out so far I thought they'd explode.

I laughed. "Man, you look like you was tryin to shit a brick!"

Doug laughed too, sitting up and stretching his arms. "C'mon, the bell's about to ring." We put away the weights and went to the locker room to shower.

"So what's up for tonight?" I yelled over the sound of the showers.

"I think Bill O'Keefe's havin a party!"

"Again?" Bill had a party last night but it only lasted a half hour cuz a bunch of the MG set showed up and started scrapping so the cops came and broke it up.

"Yeah, I guess—" Doug turned off his shower and went to his locker. I did, too. "Y'know, if Erika's actin bitchy you should go for, God, what's her name, the blonde—"

I laughed. "Kelli? Erika'd kick my ass!"

"You'd be showin her up!"

"Nah, not Kelli. Kelli too stupid. Y'know, you and her might get along pretty good!"

Doug slugged me in the shoulder, then he laughed. "Y'know, I just might go for her. Jamil says she's pretty good. Besides, no chick can resist the Vike!"

I laughed. "You ain't kiddin!" We all call Doug the Vike cuz he's so pale and got light blond hair. But we also call him that cuz he's a vicious blocker. He made All-State playing center. We went to meet the fellas in the cafeteria, seeing them in our usual corner. Doug yelled "Yo FELLAS!" so the whole cafeteria could hear.

"It's the Vike and the Dream!" I heard Jamil yell over the crowd noise. We pushed our way through the crowd over to the guys. Yeah, we was obnoxious but what the hell.

One thing about us fellas is that we all play football, but we ain't one of them stupid football cliques you see at the white schools with the cheerleaders and all that. For one, our cheerleaders are a bunch of cows and two, we all been hanging together since junior high and grade school. Doug and Kevin's the only white dudes who hang with us but they're down with us so they're okay. The rest of us is brothers. Me, Wakeen, Jamil, and Ray.

Jamil slapped hands with me and Doug. "Whassup, man?"

"Nothin—" I said. "So the action's at Bill's tonight?"

"Yeah, free beer!" said Kevin.

"Hey, any of y'all going to plyometrics?" asked Wakeen. All of us was gonna be on the track team this spring and we was already starting conditioning.

All of us looked at each other and shook our heads.

Wakeen shook his head at us. "Y'all better start gettin in shape again!"

Kevin laughed. "You're the only one who gives a shit about track, man!"

"Hey, you won't be laughin when I win state in the one hundred and two hundred this year!" Wakeen said proudly. All them sports analysts was already picking him to win cuz he went to some national indoor meet last month and kicked ass.

"Nah, I ain't going," I said. "My legs is sore enough already!"

"You guys workin too hard or somethin?" I heard this sexy voice behind us. We all turned around and saw all Erika's girls, Monica, Kelli, Michella and Imani.

"Erika went home," Imani told me. "I don't think she was feelin too good."

"Girl, I already told him!" Kelli said. "Yeah, she left after we started up with them Black Cows this morning!"

Wakeen laughed. "Man, you girls is worse than us!"

She grinned. "You know it!"

I looked at Doug and laughed. He was scoping her out in a big way. "Yo Kelli, you should come with us tonight!"

"You guys going to Bill's party?" she asked.

Doug got up all close to her. "Yeah. You going?" He looked funny next to her cuz he's six four and she's barely

38

five feet tall.

Kelli grinned back like the flirt she was. "I'll be there!"

She and Doug started flirting and Jamil started talking shit as usual so I tuned them all out and looked around the cafeteria, watching everybody leave for the weekend. I saw Ruthie with some redhead girl and that white dude Christian somebody. Christian's one of those rich dudes from the Hill.

Wakeen must've saw him too cuz he said, "Hey, that's the chick you almost made go blind!"

"Shut up!" They wasn't never gonna let me live that down!

"Man, she always with that white dude!"

Kevin got in on it, too. "Who Christian? Yeah, she is."

"I don't get it. Do they got somethin going?" I asked.

Kevin shrugged. "I dunno."

Now all Erika's girls started glaring at me.

I was confused as hell. "But I know all them rich white chicks hang all over him!"

Kevin looked pissed off. "I'm gonna kick his snobby ass before we graduate, man!"

Ray laughed. "What's he done to you?"

Kevin's eyes narrowed at Christian. "I'll think of somethin!"

I laughed, too. Kevin's crazy. "Well you stay here thinkin, I gotta get going. Ray, take me home, willya?"

Ray picked up his duffle bag. "Yeah, let's go." Me and Ray left the cafeteria. "You getting sick of Erika or somethin?"

I shrugged. "She been gettin on my nerves."

Ray just nodded. He's real quiet. He don't say much unless he's pissed off. He's pretty small, too. That's why he didn't get recruited much, even though he's real strong and a fast runner.

We was at my house in no time. I live east of the school in a little brick house on the corner of Niagara and twenty-

39

third. Ray lives on the next street. My neighborhood ain't the slums but it ain't that nice, either. It's pretty old, I mean, it's been around a long time, so everything looks sort of old. There's a lot of drugs and shit cuz of the gangs, but I guess it could be worse. Ray dropped me off and I ran up to the front door. The second I opened the door I got squirted with a water pistol.

"Where are you, you little shit!" I hollered, throwing down my bag. I could hear giggling behind the door. I shut the door and saw my little brother Anthony standing there with a watergun.

I picked him up. "Didn't I tell you not to squirt me with that?"

"Hey, put me down!" he squealed.

I carried him upside down to my room and threw him on the bed. I tackled him and put his head in a neck lock. "You ain't supposed to be playin with that in the house, anyway! C'mon, say you're sorry—"

"No way!"

"C'mon—" I squeezed his head a little.

"Okay, okay! Sorry!"

I let go of him and he rubbed his neck. "Geez!" he said. I laughed. He's always playing jokes on me.

"So what'd you do today?" I asked.

He looked serious. "I broke up with Sara."

I laughed. He's only six and already got girlfriends. "Why?"

"She wanted to wear my necklace but I said no!"

"Good. You don't need to be gettin serious about girls yet."

Anthony shook his head. "No way! Girls is stupid! All they like to do is play chase!"

I grinned. "Well that don't change, kid!"

He picked up his squirt gun and aimed it at me. I took

it from him. "Dad'll kick your little ass if he see you with this in the house!"

"I squirted Franco and he yelled at me!"

I sighed. "You know better than messin with Franco. What was he doing here, anyway?"

"His homeboys was here with him. They had lots and lots of money!"

I sucked in my breath.

Anthony crawled onto my lap and looked in my face. "Whassup, bro?"

I chuckled. "Nothin, kid—" I sat him so that he was facing me. "Hey...you know how Franco gets all that money, don't you?"

Anthony nodded. "He sell dope!"

I took a deep breath. "And you know that's bad news, right?"

Anthony shrugged. "Franco don't think so!"

I looked at Anthony real hard. "You listen to me real good. Don't listen to Franco, okay?"

"Let's go to the movies tonight!" Anthony said. He's got kind of a short attention span. But I guess all little kids do. For a second I thought about calling up Ray and telling him I wasn't going out tonight, but I kinda felt like getting trashed. "Nah, we'll go out tom rrow night, okay?"

Anthony jumped down from my lap. "Okay!"

"Where you going?"

"Outside to play with Gary!"

"You gotta eat dinner first!"

"I'll eat at Gary's!"

"Okay. Come back early!" I yelled after him. I watched him run out, then I thought about Franco. Franco's a dopeman high roller whatever you wanna call it. He's nineteen. Or maybe he's twenty, I dunno. He hasn't been living at home ever since he got in with the Compton Posse

41

three years ago. He just comes around whenever he feel like it. The Compton Posse is probably the most vicious gang in Denver. They fight the MG's, run crack houses, get in all kinds of trouble. A couple of years ago I was down with them too, mainly cuz of Franco. But I never went in all the way cuz of football. Me and Franco used to be real close too but now I think he's nothing but trouble. We share a room but like I said, he's hardly ever home. And when he is home we don't talk.

But I told him to keep his shit away from Anthony! Anthony's a little kid, he don't need to be seeing all that! And I'm the only one here to make sure Anthony stays outta trouble cuz Mom died three years ago. And Dad's always been kinda lazy when it comes to us kids. I mean, he pays the bills and shit but he don't pay us much attention. I guess he thinks we can take care of ourselves. I went to the fridge to get something to eat, then back to my room to watch some TV before I went over to Ray's. Franco came walking in about fifteen minutes before I was gonna leave. I looked at him, not saying nothing. Usually he's high but today he was looking pretty mellow. He must've got in a fight recently cuz there's this long scar down his face that I never seen before. Franco's gotta be the most scarred-up guy I ever saw! He's been stabbed, shot at, hit with crowbars, you name it. He'd be real good-looking if he wasn't so scarred up. He's built like a linebacker. Six feet tall like me, but over two hundred pounds.

"Whassup?" he said.

"Nothin. I'm on my way out."

"Hmm," he said and sat down next to me on the bed, looking at the TV. I kept looking at him but he didn't notice.

"I thought I told you to stay away from Anthony!" I said to get his attention.

Franco shrugged. "So?"

I didn't say nothing else. I wasn't up for a fight with him tonight, especially when he was looking so mellow. But I knew I had to hurry up and get outta there before I did start up with him. I changed my shirt and walked up the street to Ray's.

Ray came to the door. "Whassup?"

"Franco's home," I muttered, going inside and sitting on the couch.

"Was he startin up shit?"

"Nah, he was chilled out. But he been talkin shit to Anthony. Man, I don't want him to start puttin ideas into Anthony's head! He just a little kid!"

Ray didn't say nothing else. I wasn't feeling no better.

We sat around his house until nine or so, then headed over to Bill's house. Bill lived on the west side in a shithole of a house near the projects. There was already a ton of cars outside his house when we got there and you could hear the music from outside.

Bill opened the door, looking drunk. "It's the Dream!" he shouted. "Whassup, man? Go on downstairs!" He was standing so close to me I could smell his breath, which stank like you wouldn't believe. We went down to the basement where everyone was packed in, dancing and drinking beer. I saw the fellas standing over by the keg. "It's the Dream!" yelled Kevin. Me and Ray pushed our way over to them.

I slapped hands with Doug and Jamil and Kevin and Wakeen. "Whassup?"

"Erika's here," Doug said. "She's lookin good!"

"Yeah?" I looked around for a clean cup on the table, then got myself some beer.

"I saw some MG's too!" said Jamil.

I shook my head. The MG's, or Mafia Gangsters or something like that, is Compton rivals. Some of them try to start up shit with me cuz of my brother and cuz they know

I used to be down with the Compton Posse.

"Yeah, I'd like to see them try to start some shit with me!" Jamil was already sounding drunk. "Cuz I feel like hurtin somebody!"

Ray chuckled. "You full of shit, Jamil!"

"Oh shit—" said Kevin.

We all looked at him. "What?"

Kevin pointed across the room. "Look, man!"

I saw Erika getting close to one of those MG's. I narrowed my eyes at her. "Bitch!" I downed my beer, got myself some more, then pushed my way over to her. "Whassup, Erika!" I said, glaring at her.

She turned around and grinned at me. She was looking good, wearing a tight skirt. "AJ, do you know Rajean?" When she opened her mouth I could tell she'd been drinking.

I grabbed her arm and yanked her away from that guy.

"Let go of me, AJ!" She tried to pull away from me, looking pissed off. "Now you know what it feel like, huh?"

I glared at her. "So this is the game you gonna play?"

She didn't say nothing. Just glared back at me.

So I pushed her aside and said, "Go ahead, then!"

She turned and strutted back over to that MG dude. He put his hand on her ass and started getting up close to her. For a second, I wanted to go over there and knock him out. Every now and then she looked over at me like she had me beat or something. So I said forget her. I wasn't gonna put up with her shit!

Then I saw Trina Ash, this stupid white chick I know from Economics. We used to get together a lot last year at Gucci's, this nightclub. And nothing pissed off Erika more than when I flirted with white chicks.

"Hey Trina, whassup?" I said.

She looked at me and grinned. "Well if it isn't the Dream!"

"You know it!" I grinned back and let her put her arms around my neck. All white chicks was the same. They just liked me cuz I played football and got a lot of attention. But I don't care cuz white chicks can be kinda fun sometimes. "You been waitin for me? Cuz you look like you was waitin for somebody—"

She giggled. "Yeah, I've been saving myself for you, AJ!" She was pretty drunk. I turned to look at Erika and saw her glaring at me. She'll probably kick Trina's ass Monday. Erika's done that before. Then I saw Erika pull that MG guy close and start kissing him. That pissed me off so bad I had to turn back to Trina so I wouldn't go over there and kick some ass.

"Let's sit down somewhere," I said.

She giggled and nodded.

We found an empty couch and I started kissing her. The girl must've been pretty gone cuz she was letting me do all sorts of stuff I shouldn't have been doing.

"Go AJ!" I heard some of the fellas yell. I know Erika was pissed as hell.

Trina started biting on my ear. "Is anyone in Bill's room?"

I laughed. This girl was too much! I looked up and saw Doug and some other dude talking shit and knew they'd start fighting pretty soon. I sat there on the couch with Trina, watching Doug and this dude start scrapping. Then Jamil and this other dude jumped in. I guess the party was just about over cuz Bill was starting to get mad and throw people out of his house.

I turned to Trina. "I gotta get going, okay?"

She pouted. "Okay. Call me."

"Yeah." I stood up, knowing I wouldn't. I went to find the fellas so we could get outta here before the cops came. Cops and athletes don't mix. Especially cops and black athletes.

# RUTHIE

"Did that Erika girl ever threaten your life?" Christian asked me in student council one day in early February.

I smiled. It'd been three weeks since my accident and all of the furor had died down. "No. AJ and I don't talk anymore so she's probably feeling pretty secure."

"Why don't you?" asked Andrea.

I shrugged. "Why should we?"

"I think the two of you would make an interesting couple!"

I laughed. "Yeah, sure. We have nothing in common!"

"Well, it would be interesting—" she said, then turned to Christian. "What about you? Are you ever going to find a girl? Not that you couldn't have any girl you wanted—" I had to agree with her. Christian's probably the best looking guy at Centennial.

"I doubt it," he said casually. "But I'm not looking so big deal, right?"

"Why are you so elusive, huh?" I asked him. "Why can't

anyone ever figure you out?"

He grinned but I think the fact that he was good-looking really bothered him. He rarely dated any girl from Centennial or any girl for that matter. "I guess I like being that way."

Andrea elbowed him. "Being a mystery man adds to his charm!"

I shook my head. Andrea and I were closer to him than anyone else at school and sometimes we felt like we didn't know him all that well. He was as close to perfect as guys came; great-looking, polite, intelligent. Even I sometimes felt twinges of attraction toward him, though I'd never show it. I would never want to be anything more than his friend. Those twinges made me feel painfully guilty because I really shouldn't be attracted to white guys. I suppose when it comes down to it, I'm not against interracial relationships, but isn't there something wrong when you're almost never attracted to guys of your own race? But the majority of the black guys around here were egotistical jocks or just plain thugs. And why do I have to associate with that? That's why I sometimes feel a little jealous of Andrea, who has such a nice boyfriend. Her boyfriend Ted's a freshman at Denver University. Someone with goals and dreams and ambitions. Someone who can do more than play ball and boast and fight.

"What's up Ruthie? You look like you're in another world," Andrea said, breaking my daze.

I shook my head and smiled. "Oh. . .nothing." The bell rang and I gathered my books. "I'll see you guys at lunch!"

"Okay, see you!" they called after me.

I left the classroom and walked down the hall, my mind still on my situation. I passed a group of black girls talking and laughing and thought, why am I so different? I felt guilty because I couldn't really associate with black people and even guiltier because I wasn't sure if I wanted to. I hear all of the problems of the black community, the drugs, the gangs, the breakdown of the family, and it all angers me because I know that as a black person, I have to carry that stigma and that stereotype in front of me. But why did it have to be that way? Why couldn't I be seen as a human being first and a black person second? Then I read about all of the blacks who are doing good things in the community, the philanthropists and the activists, though I have to go out of my way to read about them when I can pick up any newspaper and read about the multitudes of "black problems." So added up, what does this all mean? Is being black the least or the most important thing about me?

My parents aren't much help. Both of them grew up in black communities, then decided to live in white communities so that my brother and I would have better opportunities than they did. So they can't quite understand why I'm so confused. And I'm not sure if they even want to. Both of my parents have a tendency to stick their heads in the sand and pretend not to see anything they can't understand. As you grow older, you begin to realize that your parents aren't the all-knowing, fix-everything people you once thought they were, but have fears and weaknesses just like everyone else.

They especially don't understand, or don't want to understand, why I no longer enjoy going to church when I had no problem with church when we lived in Littleton. As usual, I approached my mother in the kitchen Saturday afternoon and tried to make up an excuse to avoid it. "Mom, I'm going out with Andrea tonight," I told her. "I'll probably stay the night at her house."

Mom sighed. "Ruthie, you haven't been to church in over a month. You need to go this week."

I sat down at the kitchen table. "I don't like church."

She shrugged. "You never had a problem with church before."

"Our other church was . . . different. It was only an hour.

This one's three hours! It's a waste of a whole morning!''

Though I wasn't looking at her, I could feel my mother's eyes on me. For a while she said nothing and I stared at the floor sullenly.

Finally, Mom asked softly, ''Is that really it?''

I sighed. ''I. . .just don't like it!''

Mom's voice stayed soft. ''Ruthie, you were the one who wanted to make the change. You were the one who wanted more black influence in your life. Remember that? Ruthie, we did all of this for you.''

I felt my brow furrow and her words weighed heavily on my heart. Her voice held no indication of anger but I was disappointed with myself nonetheless. Was I really so ungrateful?

''But—'' I sputtered in protest. ''They don't even like us at Zion!''

''How do you know that?''

''We've been going to that church for over a year and a half! Every Sunday we come in with our perfect two-parent family in our perfect Beretta and sit in the second row pew. Has anyone ever once come up and attempted to get to know us? Really get to know us? Yeah, they're nice when they want money for this and that, but do they really act like they want us to be there?''

Mom said nothing.

I went on, my voice rising with my frustration. ''None of the ladies have ever asked you to join their cliques. And you and Dad do so much for that stupid church! You teach Sunday School and the kids are actually learning something!''

Mom went to put a batch of cookies in the oven.

''Then you indulge them,'' I muttered. ''Giving them cookies and stuff. None of the other teachers give their kids cookies!''

Mom smiled gently. ''You're misunderstanding the point,

Ruthie.''

"What?"

"The point of a church isn't belonging to the clubs. It's the—spiritual fellowship, I'll say for the lack of a better word. And I enjoy teaching Sunday school. So does your father. And I like to reward the kids for learning their lessons.''

I nodded slowly. I went downstairs to my room, more confused than ever. I tried calling Andrea and Christian but neither of them was home, so I lay on my bed and tried to think of a way to ease my confusion. Maybe I'll stay the night at Andrea's and get up early enough to go to church in the morning. Or maybe I'll just avoid it again. Because by avoiding it I wouldn't have to deal with all of my questions. I wasn't sure if I believed in God, anyway.

If there is a God, I really wish He'd give me some answers.

# ERIKA

I met God three years ago, when I first came out here to live with Mom. I mean, I was brought up in the church but it wasn't till I moved in with Mom that I really got to know God. One Saturday night me and Mom was fightin cuz I was seein this nineteen year old guy and she was mad about it. I was still feelin like shit on Sunday but Troy came by cuz he wanted to take me to his church, Zion African Methodist Episcopal. And something at that church just... touched me. I don't know what it was to this day. After that I went to that church every Sunday, even after I broke up with Troy. It was at church I found out I could sing. Now I'm student director of the church youth choir. It's the only thing I do that I'm really proud of, I guess.

Most of the black kids at school go to Zion. AJ show up sometime. But he gonna be here today. I'm gonna sing solo and he gonna hear me. Me and Imani are in the bathroom, fixin up our hair before service. Imani in the choir too but she can't sing worth a shit. "Whassup girl, you ain't never this quiet!"

I shrug and we go to the warm-up room. "Kinda nervous—"

Now Ronell come over to stick his nose in. "Nervous! You sang this a hundred times before! Why you nervous?"

"AJ comin today."

Ronell look surprised. "AJ! Man, he ain't come to church since Christmas! Why don't he come, anyway?"

"Lazy." AJ sleep off his hangovers on Sundays. But I always come to church, hangover or not.

Ronell laugh. "He was trippin last night! He started up with this white dude at Jamil's party! I almost had to jump in, but—"

Imani roll her eyes. "Oh hush Ronell, you couldn't break up a cat fight!"

I laugh at that.

Ronell mumble somethin under his breath but then he smile at Imani. "I know you got yours last night!"

Imani flip her hair. "Damn straight! Them Black Cows showed up at Monica's and we kicked some ass, right Erika?"

"Yeah—" I wonder if Shanice'll be here this morning cuz she in the choir too. But I whipped her ass good last night. She called me a slut once too often.

At seven thirty the church regulars start showin up. Service don't start for another fifteen minutes but most folks show up late anyway. Black folk ain't never on time no where.

"Hi Sister Simmons, Sister Mohan," I say to two old ladies comin in.

Sister Simmons smile at me. "Well hello Erika! How are you this morning?"

"Fine," I say and smile. They such sweet old ladies.

"And Ronell, how you doing this morning?" say Sister

Mōhan.

Ronell smile, all gentlemanly. "Fine. It's a nice morning, isn't it!"

Imani roll her eyes. I do too. I wonder what these old ladies'd think if they knew all the shit Ronell into.

As soon as the ladies walk away Ronell mutter, "Old bats!"

"Don't say that!" say Imani. "They nice little old ladies!" Then her eyes narrow. "Hey, there's that Ruthie!"

I see Ruthie and her folks come in and roll my eyes. Her and her prissy folks come to church every Sunday. I just never knew who she was before all that shit with her and AJ.

Ronell watch her go into the sanctuary. "Man, she somethin!"

"She dark," Imani mumble. "Erika, you should start some shit with her!"

"Man, she'll probably sic her lawyer on your ass," say Ronell. "That bitch is loaded!"

"Yeah?" I say. AJ hasn't been talkin to her lately. I guess my yellin finally sank in.

"She a wannabe," say Imani. "She don't even sound black."

All the choir line up behind the ministers and laypeople for the processional. There's only twelve of us here, the other eight'll show up late, I know it. They always do.

I sit there watchin Ruthie through the whole first part of the service. She look like she don't want to be here. She don't sing the hymns or repeat any of the responses. I guess she think she too good for church or somethin. But her folks look like nice people. I seen them talkin to the pastor and stuff. It must be nice to have nice folks. But it ain't done nothin for Ruthie but make her uppity. Maybe she do need to get the shit kicked outta her, like Imani say. That might be kinda fun.

I keep lookin toward the door, watchin for AJ to come walkin in. But I don't see him. Shanice come in right before we have to sing. She give me a dirty look. I want to laugh. Her face is still scratched up from last night. Bitch.

Ronell sing solo in our first choir selection. Man, do that boy got a voice! If I didn't know him and just saw him singin like that I could probably fall in love him. Too bad the rest of the church don't know what a fool he is.

I keep watchin the door, lookin for AJ. I don't see him and he still ain't here when it come time for the second choir selection, my solo. Now I'm pissed off instead of nervous. I sang this song a hundred times before.

So I go down to the mike and start singin, trying not to let it show that I'm mad. As I sing I feel all my madness lift off. Cuz what I'm singin is true. I'm glad I'm a Christian and I know God's way. Cuz God don't give a shit that I'm a half-breed or that my mom's a bitch.

By the end of the song the whole church is clappin and sayin Amen and I get this good feelin deep inside. On my way back to my seat I look at Ruthie. She lookin back at me with this weird look on her face. Snob bitch. Then I look around the sanctuary one more time for AJ. He still hasn't showed.

# AJ

I was expecting Erika to get on my ass Monday morning cuz I didn't go listen to her sing at church. I got home at six Sunday morning and she expected me to be at church at eight? No way!

She came up to my locker and just stood there. I was expecting her to start bitching but she didn't say nothing. So finally I just looked at her and said, "What?"

"AJ, can I ask you somethin?"

I shrugged. "What?"

"Do you love me?"

That about knocked the wind right out of me. I couldn't say nothing. I shut my locker and stared at the floor.

"AJ?" For once, her voice was soft and she sounded sweet.

I laughed, and my laugh sounded nervous. "Man, I never expected you to ask me that!"

"Why not? We been going out a year now and you never

told me if you love me or not.''

I rolled my eyes. ''Oh yeah, Valentine's Day's comin up—''

''This don't got nothin to do with Valentine's Day! I just wanna know if you love me or not.''

''Well—'' I really didn't know what to say. I honestly never thought about it before. Yeah she was my girl, but I dunno

Erika was starting to look impatient. ''AJ?''

''Hey, do you love me?'' Erika took a deep breath, then she looked into my eyes. ''Well, you do a lotta shit that piss me off. You flirt with other chicks too much, you fight too much—''

''Hey, look who's talkin about fightin!''

Erika shrugged. ''And you conceited as hell. But—'' She stopped and took another deep breath. ''Then I think about the times you was there for me when I fight with my mom, and how you hold me in your arms after we...well, you know, stuff like that.''

''And?''

Now she grinned at me. ''I guess yeah, I do love you.''

I grinned back but inside I was nervous as hell. I didn't know what to say. So I just pulled her to me and kissed her. Maybe that'd be enough of an answer for her. ''I gotta go. I'll see you later.''

''Okay.'' She was looking so pretty I kissed her again. It's too bad she ain't sweet like this all the time.

I left her and went to chemistry, even though I didn't feel like going. But I didn't go all last week and I gotta make sure I pass the class. I can't fail nothing if I wanna graduate. I failed a bunch of classes when I was a sophomore so I gotta be careful now.

I sat down in my seat behind Ruthie. She turned around when she saw me and said, ''Wow, I actually have a lab partner after all!'' I didn't know if she was being stuck-up or what so I didn't say nothing. As usual, she was dressed like a businesswoman or something, wearing a nice sweater with this scarf thing tied around it.

"Did I miss a lot?"

She nodded. "Where've you been?"

"Busy." I didn't wanna tell her I just didn't feel like coming.

"We've been doing worksheets. You can get them from Mrs. Fleener. That's what we're going to be doing today, too."

I nodded but I was still thinking about Erika and what she said. Do I love her? I dunno. I mean, I think she's sexy and she can be nice sometimes. Is that love?

"Are you okay?"

I looked at Ruthie and saw her looking at me. "What? Yeah—"

"Then let's get started." She took out some worksheets and started working on them. I just sat there.

"I went ahead and did these on my own," she said. "You might want to ask Mrs. Fleener how to do them."

"Nah, I ain't askin her nothin." She still hadn't forgiven me for Ruthie's accident. "Hey Ruthie, can I ask you somethin?"

She put down her pencil and looked at me. "What?"

I took a deep breath. "What, I mean, how do you know if you...love somebody?"

She grinned. "Why are you asking me this?"

I felt kinda stupid. "Shoot, you smart, you know this stuff!"

"I've never been in love."

"Get outta here!"

"I'm serious!"

"Why not?"

57

"I'm not implying that I've never had boyfriends. I just haven't loved any of them."

"Why not?" I don't know why I asked this. I guess it would be hard for a guy to love a girl as prissy as her.

"I just didn't. Why are you asking?"

"Cuz Erika came up to me today and asked me if I love her."

"And what did you say?"

I shrugged. "Nothin, really."

"Well—" Ruthie looked me straight in the eye. That made me uncomfortable as shit. "I guess when you love a person, you get this...wonderful feeling whenever that person's around. Even when he's not around, just thinking about that person makes you feel good." She had this dreamy look on her face.

I was confused. "You said you never been in love before!"

She shrugged. "I can dream, can't I?"

"Well, that stuff you said...I don't know if I feel like that about Erika."

"Well, you were right in not saying anything," Ruthie said. "It's not good to lie, especially to someone you care about."

I sighed. She sure could make things complicated! I was even more confused. So I decided to forget about it and looked at the worksheets we was supposed to be doing. "Let me copy this stuff."

"No way!"

I looked at her, surprised. "Why not?"

She stared back. "You weren't here to help me do these so I had to do them by myself. I'm not to let you just copy them!"

I rolled my eyes. What a priss! "Fine, I'll copy somebody else's then!" There was some girls in this class who'd love to give me the assignment!

58

"But I'll help you if you want," she said softly. "Show you how to do them."

"Whatever," I mumbled.

Five minutes before the end of class, I was confused as hell. "This is stupid, I can't do this!"

"Sure you can. Do you want me to help you some other time? Some evening or something?"

"I ain't into that homework shit!"

She shrugged, all uppity. "Well it's up to you—"

I didn't like the way she was looking at me so I sighed and said, "Can you come over tonight?"

"What time?"

I shrugged. "I dunno. I get home from practice at four. Come over after that."

"I'll be over at five." Ruthie took out an appointment book from her purse. "Where do you live?"

I laughed at that. "Man, you got a schedule and shit?"

"Where do you live?"

I gave her directions to my house. Then the bell rang and she got up and left. I watched her go and laughed. What a priss!

# RUTHIE

I really wasn't up to tutoring tonight. I had my own homework to do, plus I'd wanted to go to aerobics with Andrea. But I'd told AJ I'd tutor him, so I would.

AJ lived east of the school in a neighborhood that'd seen better days. I grew somewhat dismayed as I drove down the streets. His neighborhood was predominantly black and working-class, quite different from mine. Perhaps in its earlier days it was a close-knit community, with grandmothers sitting on front stoops and children playing ball in the streets. But everyone I saw looked almost . . . cautious. I knew this area had a lot of gang activity; I'd read many stories of drive-by shootings and drug busts on these streets.

AJ lived on the corner of Niagara street in a small brick house that could have been quite pretty with a little better landscaping. I parked my car on the side of his house, careful to lock all of the doors. I saw a group of young black men standing on a corner and gulped, walking up to his doorstep in quick steps. I suppose my suspicions were somewhat irrational, but I did feel better once someone'd let me into the house.

It took a few minutes for someone to come to the door. Finally the door opened and a tall, heavy-set man with bloodshot eyes stood in front of me.

"Hi—" I said, feeling foolish. "I'm here to see AJ—"

"Well come on in, pretty lady!" He moved aside and I stepped into a small living room. "I'm AJ's pop!"

I shook his hand. "It's nice to meet you."

"AJ!" he shouted. "There's a pretty lady here for you!"

I felt even more foolish.

When there came no reply, the man turned to me. "He in his room. You can go on back, first door on the left there."

I nodded and walked down a short hall and stood in front of a closed door, hearing loud rap music coming from inside. I knocked but there was no answer. So I turned the doorknob.

"Get the hell away from my door!" I heard him shout from inside. I heard some other voices inside as well. I rolled my eyes and opened the door anyway.

AJ was sitting on the floor with three other black guys from the football team. When I stepped into the room they all turned and looked at me. One of them looked me up and down and whistled. I rolled my eyes.

AJ looked surprised. "Oh, it's you!"

"Who is this!" exclaimed the guy who'd been ogling me.

"That's Ruthie," AJ said, going to turn down his stereo.

I didn't know what to do or say, so I crossed my arms and looked around his room. The room was small, appearing even smaller because the walls were painted black. Album covers and posters of swimsuit-clad girls bedecked the walls and I saw several beer cans on the floor.

"Ruthie, huh!" said the ogler, getting up to walk over to me. He looked me up and down and I could feel my mouth

61

tightening.

"Ruthie, these're my boys Wakeen, Jamil, and Ray," AJ told me.

"Well hello," said the ogler suavely, who I guess was Jamil.

"Hi," I replied. He was still looking at me as if I was wearing a price tag.

AJ grinned sheepishly. "Man, I forgot you was comin over! Me and the fellas was playin cards—"

"Maybe you can finish your game some other time."

AJ rolled his eyes. "Yeah, sure. Y'all get outta here!"

The other two guys got up to leave but that Jamil guy kept standing there.

Finally, I grew so annoyed that I turned to him and said, "What!"

He shook his head with a half smile on his face, looking at me as if he was the greatest thing on earth and I should appreciate the fact that he was talking to me. "You have got to give me your phone number!"

"It's 1-800-Get-Lost!"

AJ grinned. Jamil looked surprised, then embarrassed, then angry. "Oh, so you a snob!" he muttered.

I didn't answer. He turned around and stormed out.

Now AJ laughed. "Man, that was cold!"

"I refuse to be treated like a piece of merchandise!"

AJ nodded, still grinning. "I see. Wanna beer?"

"No," I told him and went to sit on a chair. He shrugged and opened one for himself.

I took out my chemistry notebook. "Okay, let's get started. Where's your book?"

AJ looked through his duffle bag. "Oh man. . .I left it at school!"

I rolled my eyes. "You knew we'd be working on chemistry tonight!"

He shrugged. "Like I said, I forgot."

I sighed, closing my book. "This did me a lot of good. You know, I missed my aerobics class so I could come help you!"

"What, do you want me to pay you for your time or something?" he snapped. "I said I forgot!"

"Well your irresponsibility shouldn't come at the expense of others!"

He rolled his eyes.

"You're just too used to having everyone bow down to you!" I muttered.

"And you're too stuck-up for your own good!" he mumbled, finishing off his beer.

I shook my head in disgust. "So what now?"

He shrugged. "Do whatever you want."

I gathered my books. "Well if you left your stuff at school, there isn't much we can do."

He didn't answer.

There was a knock on his door. "Get the hell away from my door!" AJ yelled.

"It's Anthony!" came a child's voice. The door opened and in ran a little boy who was a miniature copy of AJ, down to the same flattop haircut. The boy stopped and looked at me with large eyes. "Who this?"

"This is Ruthie," AJ said. "Ruthie, this is my brother Anthony."

I smiled at him. "Hi!"

The little boy looked confused. "But I thought Erika was your girlfriend!"

AJ threw back his head and laughed. "Erika is my girlfriend. Ruthie's a girl I know from school."

The little boy looked at me. "Is she your girlfriend, too?"

I tried not to laugh.

"Nah," AJ told him.

Anthony turned to me. "So if you ain't his girlfriend, what you doing here?"

"I was supposed to help him with his schoolwork," I replied.

"His girlfriend never do that!" declared Anthony. "She usually come in here and take her clothes off!"

My eyes widened and I looked at AJ. He looked embarrassed. "Anthony, you gonna die!" He picked up his brother and held him upside down.

Anthony giggled. "She do! I know cuz one day there was girl's underwear in here! Hey, put me down!"

AJ set him down on the floor and gave him a little shove. "Get outta here, kid!"

"I wanna go to McDonalds!"

"Later! Out!"

Anthony pouted and stomped out of the room. Now I laughed. AJ grinned also.

"How old is he?" I asked.

"Six. Don't be listenin to him!"

I smiled. "I don't know. Children are pretty honest."

AJ looked embarrassed.

"I suppose I should get going. Maybe I'll help you sometime when you remember your books!"

"Yeah sure," AJ muttered. "I guess I should walk you out to your car."

"I'd appreciate it," I said. Without a word, he led me out of his room and walked me out to my car. I felt much safer, especially now that it was dark outside.

"See ya tomorrow," he said, shutting my car door for me.

I nodded. "Goodbye."

I turned on my lights and headed home, feeling better once I reached the safety of my own neighborhood.

# PART II

# AJ

Everybody's waiting for me to decide where I want to go to college and I mean everybody! People at school I don't even know've been coming up to me, asking me where I'm gonna go and stuff. And people from the newspapers and TV and all the college recruiters've been coming to my house every day for the past week. Anthony really liked the TV cameras. One of the camerapeople even taped him goofing around with me cuz he's so cute. There's even been articles in the paper about me every day. Big ones, with pictures and headlines like Centennial Star Has Yet To Make Up His Mind and Major Division I Colleges Flock For The Attention Of Star Defender AJ Johnson. I didn't verbally commit with anybody like Kevin and Wakeen did but now, two days before signing day, I figured I better make up my mind pretty quick.

Just to see what she'd say, I thought I'd ask Ruthie about it in chemistry. But she brought it up first. We was doing a lab when she asked, "So how does it feel, being famous?"

I grinned. "Pretty good. There's all these people I don't know asking me about college and football and stuff." I didn't tell her the girls was starting to hang on me like never before. Especially the white girls. Erika was getting pretty pissed off.

She nodded.

"Hey Ruthie, where you think I should sign?"

She shrugged. "It's not my decision."

"But I want your opinion."

"Why?"

I shrugged, grinning. "Why not?"

"Where are you considering?"

"CU, Florida State, Michigan, Southern Cal, and Auburn."

"Wherever you go you'll be treated like a god—" Ruthie sounded pissed off. "So you basically have to decide what part of the country you want to be in."

"You sound pissed off."

She shrugged. "It's just ironic how some people have to work their butts off to get into college while for others it's so easy."

"And it's my fault?"

"No, it's not your fault. I just think it's...ironic."

Ironic? Whatever. "Where do you wanna go to college?"

"Stanford."

I whistled. "Man, that's tough!"

She shrugged. "You really want my advice?"

I grinned. "Yeah, why not?"

"What do you want to do in college?"

"Play football."

She rolled her eyes. "Besides that!"

"I dunno. I'll just go to the pros."

She looked at me in a weird way. "You think you're going

to make it to the pros?''

"Yeah, why not?"

She looked at me like I was stupid. "Only one in a thousand college players makes it to the pros!"

"But I'm good!"

"So's everybody else."

I rolled my eyes starting to get mad.

"I don't mean to rain on your parade but this is real life. I'm just saying you need to have a back-up plan, in case you don't make the pros."

I didn't say nothing.

"Are you mad because I'm telling you the truth?"

I sighed, annoyed. "Why you always so...righteous?"

"Somebody has to take your head out of the clouds."

"It don't gotta be you!"

"If you didn't want my opinion you shouldn't have asked for it." She sounded all prim and proper.

I shook my head. "Forget you!"

Now Ruthie's eyes widened. "Oh, I almost forgot!"

"What," I muttered, still mad.

"Guess who I'm tutoring, starting next week?"

I shrugged. "Why should I care?"

"Anthony Johnson, first grader at Carver Elementary."

I looked at her, surprised. "Anthony?"

She nodded. "We tutor elementary kids in National Honor Society. Anthony's name was on the list so I picked him."

"Why'd you pick Anthony?"

She shrugged. "I recognized the name. Why not?"

I shook my head. Now she'd be trying to put them righteous ideas in Anthony's head! "Why he need a tutor anyway?"

"I think he needs help with his reading comprehension."

I rolled my eyes. "Yeah, I guess you could help him, Miss Know-it-all!"

She shrugged. "Help me finish this problem."

I just looked at her. Couldn't she tell I was pissed off at her?

"Come on!"

"Let me tell you, you ain't my favorite person in the world right now!"

"So!"

Man, I couldn't wait for this period to be over so I could get away from her! When the bell rang I got out of that room as quick as I could.

"Yo AJ!"

I turned and looked down the hall, seeing Ronell Woods, this thug who hang with my brother and the Comptons. He ran to catch up with me. "So I hear all them college's scopin you out! Where you gonna go, man?"

"I dunno yet."

"You gonna go to Texas with Kevin?"

"No."

"Man, you know where you should go? Miami! Lotsa women in Miami!"

"I said I don't know yet!"

"Or Notre Dame. Nah, that's a stiff-assed Catholic school—"

I rolled my eyes. Ronell was really starting to piss me off.

"Man, you shoulda seen the scrap your bro was in last night!" said Ronell, flying up in my face. "This white dude in the movie theater started talkin shit and Franco haul off and knock him out! You shoulda—"

"I gotta get going, man," I tell him and go to my locker. I don't give a shit what my brother do.

Ronell was right behind me. "Man, I got myself a twelve gage yesterday after that MG—"

I got so sick of him I turned around and yelled "GET OUTTA MY FACE YOU BLACK-ASS FOOL!"

Now Ronell copped an attitude. "What's your problem, man!" He threw down his books. "What, Erika ain't givin you enough?"

I rolled my eyes cuz I knew he was just trying to start up shit with me for attention. "You know I'll kick your ass in a minute so don't even try it!"

"Kick my ass!" Ronell said all loud so people would stop and look at us. "Kick my ass! I'll kick your ass you stuck-up high jumpin son of a bitch!"

I walked away before he pissed me off some more and we really did start scrapping. I wasn't in the mood for his shit.

# RONELL

AJ walk away and I stand there feelin stupid cuz there's all these people lookin at me. "What you lookin at!" I yell especially at all them stupid white people who start lookin scared and run away. I pick up my books.

I don't wanna go to choir so I say to hell with it and go over to City Park. City Park's right across the street from the school where all the brothers be hangin out and shit.

Franco there with some more of our set, the Compton Posse. He sittin under a tree smokin on a pipe. The cops come here all the time cuz they don't like us niggers but Franco, he don't give a shit. He smooth.

"Man, you need to kick your brother's ass!" I tell Franco. He lean up against the tree and laugh. "What's he doing?"

"Startin up shit with me. I shoulda kicked his ass myself!"

Franco don't say nothin and hit the pipe again. One of my homies is smokin a joint so I go smoke on it too. I figure then I'll head over to my corner on Vine and Twenty-fourth

72

and start clockin. I got myself a regular set of junkies who come every day to buy shit from me. White, black, Mexican, business suits, bums, you name it. And one of these days I'm gonna be pullin in as much as Franco. But I get good and high before I head on over my corner. You gotta be high to run this shit.

# AJ

Ten o'clock Valentine's Day I signed my letter of intent with Florida State University. Everyone made a big deal about it. The newspaper and TV people was there. So was my recruiter, Coach and Mr. Ferris. Kevin was signing with Texas and Wakeen and Doug with Colorado and their recruiters was there too. The four of us sat at a table in the spotlight. Man, it was great! Then Erika ran over to me and gave me a big hug and kiss. The newspapers got a picture of us.

"I'm so proud of you AJ!" she squealed, jumping up and down. "You'll be this big football star and I'll be your wife—"

I laughed. "Wife!"

"Y'know, we should get married, go out to Florida together—"

"Get outta here!" I said, still laughing.

"I'm takin you out to dinner tonight to celebrate! Oh look,

74

the television guy wanna talk to me!"

I laughed, watching her run over to the TV guy. I looked over at Coach, who looked as happy as could be. He was making this big speech to the reporters about how excited he was and blah, blah, blah. I looked over at Kevin, who was looking over his letter and grinning like a fool. So was Doug and Wakeen. Then I looked over at Mr. Ferris, who was just standing there like he was at a board meeting or something. I wanted to yell "in your face!" for all the times he said shit to me.

After Coach finished his speech the newspeople turned to Ferris. "And what do you have to say about your four exciting college prospects?" asked some ditso newslady.

He cleared his throat. "I wish them the best of luck, and I hope they perform just as well in the classroom as they do on the football field."

Kevin rolled his eyes. I chuckled.

The newslady turned to me. "So how are you feeling right now, signing with a major Division I school, named an All-America—"

"Well, I'm like feeling really good, you know," I said. "I'm really looking forward to, you know, going to college and playing at Florida State. They got a great football program, you know, and I hope I can, you know, contribute."

She grinned. "We all wish you the best of luck!" Then she turned to Doug.

All the activity died down around twelve and the four of us went into the locker room to get ready for gym class.

"WHOOOOEEE!" Kevin yelled out.

"That's what it's gonna be like in college!" shouted Wakeen, doing a front flip over the bench. "Everyone droppin at our feet!"

Doug got in on the act, jumping over a bench. "Man, I

75

wanna go right now!'' We was all hollering and making noise.

"Man, let's skip the rest of the day!'' said Kevin. "Drink some beers and celebrate! To the Dream, the Vike, the Bullet and the Master!''

Doug jabbed him in the ribs. "Last and least!''

Kevin punched him back. "No way, man!''

"We celebratin at my house!'' I told them. "So let's get movin!'' Wakeen did another flip as we went running out of the locker room and down the hallway. Everyone was stopping and looking at us like we was gods. We all jumped into Kevin's truck and he did ninety all the way to my house. Then we went to my room, where I took two cases of beer from under my bed.

Kevin jumped onto my bed and sighed, opening his beer. "Man, nothin like a brewski on a cold afternoon!''

Wakeen shook his head. "Man, him and that white talk!''

"Shut up!'' Kevin said, then downed his beer. He let out a loud belch and leaned against the wall. "Man, this is the life!''

I saw Doug staring into space. "Yo Vike, whassup?'' I asked him.

He shrugged. "I was just thinkin, man—''

Wakeen finished his beer and yelled, "So you can think!''

"Shut up!'' Doug said and chuckled. "Yeah, I was thinkin about all us. The fellas.''

Kevin started on his second beer. "What about us, man?''

"We been hangin together a long time! Since freshman year!''

"Shoot, it's been longer than that,'' Wakeen said softly. "We been playin ball together since little leagues.''

I laughed. "And going out drinkin and fightin on weekends—''

Doug shook his head. "But this is it, man! I mean, what

76

happens after this year?''

We all got quiet. I guess none of us had ever really thought about that.

Kevin shrugged. ''I dunno, man—''

I looked at Kevin, Doug, and Wakeen, remembering all the crap we been through together. How they was there for me when Mom died, how we was there for Kevin when his folks got divorced. I remember, he got so fed up with his folks' shit he hung around at my house for three months.

Wakeen got a thoughtful look on his face as he popped open another beer. ''Are y'all ever afraid of things...changing?''

Nobody said nothing.

''I am,'' Wakeen said. ''I wanna go to college and shit but man, I'm scared, too.''

''Me too,'' said Doug.

I didn't say nothing, but so was I.

Kevin reached for another beer, then threw up his arms. ''We're gonna start soundin like a bunch of girls if we don't stop this shit! What's with you guys? Right now we're still number one and that's what matters! Right now! Not next year!''

Doug held up his beer. ''To us, man!''

''To us,'' I repeated, downing my beer. We sat there drinking and laughing about old times until about three.

Wakeen rolled on his stomach and looked at the clock. ''Man, we gotta go to track today—''

Kevin laughed hysterically. ''Like this? Man, that'd be somethin! We all show up to practice tore up the same day we sign our letters of intent!''

''I ain't drunk!'' Wakeen said, still lying on the floor.

I laughed. ''Man, you is too drunk!'' Wakeen's always been kind of a lightweight.

Anthony came running into my room.

Doug held up his beer to him. "It's the Little Dream!"

Anthony went to slap his hand. "What's happenin man?" Then he turned to Kevin. "It's the Master!"

I laughed. Anthony's pretty smooth.

Now he looked down at Wakeen. "What's wrong with him?"

Doug laughed. "He's drunk!"

Anthony giggled.

Now I picked him up. "What you doing, little guy?"

Anthony squealed. "Nothin! Put me down!"

I held him over my head. "No way!"

Anthony kicked and bucked but he was still giggling. I put him down and started tickling him. The kid was ticklish like nobody I ever seen! He was hollering and laughing.

The fellas was laughing, too. "Give the boy a beer!" cried Kevin.

"No way!"

Anthony looked at me with them big owl eyes of his. "Can I have beer next year?"

"No!" I put him in a neck lock and scruffed his head.

Anthony pulled out and shook his head. "Geez!" he said. "Guess what! You guys was on TV today!"

"How'd you know?" asked Doug.

"Cuz I made my class watch it! We was supposed to be watchin some dumb show but I told my teacher we had to watch cuz AJ's my brother! And you know what they said?"

"What?"

"My class asked if they could have your autographs! But I told them you had to check with me first!"

I looked at Anthony and grinned.

He threw his arms around my neck. "You know what!"

I patted him on the head. "What, kid."

"You're the best big brother I ever had!"

I hugged him back. "You're the best little brother I ever

78

had!''

He looked at me crazily. "Silly! I'm the only little brother you got!"

I tickled him again and he giggled.

"Aw, ain't that cute!" Doug said but he was only half-kidding. It was one of those moments you wish you could hold onto forever, you know?

I heard the doorbell ring.

"I'll get it!" Anthony went running from the room.

Kevin looked after him. "Man, he's a good little kid."

I grinned. There wasn't no one else like him. Anthony was special.

He stuck his head in my door, grinning. "Guess who's here!"

Now Erika came walking into my room. All the fellas started whistling. She flipped them off and came over to give me a big kiss.

"Go AJ!" yelled Kevin.

Erika laughed. "Oh shut up, I know you get yours!"

Kevin grinned. "You know it!"

Anthony made a face. "Oh yuck!"

"Then get out!" I told him.

"Is she gonna take her clothes off?"

The fellas burst out laughing. Erika looked surprised. "What?"

"Get outta here!" I said. Anthony went running out.

Erika shook her head. "Where do he get stuff like that?"

I shrugged, touching her face.

"I love you, AJ," she said softly.

Kevin sighed dramatically. "Oh, how sweet!"

I laughed. "Get outta here!"

Doug stood up. "Yeah, we better! Get up Wakeen, we're leavin!"

They helped Wakeen up and shut the door behind them.

I turned to Erika and grinned at her. "Didn't you say you wanted to take the Dream out to dinner to celebrate?"

Erika grinned back, puttin her arms around me. "Yeah, but not now. Later."

I chuckled. "Later?"

"Much later—" she sighed, unbuttoning my shirt. I lay back and stared at the ceiling. Man, this was the life!

# RUTHIE

My life was driving me crazy! I had a major history project due Monday, I had to start tutoring after school, plus my mother needed me to teach her Sunday School class this week so I had to make up a lesson plan. We had a free day Friday in student council but I was so burnt-out I couldn't get anything done. So I just sat with Andrea and Christian and talked.

"Hey Ruthie, this pass just came for you," said one of the freshman officers about halfway though the class. "They want you in the office."

"Uh-oh!" singsonged Andrea.

Christian whistled. "Go on down, you troublemaker!"

"Yeah, sure," I said wryly. I took my notice and left the room. I was wanted in the principal's office immediately. I wondered what he wanted. I hoped he didn't want me to do anything for him. I was swamped enough as it was.

I went into the main office and one of the secretaries looked up at me and smiled. "Hi Ruthie. Mr. Ferris is expecting you."

I nodded and went back to his office. There were a few sullen-looking black guys sitting outside the door, probably in trouble for something or another. One of them whistled as I passed, adding some other comments I won't repeat. I rolled my eyes.

Mr. Ferris was sitting at his desk when I entered the room. "Excuse me," I said to get his attention. "You called for me?"

He looked up and smiled. "Yes, I did!" He stood up and shook my hand. "How are you today?"

"Fine," I said, sitting down.

He rummaged through some papers on his desk. "I have some good news for you."

"What?"

He picked up a letter and began to read. "To Miss Ruthie Bates. You have been selected as a finalist in the 1990 National Achievement Scholarship for Outstanding Negro Students competition."

"I'm a finalist?" I exclaimed.

He handed me the letter. "Yes, you are."

I skimmed it quickly. "This is great!"

Mr. Ferris was smiling. "Congratulations. It always makes me so proud when our black students do well."

"Wow, this is wonderful!" The scholarship competition is run by the same people who run the National Merit competition, and being a selected as a finalist meant a good chance for a college scholarship. You can bet my parents would be thrilled.

"Would you like to call your parents and tell them the good news?" he asked, offering me the phone.

I called Mom first, who put me on hold while she told all of her co-workers. She's always bragging about me to them.

Dad was thrilled, too. That made me even more happy. My father's one of those ultra-dedicated, ultra-smart people whose very presence is enough to motivate anybody. So any time I can make him feel proud of me is extra special.

"I take it the folks are proud," said Mr. Ferris after I finished talking to my father.

I smiled and nodded. "They've always put so much importance on education. They're glad to see it paying off."

Mr. Ferris nodded. "That's good. Real good. I wish more of our youngsters would place a greater value on education."

"I was raised on it. Not everyone is."

Mr. Ferris shook his head. "No, and it's a shame to see so many minds going to waste. We need more kids like you, Ruthie. Kids who can maybe influence some of the unlucky ones. I know I can't think of anything more I can do—"

"By now it's too late," I said softly.

He nodded slowly. "But kids like you are our only hope—"

I took a deep breath, feeling uncomfortable. I kept hearing this message from Mr. Ferris, my parents, adults in general, that it's up to me and kids like me to change everything. But what can I do? What am I supposed to do? Especially knowing the average black person at this school wouldn't give me the time of day if I asked.

"Well congratulations again," said Mr. Ferris. "I'll write you a pass back to class."

"Thanks," I said, but my mind was still on what he'd said. Was it really up to people like me to turn things around? I wished there was someone I could talk to about it. Andrea and Christian wouldn't understand. It must be so much easier, being white. White people don't have to deal with half of the things black people have to deal with. I don't wish I was white or anything. I just wish there were more things for black people to be proud of.

Second hour had long since started so I went to chemistry and took my seat in front of AJ. He'd been acting relatively cold toward me lately. Probably because I refused to be one of his worshippers.

"Where you been?" he whispered as I sat down.

"I just found out I made National Achievement finalist."

"Ain't we movin up in the world!"

I couldn't tell if he was being sarcastic so I turned to listen to the lecture. But Mr. Ferris's statements were still pervading my thoughts. Could I really do something to influence someone else? Could I?

That question was still on my mind when I went to Carver Elementary school at three o'clock. Every year our Honor Society "adopts" an elementary school and we tutor kids, help grade papers, or just volunteer where needed. This was the first time I'd ever signed up to tutor. I tutor high school kids all the time but I've never tutored a younger person. So I felt somewhat nervous as I entered the building.

At about five after three, a tired-looking teacher and about twenty young children paraded into the cafeteria. I saw AJ's little brother among them. He had the type of face you know will grow handsome as he grows older, with large, deer-shaped eyes. The teacher clapped her hands together. "Children, stay in line!" I heard a few chuckles from my fellow Honor Society members.

The teacher turned to us. "I'm Mrs. Huarez, coordinator of our school's tutoring program. You all know that you'll be working closely with one student for the next two months and you've already been given their names. So why don't we all introduce ourselves and have some cookies and juice."

"Cookies!" cried one snaggle-toothed first grader. The kids all cheered. I then noticed that fifteen of the twenty children were black or hispanic. And I was the only black tutor.

Anthony was standing with a few other little boys. I went over to introduce myself.

"Hi Anthony," I said, smiling. "Remember me?"

His large eyes grew even larger. "Yeah, you was over at my house with AJ! What's your name?"

"Ruthie."

He wrinkled his nose. "Ruthie! That's a stupid name!"

"Hey, that wasn't very nice."

He shrugged. "Well it is!"

I put on a serious face. "But you hurt my feelings. People's feelings get hurt when you say things like that."

He sombered and hung his head. "I'm sorry."

I smiled and put a hand on his shoulder. "It's okay."

I stood up and he looked up at me. "So you gonna be my tutor?"

"Yes."

Anthony put his hands in his pockets. "AJ talk about you!"

I smiled again. "What did he say?"

"He say you a priss!"

I laughed. "Oh did he?"

"Yeah!"

"Do you think I'm a priss?"

He threw up his hands. "I dunno! I just met you!"

I laughed. "How old are you, Anthony?"

"Six!"

"I hear you're having a little trouble with your reading."

Now his little face wore a scowl. "I ain't havin no trouble!"

"Let's discuss it over juice and cookies," I suggested.

"Okay!" He ran to the refreshment table and took six cookies.

"That's a lot, don't you think?"

Anthony chomped on a cookie. "So?"

"If you eat all those there won't be enough for everyone

else.''

He sighed and put three back. "You is a priss!"

I shrugged and we sat down. "So how do you like school?''

"I don't like it!" he declared. "School's dumb!"

"Who told you that?''

"AJ!''

"Figures," I muttered, then looked at him. "Anthony, what if I told you school could be fun?''

"I'd know you was lyin'," he replied, then turned to gab with another first grader. I sighed. So he was going to be a challenge. I wasn't sure how up to a challenge I was. "Anthony!" He turned to look at me.

"Do you like to read?''

"Nope!''

"Why not?''

"Cuz—''

"What do you like to do, Anthony?''

"Play!''

"Play what?''

He thought for a moment. "Lotsa stuff! Nintendo, Teenage Mutant Ninja Turtles, GI Joe—" He rattled off some more things. I nodded slowly, a wonderful idea coming to my head. I could help Anthony with his reading. And I knew exactly how I'd do it.

# ERIKA

I go to choir Monday morning and find out I got the lead in the school musical *Porgy And Bess*. "All right, huh!" Ronell come up behind me and put his arms around me. I turn around and smile. Even stupid Ronell can't piss me off today.

"All right!" I say and hug him. He got Porgy, opposite me. I knew he would, he the best in the choir.

Imani and Kelli come runnin up to me. "All right Erika, you got Bess!" Imani scream and hug me. All the people in the choir crowd around me and Ronell, congratulatin us and huggin us and stuff.

"This is gonna be the best musical this school ever seen!" I been dreamin about gettin the lead in the musical ever since I was a freshman. Even Mom is gonna be impressed!

"Oh shit—" say Kelli.

I look at her. "What?"

She smirk. "Guess who got Bess opposite you?"

I shrug. I hadn't looked at the cast list really. I just saw my own name and got happy. Now I look at the cast list and see Shanice Taylor's name next to mine. Black Cow bitch. My happiness fizzle out real quick.

Ronell chuckle. "Man, this musical's gonna be fun! The two girl leads beatin each other up—"

"Shut up!" The bell ring and everyone go into the room. I stand outside by myself, still starin at the cast list. And I get this nervous, jittery feelin in my stomach. I got the lead. I'm gonna be the one everyone's clappin for. I'm gonna do it. I worked my ass off for the audition, practicin with the videotape, singin in front of the mirror. I deserve it, really. I earned it.

I'm still standin there when the Black Cows come walkin up to the door, late as usual. I feel my jaw tighten but I don't turn around or say nothin.

Shanice stand next to me and look at the list. When she see her name next to mine she let out a loud whoop and start huggin her girls. "I got the lead!" she keep sayin over and over. I roll my eyes, feelin jealous. I don't wanna share the glory with nobody!

Finally one of her girls Patrice say, "Look who you sharin the lead with!"

Now all them Black Cows start glarin at me. I glare back at all them. Shanice look me up and down like I'm dirt.

"Girl, they gonna have to color you in or somethin!" Patrice say and start laughin.

"Shut up, black bitch," I mutter and go into the room. The choir is sittin around doing nothin, as usual. When Shanice come in everyone crowd around her, congratulatin her and all that. I go sit down and Imani and Kelli sit down with me.

"What she say to you?" ask Imani.

I shake my head, frownin. "We'll see who the best!"

Kelli roll her eyes. "Girl, she don't hold a candle to you!"

I don't say nothin cuz I know she do hold a candle to me. That girl can sing like you wouldn't believe. As much as I don't want to say it, I know she'll be a good Bess. Was she right? Am I too light to be a good Bess? That's been in the back of my mind since auditions Friday. I was worried I wouldn't get the lead cuz I'm too light. Our choir director Mr. Pauly is charcoal black and I know he got a likin for dark folk. He love Shanice to death. I can barely get a good word out of him even though I'm always doing shit for him.

"Whassup, Erika?" say Imani. "You ain't supposed to be sad, girl! You got the lead in the musical!"

I look and see Mr. Pauly over talkin with Shanice about the musical. He'll probably give her opening night. I know he will. I narrow my eyes at her. Black cow bitch.

After all the commotion die down we all take out seats and warm up. I sing first soprano so I sit in front. We got a pretty big concert choir, over a hundred kids. Our school might be only twenty-five percent black but the choir about eighty percent. That's why we always do black musicals, like *The Wiz* and *Porgy And Bess*. But Centennial musicals is always good.

I watch Shanice as we warm up. She sit a few seats down from me cuz she sing second soprano. I can hear her voice over everybody's. She sing real loud. But I'm gonna be a better Bess than her. I'm gonna make Mr. Pauly notice me, show him this half-breed can sing just as good any dark sister. I will.

# AJ

There was a blue Ford Escort parked in front of my house when Ray dropped me off Monday after track. I was confused cuz none of the fellas drive Ford Escorts. And Franco's boys drive stuff like Mercedes. I walked in the house and saw Ruthie and Anthony sitting on the couch. They was sitting close, sharing a book in their laps. Anthony had this real serious look on his face, like he was concentrating hard. He was reading to her. Every once in a while Ruthie would say something in a soft voice that only he could hear. And Anthony would grin and start reading again.

I stood there watching them, getting this strange feeling in my chest. For a minute I couldn't tell what it was. But as I watched them I started thinking about Mom, something I hadn't done in a long time. I gulped, feeling something hard in my throat.

Now Ruthie looked up and saw me. "AJ!"

Anthony got up and threw his arms around my legs. "Yo

AJ!''

I patted his head. "Whassup, kid?"

Anthony held up a book. "Look what Ruthie got me!"

I took it from him and read the cover. "The Adventures of the Teenage Mutant Ninja Turtles?"

Anthony took it from me, looking serious. "But she said she'd only let me have it if I read it to her. So I'm readin it to her!"

Now I looked at Ruthie, who was still sitting on the couch all prim and proper. And I got this really cold feeling. "Oh yeah?"

"Yeah!" Anthony's eyes was wide and excited-looking.

"Go fix yourself a snack or somethin," I told him, my eyes still on Ruthie.

"Ruthie gonna take me out for ice cream after we're done readin!" Anthony told me.

I narrowed me eyes at Ruthie. "No she ain't."

Anthony pouted. "Why not?"

"Cuz I said so! Go outside and play or somethin!"

Anthony shook his head. "I'm supposed to be readin! Why can't I get ice cream with Ruthie? I wanna go get ice cream with Ruthie!"

"I'm gonna kick your little black ass if you don't shut up!"

Anthony glared at me. "Jerk!" He ran to his room and slammed the door.

Now I turned to look at Ruthie again. She had this annoyed look on her face. "Was all that really necessary?"

"What's with this?" I snapped, holding up the book. "What you doing, buyin him stuff and takin him out?"

She didn't answer me. Just looked straight into my eyes.

"What, you tryin to give him charity?"

Ruthie rolled her eyes. That made me madder. I stood there, crossing my arms and glaring at her. I wanted her to get mad and start yelling back at me. I wanted to see Little

Miss Perfect swear and come down off her high horse.

"You doing your duty to the little people, is that it? Well, I don't want you messin with Anthony! So you can take your books and ice cream and shove 'em up your ass!"

Now she stood up, still looking me in the eyes. I thought she'd start yelling back but she just stood there. I was getting uncomfortable. But I wasn't gonna let her stare me down so I stared right back.

Finally Ruthie spoke. "Why do you have so much pride, AJ?"

I didn't know what she was getting at but I wasn't gonna let down my guard. "What you talkin about?"

"You know what I'm talking about. Why does everything have to be an insult to your pride? You feel like I'm threatening you, don't you!" She kept looking me in the eyes. "I don't know why, but you do, don't you."

"What? That's a crock of shit!"

"Is it?"

I didn't know what to say to that so I just said "Yeah!"

She looked at me like she knew otherwise. Man, I wanted to ring that little clean neck of hers!

"For your information, Anthony needs help with his reading," Ruthie said evenly. "Your parents never come to his teacher conferences so his teacher referred him to our program."

"Yeah, so?" I muttered.

Her voice grew soft. "All he needs is someone to spend some extra time with him. He's a great kid, but he's also in trouble."

"Trouble?"

"If he doesn't get help now, he'll be put in remedial classes where he'll never be able to challenge himself. Kids his age need to be taught to believe in themselves, because if they don't learn now they might never learn!"

I rolled my eyes. "And you supposed to help him do that?"

"Yes! That's why I bought him the book. He told me he likes the Teenage Mutant Ninja Turtles, so I figured he'd be most responsive to something he likes!"

I didn't say nothing.

"Most of the times I'll get his books from the library," she went on. "And I wanted to take him out for ice cream to reward him for doing well. Don't you see? I'm starting to get him to trust me! Well, until you came along and messed everything up!"

I stared at the ground so she couldn't see my face. I was feeling pretty stupid. It seemed like she really cared about Anthony. But I wasn't sure if I wanted her to. He's my little brother. Not hers.

I looked up and saw her looking at me.

"Hey, why you do that?"

"Do what?"

"Look people in the eye and shit!"

She shrugged. "I guess it's a habit."

"It's a bad habit," I muttered.

Right then the door opened and in walked Franco. He looked Ruthie up and down. "Who this?"

"This's Ruthie. She go to my school," I muttered. "Ruthie, this's my brother Franco."

She looked him in the eye, too. "Hi."

He raised his eyebrows. "Hi yourself. What brings you here?"

"She was just fixin to take Anthony out for ice cream," I told him.

Ruthie grinned at me. I didn't grin back.

"Anthony!" I yelled. He ran out of his room and over to slap hands with Franco.

"If it ain't my man Franco!"

"Hey hey, little buddy!" Franco picked him up and swung

him around. I looked at Ruthie and saw her looking from me to Franco to Anthony in a weird way.

"You and Ruthie's going out for ice cream," I told him.

Anthony jumped up and down. "All right! Let's go!" He took Ruthie's hand and dragged her out of the house.

Franco looked after her. "So where'd you find her?"

"She my science partner," I muttered.

Franco nodded slowly and whistled. "Whatever happened to that one light-skinned girl?"

"Erika? She still my girl."

"So what's with this chick? She on the side or somethin?"

"No!" I didn't wanna be in the house with him so I went over to Ray's and hung out there.

# RUTHIE

If I had a hit-list, AJ Johnson would certainly be on top of it! For the past two weeks he's made my life hell! Well chemistry at least. He never helped me with any of the labwork and always found something to criticize about me; my hair, my clothes, my speech, you name it! And he grew especially cold whenever I tutored Anthony. Anthony asked me about it one Tuesday early in March. We were at the library, reading *Green Eggs And Ham* when he looked up at me and asked, "Why AJ so mean to you?"

I took a deep breath, surprised that he'd asked. "I don't think he likes me very much."

Anthony looked confused. "Why not? I like you!"

I smiled. "I like you, too."

"He say you a priss and a wannabe—"

"He says," I corrected him.

He rolled his eyes. "He says! Why you talk so proper?"

I smiled again. "Do you want me to speak improperly?"

He giggled. "No!"

I picked up the book. "Let's see what happens to Sam-I-am."

"Why he keep tryin to feed that guy green eggs and ham?"

"I don't know. Maybe we'll find out in the end."

Anthony shook his head. "I don't want to."

"Why not?"

He pouted. "I wanna read Teenage Mutant Ninja Turtles again!"

I groaned. We'd read that twice already. "Maybe we'll read it again after we finish this book."

He sighed, picked up the book, and set it down again. "Ruthie, do you have a mama?"

I was taken aback. "Of course I do."

"What's she like?"

"Well—" I thought for a moment. "She's very loving, warm—"

"Warm?"

"Yes. She's not cold."

Anthony giggled.

"Why do you ask? Don't you have a mom?"

He shook his head, his large eyes solemn.

"Where is she?"

"Dead!"

I looked at him for a moment, surprised at his nonchalance. "When did she die, Anthony?" I asked softly.

"A long time ago."

"Do you remember her?"

Again, he shook his head. "AJ do though. So do Franco."

I nodded slowly. "Do you know how she died, Anthony?"

He nodded.

"How?"

"She killed herself! Franco told me so." Then as quickly as he'd mentioned it, he picked up the book again and began

96

reading as if the conversation had never taken place.

I tried not to show the shock on my face but my mind was in turmoil. I suddenly thought about AJ . . . how distant and cold he was.

"Hey Ruthie!"

I snapped out of my daze and smiled at Anthony. "What? Sorry."

"I'm finished. The guy likes green eggs and ham!"

"Yes, I know."

"So what?" He was looking at me with large, inquiring eyes. I felt an urge to take him into my arms and hug him.

"I think . . . the book's trying to say that sometimes people say they don't like things without giving them a try."

He looked confused. "What?"

"Well, like spinach. Do you like spinach?"

Anthony made a face. "No! Yech!"

"What about kiwi fruit?"

"What's that?"

"It's really good, but it's kind of funny-looking."

"Funny looking?"

"And sometimes people won't taste it because it looks so funny, but once they taste it, they like it!"

Anthony nodded solemnly. "I'll eat kiwi fruit then!"

I laughed. "I'll get you some for next time. C'mon, I'll take you home."

"Can we come back to the library tomorrow?"

I shook my head. "I have some things I have to do tomorrow."

He hung his head. I was so touched that I added, "I'll stop by later in the week, okay?"

He grinned. "Okay!"

I drove him home, listening to his chatter. In just three weeks tutoring him I was already feeling a closeness toward him I never thought I'd feel. And in some strange way I knew he was helping me just as much as I was helping him.

I parked my car in front of his house and saw AJ sitting on the front porch with some of his friends who, as I'd expected, began to talk about me as I walked up.

"I'll see you later, Anthony," I told him.

He gave me a hug. "Okay! I like Green Eggs And Ham!"

I smiled. "I'm glad you do."

I walked him to the door, past AJ and his friends. Anthony ran inside and I turned to walk back to my car self-consciously, feeling several pairs of eyes on my back.

"Hey Ruthie!" AJ called.

I stopped, but didn't turn around.

"What kinda shit'd you put in Anthony's head today? I gotta, like, wash it out and shit—" His friends chuckled.

I turned to look him in the face, suddenly remembering what Anthony'd told me. My eyes lowered to the ground. No wonder . . .

"Hey, what's your problem?"

I looked up to see AJ grinning at me in a very self-satisfied way. He was waiting for me to get mad, I knew it. But I kept seeing Anthony's solemn little face, those large eyes, when he told me about his mother, and I couldn't say a word.

"Hey, I think Miss Cuteness's finally cracked, man!" cried one of his friends.

"Is she gonna cry?"

I ignored them, staring at AJ. He caught my gaze and the self-satisfied expression dissolved from his face. The muscles in his face tensed, as if he knew I knew something about him. The most important secret he kept. Without a word, I turned to walk to my car, feeling AJ's eyes on my back.

AJ seemed restless the next morning in chemistry as well. He was distant and inattentive as we worked on our lab and near the end of our experiment (which I had run by myself), he gripped our two tests tubes so hard they both shattered and our precipitate spilled onto the floor.

"Shit," he muttered.

I sighed. "Don't worry about it. I'll redo it."

"Yeah, Ruthie Bates to the rescue!" he snapped.

"Watch it! I'm the reason you have a B in this class!"

"So I should bow down to you!"

I looked him in the eye. He usually stared back, as if contesting me but today he couldn't even look at me. His eyes shifted all over the room.

"You know, it doesn't feel too good to be used as a scapegoat for other people's problems!"

He looked bored. "Speak English!"

"You know what I'm saying! Something in your life isn't going right and you're taking it out on me!"

Now he glared at me. "Oh am I?"

I threw up my hands. "Maybe I'm an easy scapegoat! I'm different, I don't fit in! That makes me easy to pick on, right?"

"Get outta here—" he muttered.

"I'm serious!"

Now he looked at me, challenging me. "What do I got to be down about? I'm the best football player in this whole goddamn state and I'm about to graduate and get outta this stinkin school—"

I returned his gaze. "You tell me."

"And I especially can't wait to get away from you!"

"Why?"

"Cuz you a pain! And you puttin messed-up ideas in Anthony's head!"

"By getting him to believe in himself?"

AJ rolled his eyes. "Then you got a smart answer for everything!"

"I'm telling the truth! I'm getting tired of your attitude!"

He threw up his hands. "MY attitude!"

"I don't care if you don't like me, I really don't, but you don't have to throw it in my face every day! We still have to work together for the rest of the semester!"

"Let's all take pity on poor Ruthie Bates!"

"God—" I muttered. "I don't know what it is with you, if it's your mom or—" I stopped and put a hand over my mouth.

AJ stared at me in disbelief. Then his mouth tightened and his eyes narrowed to angry slits. I sucked in my breath and opened my mouth, finding myself unable to speak.

AJ took a deep breath, as if he was trying to control himself. "What do you know about that?"

I tried to feign nonchalance. "About what?"

He gripped my shoulders, as if he were about to shake me. I winced from his hard grasp and tried to shake free. "What do you know about my mom?"

"That she committed suicide—" I said feebly. "Anthony told me—"

His mouth grew tighter and his brow furrowed deeper. He let go of me harshly, taking deep breaths. I've never seen him so mad. "I'm gonna kill that little—" he mumbled, adding some more names.

"No! He didn't know he wasn't supposed to tell me!"

"Shut up!"

"Ruthie and AJ!" screeched Mrs. Fleener.

AJ threw me a hateful glare, then threw down his books and stormed out of the room. The entire class stared after him, openmouthed. For a moment I stood where I was, paralyzed.

Then I ran after him. "AJ!" I called, running to catch up with him. I grabbed his arm but he shook me away, storming down the hall.

I jumped in front of him. "You're not going to hurt Anthony, are you? Like I said, he didn't know—"

AJ pushed me aside. "I'm gonna kick his ass—"

Undaunted, I stood before him. "And what's the big deal if I know? I won't tell anybody!" I could practically feel the anger blazing from his eyes. "Want me to kick your ass, too?"

"Would you?" I asked, probably foolishly.

"If you don't leave me alone!"

"Well I'm not going to!" I heard my voice wavering. It probably wasn't a good idea to challenge him, but I couldn't stop myself. We now stood facing each other, staring at each other suspiciously, not saying a word.

"Get the hell outta my way!" he finally shouted.

I stood right where I was, though I could feel myself trembling. He was trying to scare me and to be honest, it was working, but my stubborn pride wouldn't let me retreat. This was one battle of wills I was determined to win.

"I'm really sorry about your mother—"

"Shut up about my mother!"

I took a deep, quivering breath. From the corners of my eye I could see people staring curiously out of classroom doors. I composed myself. "I'm not trying to—"

"Get the hell away from me, bitch!"

I got mad. "So you're trying to make me hate you, is that it?"

His look grew malicious. "Yeah. Hate me!" As if to prove what he'd said, he gave me a hard shove.

I was stunned not so much from the impact of the shove, but by the fact that he'd used physical force at all. Was I foolish in trying to break down the aegis he'd built around himself? Probably so, but now more than ever I couldn't back down.

So I did the only thing I could do. I shoved him back, though my shove probably had no impact on him at all. "So you think pushing me around is going to make me back down?'' I pushed him again, provoking him even more. ''You may be bigger and stronger than me but I'll make it a fair fight! I will!''

He looked me up and down and laughed. ''Get outta here!''

''No! You started this, you finish it! You are really something, you know that? You think that just because you're hurting inside you're perfectly justified in walking over other people's feelings! Who the hell do you think you are?''

''Oh my God, they're gonna fight!'' I heard someone shriek.

''Who the hell you think you are!'' AJ shouted back. ''Why the hell you think you got the right to interfere in my life, huh?''

''I'm not interfering in your life! I'm just saying you can't treat other people like it's their fault things in your life aren't going right! Like Anthony! You better leave him alone!''

''You stay away from my brother!'' he yelled. ''And don't be tellin me what to do!''

''But you better not hurt him just because you're mad!''

His eyes narrowed at me. ''Girl, don't get me mad—''

''I already have you mad! Afraid I'm getting to close to you? That I know more than I should?''

''Shut up!''

''You want me to hate you because you'd rather have me hate you than be close to you, right? Well, I'm not going to hate you!''

The bell rang and the hall grew crowded with students, many of whom stopped to watch our shouting match.

AJ held up a fist, threatening me.

''Omigod he'll kill her!'' shrieked a teacher.

''Somebody stop him—''

Mr. Ferris suddenly ran between us, amid all the commotion. ''What the hell's going on here?''

In his blind anger, AJ pushed Mr. Ferris away from him

and Mr. Ferris went staggering into the crowd.

"AJ!" Now his girlfriend Erika ran to him, looking from me to AJ in surprise and disbelief. But AJ pushed her away also.

Now Mr. Ferris turned to AJ again, eyes blazing. "Boy, you gonna—"

"No!" I said suddenly.

All of the attention turned to me.

I cleared my fault. "It's okay."

"Okay!" shrieked a girl. "He was going to hit you!"

I sighed. "No, he wasn't. He wouldn't have. We were arguing. I started it."

Now everyone's expression turned to surprise. AJ glared at me suspiciously.

"Mr. Ferris, AJ was just reacting to some of the things I'd said. He didn't mean to push you. We'll, um, take our argument outside." I took AJ's hand and dragged him outside, away from the disbelieving crowd.

He shook his head, bewildered.

I stood facing him. "Okay, I saved your neck. Mr. Ferris would've made your life miserable."

"He hates me," AJ muttered.

"I know."

He looked at me, then chuckled. But the chuckle was more of a frustrated laugh. "So I can't get you out of my life?"

"Somehow or another I'm in there at least for now," I said softly. "You won't bother Anthony for telling me, will you?"

He said nothing. He turned to walk away from me.

I ran to catch up with him. "Hey AJ!"

"What!"

"You can kill yourself keeping everything inside, you know. Depression can make you do things you really regret."

"I ain't depressed!"

"Depression is anger turned inward. You're obviously angry."

He rolled his eyes. "Right, Miss Psychiatrist!"

Though he still looked angry, I felt myself softening toward him. "Want to go to my house to talk?"

He glared at me. "You're really somethin, you know that!"

"What do you mean?"

"You piss me off so bad I almost want to kick your ass, then you got the nerve to ask me if I wanna talk?"

I thought for a moment. "What about Bennigans? We could have breakfast. My treat."

He stared at the ground, shaking his head.

"AJ?"

He looked up and grinned, though grudgingly. "Y'know, you really got a way of getting to people!"

"I know."

"And makin 'em wanna ring your neck!"

I laughed. "Let's go."

"Okay, but you ain't treatin!"

"You are?"

"Hell no, I'm treatin myself. You buy your own food!"

I laughed and followed him out to my car.

# AJ

I don't know what was going on with me, why I had all
these weird feelings swimming around in my head. For the
past few weeks I've been feeling kinda miserable. Empty.
Then Ruthie comes along, pushing all my buttons and getting
me upset. I guess I shouldn't have blown up at her like that,
especially since it caused such a commotion. But Ruthie, that
was one brave girl. Any other girl would've went running.
But not Ruthie.

She was driving to Bennigans or somewhere and I sat in
the front seat, not saying nothing. I couldn't even look at
her. She pulled up to the restaurant and we went inside and
sat in a booth. All this time we was silent.

A waitress brought us some menus and I just stared at it,
nothing registering in my head. I wasn't hungry.

Now Ruthie spoke. "Are you going to get anything?"

I shook my head.

"How about a coke?"

"Whatever."

She told the waitress to bring two cokes and sat there looking at me. I knew she was looking at me even though I was staring at the table. I could feel her eyes on me and it was making me damn uncomfortable. She was trying to move in too close. But I sure as hell wasn't gonna let her. Everybody's got secrets they gotta keep, stuff not meant for sharing with nobody.

Now I looked up at her and saw her looking right back at me. "I don't know why you wanted to come here. I don't got nothin to say."

She nodded without a word. I rolled my eyes. So she wasn't taking me serious. That made me mad. "I mean it! Why would I want to say anything to you?"

She shrugged. "Why would you?"

I looked at her suspiciously.

"Anthony's doing really well with his reading," she said. "I can already see a difference."

"So?"

"Since you don't have a mother I assume you fill that role."

I rolled my eyes. "How would you know?"

"I haven't seen your father around much and your older brother looks like he has his own life. So I assume you're the person Anthony's closest to."

I shrugged.

"He really admires you. He always talks about you."

I grinned, thinking about Anthony.

"I'm also correct to assume you feel like a parent to him—"

"Hey, why you such a know-it-all?"

She shrugged. "I take it not many people know about your mother—"

My mouth tightened. "I said I wasn't gonna talk about

that!''

She nodded quickly. "You're right."

I looked at her suspiciously. "Are you tryin to get me to talk?''

''No.''

I shook my head. I'll never understand that girl! Our cokes came and she sipped hers, keeping her eyes on me. And her stare was making me so uncomfortable I had to start talking so she wouldn't see how nervous I was getting.

"I'll bet you got this perfect family, with Mom and Pop and all that—''

She looked thoughtful. "I do have a good family. But no, it's not perfect. Nothing's perfect.''

"That's why you so high and mighty—''

"I'm not high and mighty. But why should I feel guilty about having a good family life?''

"I never said nothin about feelin guilty—''

"No, but you're trying to make me feel that way and I won't. I'm just lucky, I guess.''

"Whatever." She was starting to sound high and mighty again.

"You know, you're a really intriguing person."

She lost me there. "What?''

"Like when you were getting all that attention for football, you were the biggest jerk—''

"What?''

"I mean it. But it didn't really seem like you. You always look like you're trying to cover something up.''

"How would you know?''

"Just by the way you act around certain people. Like Mr. Ferris. You're one of the best football players Centennial's ever seen and yet I can tell he doesn't like you very much. And you and your older brother don't look like you get along, either—''

107

I was getting that nervous feeling again. This girl was moving in way too close. But I sure as hell wasn't gonna show it! So I got mad. "So now you a detective or somethin? Why is my life so important to you?"

"What do you mean?"

I rolled my eyes. "You know what I mean! Why you tryin to mess with my life?"

Now she looked kinda taken aback. "I don't know. A lot of it's circumstantial, I guess. Especially now that I've gotten close to Anthony—"

"Close to Anthony, my ass! You help him read and shit, you ain't his goddamn social worker!"

"If you think I'm trying to weasel into your life for your sake, you're mistaken!"

"Nah, I don't think that! I know you'd rather be off with the white dudes!"

She looked off guard. "What makes you say that?"

"Who is that white dude you always with?" I wanted to grin. I was getting to her.

"Christian? He's a friend of mine!"

I rolled my eyes. "A friend! Don't you wish it was more?" She didn't say nothing.

"That's sick, you know. You can't even stand by your own kind!" She still didn't say nothing. I went on, wanting to piss her off like she'd pissed me off so many times. "What, black folk ain't good enough for you? You wish you was white, don't you!"

I expected her to start yelling back cuz she was looking really mad. Her face was all drawn up and her fists clenched. But then her body relaxed and she stared at the table.

I wanted to laugh. "I'm right, huh!"

Now she looked up at me, her eyes looking strange. "You really think that about me?"

"Hell, look at you! I never see you talkin to black folks!

And you say they don't like you, that's bullshit! They don't like you cuz you don't like them!''

She folded her hands on the table. ''Then I'll be straight with you.''

''What!''

She sighed. ''No, I don't wish I was white. I guess my problem is that I just don't know who I am. And yeah, sometimes I do like Christian more than I should—''

''I knew it!''

She shook her head quickly. ''It's not like you think. But look at the black guys at Centennial! Most of them are thugs, gang members and wanna-be gang members. Why would I want to associate with that? How can I respect someone who can't even respect himself? Then there are the athletes like you, who would be thugs if you weren't so damn talented!''

I sucked in my breath, like she hit me or something.

''What am I supposed to do?'' She raised her voice. ''Sacrefice my standards just so the world can see I have a stupid boyfriend?''

''And what's your standards?''

She shrugged. ''Basically self-respect. That just about covers everything.''

I rolled my eyes. ''Nah, that can't be it. Someone like you's gotta be after looks and money and shit like that—''

''I'd hate myself if I were that shallow,'' she said softly. ''But I can't look at the guys at Centennial with much more than pity.''

''And what about me?''

''I used to look at you like that, too.''

''Used to?''

''Until I saw you with Anthony. You can be a very loving and caring person. It's too bad you aren't like that more often.''

I just looked at her, feeling like a fool cuz I wasn't prepared at all for what she just said. I was getting myself ready for a good all-out fight and she turned the tables completely. I stared at the table. "Get outta here—"

"I mean it. But I guess you can't show vulnerability when you have things to hide, can you."

"Vulnerability?"

She nodded, looking into my eyes.

And I started feeling...weird again. I didn't know what this girl was doing to me but I felt there was an earthquake going on in my head. All these things starting to come back to me. The house... so quiet...the blood—

"AJ?"

I tried to shake the pictures out of my head. "What?"

"I said something that upset you, didn't I."

I sighed, staring at the table:...seeing Anthony crying...just a baby...and Franco...I shut my eyes, trying to shut it out. But it wouldn't leave. And I thought my head just might explode.

Then I heard Ruthie's voice again. "AJ?"

"I didn't talk about it with no one. No one—" I heard myself say. I tried to stop myself but I couldn't. I had to talk. Ruthie didn't say nothing.

"I was a freshman. Anthony, he was only three. One day...it was sometime in October...I came inside and she was in the bathroom—"

Ruthie nodded slowly. "Do you know why she did it?"

I shrugged. "She was always kinda weird, you know? She slept a lot and cried a lot. She had something wrong with her...mentally—"

Ruthie didn't say nothing. She just reached across the table and took my hand. I was surprised she did that, especially after all the mean things I said to her. But she looked like she'd forgot about all that. And I didn't pull my hand away.

110

"After that, I left and didn't come back for two weeks. And Franco...he sorta went nuts, too—"

"It seems like there are a lot of things that haven't been resolved in your life."

I shrugged. "Franco's a dopeman now. He just push and stay high all the time. He run with the Compton Posse. And I try to keep that shit away from Anthony cuz I'm all he got now—"

"It must be hard—"

"I'm afraid Franco's gonna start puttin ideas in his head."

Ruthie smiled. "You said you didn't know what love was."

"What?"

"A long time ago, you asked me about love. You love Anthony, don't you."

I nodded slowly. "More than anybody alive."

"He looks like he'd be an easy little boy to love."

I grinned. "Yeah, he's great, isn't he."

She nodded. I didn't say nothing.

"So was your mom buried or cremated?"

"Buried. She in the Evergreen cemetary."

"Do you visit her a lot?"

I shook my head. "Nah."

"Maybe you should go visit her."

"Why?"

"You might find it helpful."

"I dunno—" I looked down at the table again. This whole talk had really brought me down.

"Do you want to go home now?" she asked softly.

I nodded. I hadn't even touched my coke. She pulled her hand away from mine and to my surprise, I didn't want to let go.

I didn't say nothing as she drove me home. My mind was still a mess. I was mad I'd told her stuff but in a way I was glad, too. That girl really stirred things up in me. And as much as I didn't want to, I was starting to feel like I could trust her.

I didn't even look at her when she dropped me off. I just said thanks and ran up to my front porch. I went straight to my room and got in bed, thinking I could maybe sleep all this off.

When I sat up again it was after five o'clock. I missed track. Oh well. I didn't know what the hell Ruthie did but it'd certainly gotten me down.

"Anthony!" I yelled.

He ran into my room and jumped on my bed. "Whassup, bro!"

"What you been up to?"

"I was readin my book! Ruthie can't take me to the library before tomorrow so I read by myself!"

"Good for you, kid." I guess Ruthie wasn't such a bad influence after all.

"Now I'm gonna go outside and play!"

"Go on out. I just wanted to see if you were here."

He jumped up and left. I grabbed a beer and decided to go out and sit on the porch. I thought about heading over to Ray's or Kevin's but decided I'd stay right here on the porch.

Anthony and his friends were running around in the yard, shooting each other with squirt guns. I decided to join them, roughhouse a bit. They loved it when I played with them. I snuck up behind Anthony.

"Give me that rock you MG!" Anthony screamed.

The other little kid handed him a bag of rocks. "I'm gonna tell my lieutenant and he gonna shoot you!"

I stopped dead in my tracks.

Anthony and this other kid pulled out what looked like bags of dead grass. "Take this weed across the street," Anthony told the kid. "And don't let them MG's shoot you!"

"Okay!" The kid went running across the street.

Now I grabbed Anthony by the shoulders. "What you doing?"

He shrugged. "Playin!"

"Playin?" I picked up a bag of sugar off the ground. "What the hell you playin?"

"Comptons and MG's!" Anthony said proudly. "I get to be Franco!" He giggled. "Stevie gotta be Ronell!"

I shut my eyes, trying not to lose my temper.

"Wanna play with us?"

"Go inside! Now!" I yelled. "All you kids get outta here!"

They left the yard and I marched Anthony inside.

Anthony looked confused. "What's wrong?"

"I don't want you playin that game no more. It's a bad game!"

Anthony shrugged. "It's fun!"

I knelt down so I was eye level with him and put my hands on his shoulders. "Listen kid, gangbangin's bad! It's not fun!"

Anthony rolled his eyes. "You sound like my teacher! She always say 'say no to drugs,' but that's just a bunch of bull!"

"Who told you that?"

"Franco!" Anthony grinned proudly. "And he said I could be just like him someday!"

That hit me like a ton of bricks. "I thought you wanted to be like me."

"I do. Franco too. He even let me run an errand for him!"

"What?"

"I got to take this paper bag down the block to his friend's house and he gave me ten dollars!"

"When?"

"Today!"

113

I shut my eyes for a second, feeling the hate boiling in me. I opened my eyes and looked at Anthony, who was still looking at me like nothing was wrong. "Listen kid, I don't know how to say this, but Franco's bad. Stay away from him!"

"No way, he's my bro!"

"You stay away from him or I'll—" I shouted. Anthony was looking at me with big, scared eyes. I took a deep breath and tried to control myself. "Go spend the night at Stevie's okay? Can you do that?"

Anthony shrugged. "Okay. See ya later!"

I watched him cross the street. When he was gone I threw myself down on the couch and put my head in my hands. I was gonna kill him. Franco wasn't gonna put that shit in Anthony's head! No way! He almost screwed me up and I sure as hell wasn't gonna let him screw up Anthony!

I turned on the TV, trying to clear my head. Franco'd be home tonight, I knew he would. He's been coming around a lot lately. And I was gonna make sure he stayed away from Anthony once and for all!

Franco came swaggering in around seven. I was sitting on the couch waiting for him. When he saw me he said, "Whassup, AJ?"

I stood up and glared at him. He was high, I could tell. He always was. "You let Anthony run for you."

Franco shrugged. "So?"

"Don't you be pullin that shit no more! You stay away from Anthony!"

Franco looked me up and down and laughed. "What the hell you gonna do about it?"

"Kill you," I said, getting myself ready for a fight.

Franco threw back him head and laughed out loud. "Kill me?"

"You ain't fuckin up Anthony like you fucked up

114

yourself!''

Franco grinned. ''So you want him to be a big FOOT-BALL star like you?''

My eyes narrowed at him. ''That's a hell of a lot better than what you are! Cuz you're shit! You're nothin! If you don't OD you gonna die cuz someone kill you and I won't give a shit!''

Franco shrugged again. ''I won't give a shit, neither.''

''But you ain't draggin Anthony down with you! He just a little kid, goddamnit!''

Franco nodded slowly. ''You always been a fool, AJ. Always stickin your ass where it don't belong. What difference does it make if Anthony ran a little errand for me?''

''Cuz I love Anthony!'' I screamed and slammed him against the wall. I started slugging him.

Franco threw me off and came toward me, fists clenched. I kept my eyes on him and we circled each other like two tigers ready to spring. I managed a quick one to his jaw, hearing his head snap sideways. He got me across the cheek, in the stomach, then finally bashed me in the temple, sending me reeling. I think he really was trying to kill me. He slammed me against the wall and then we fell into the coffee table. I managed to pin his arm behind his back.

''Ah, son of a bitch!'' he yelled as I pulled his arm backward. I smacked his head against the wooden table, surprising myself with my strength. But he bucked and I went flying backward into the TV set. My head was throbbing. I touched the side of my head and my hand was covered with blood.

Now Franco stood up slowly, chest heaving, eyes narrowing at me. I backed away from him, keeping my eyes on him.

He lunged for me and we went rolling across the floor.

115

He managed to close his fingers around my throat. I kicked and strugged and gasped, trying to break free. He kept choking me, his hands squeezing tighter and tighter, a fiendish grin on his face. He was really gonna kill me. I was starting to feel light-headed. Who was gonna protect Anthony?

"M-mom—" I choked. "M-mom—"

Franco let go and flew back as if something had hit him. I wheezed and gasped, sucking at the air.

We sat there on the floor, glaring at each other, hating each other. Franco wiped blood from his face, taking deep breaths. Then something in me snapped. I got up and ran for the door, running out of that house and down the street as hard as I could. Only Mom could help me now. Mom was gonna help me now...

# PART III

# RUTHIE

I've always hated the month of March. The sky's locked in a dull gray state between winter and spring and everyone is impatiently waiting for the onset of warm weather and blue skies. This March was especially stagnant for high school seniors because every senior was waiting for April, the Month of Reckoning, when college acceptance and rejection letters would fill mailboxes and when the realization that high school would soon be over finally hits.

That's what was on my mind at graduation speaker tryouts. Because I didn't have a pre-established speaking spot in the graduation ceremony, I was auditioning for one of the other speaking parts. I'm not exactly sure why I felt a need to speak at graduation. I had no idea what I would say. But I had a feeling come June, I will have discovered something meaningful and important to make sense out of this experience called high school.

I thought the tryouts were rather early, for this was only

the second week of March and graduation wasn't for another two and a half months. Nevertheless, I had an interim speech prepared, which I delivered before the panel of teachers acting as judges. Afterward I met up with Andrea and Christian, who were waiting for me outside the auditorium.

"How'd it go?" asked Andrea.

I shrugged. "Fine, I guess."

"You'll get it, I know you will," Christian told me as we walked out to his car. "All the teachers love you."

I shrugged again. "We'll see."

Christian drove us to Poor Richard's, a trendy cafe a few blocks from the school. We went there often because Christian seemed to really like it. We all ordered coffee and sat in our usual corner booth.

"It's so weird to think about graduation," Andrea declared, shaking her head. "This is all starting to hit me now—"

"It's about time," said Christian.

"And prom. That's coming up, too—"

I'd almost forgotten about prom. "When is it, anyway?"

"May fifth. It's still almost two months away, but it's not too early to start thinking about it. Are you going to ask someone, Ruthie?"

"I haven't thought about it."

Andrea turned to Christian. "What about you?"

He only shrugged.

"I suppose I should ask Ted pretty soon. I think I'm going to have my dress made this year. The prom dresses in the stores are so gross! They're all short and tight and covered with sequins!"

I laughed. "I think the designers are trying to make prom dresses more sophisticated."

"But they look silly, not sophisticated!"

Christian laughed. "You girls—"

"Hey, you're going to marry one one of these days so get used to it!" Andrea told him.

He grinned elusively. "Who says I'm going to get married?"

Andrea grinned back. "Face it honey, when it comes time for you to marry you're going to have to fight the girls off!"

He shrugged. "Maybe I'll turn into some impossible asshole so no girl'll want to talk to me."

"You? Never!" I told him. "All the little rich Yale girls'll be falling at your feet."

He laughed uncomfortably. "Yeah, sure."

Andrea shook her head. "It's ironic to think how many guys'd love to be in your shoes—"

He rolled his eyes.

"I mean it! Even though you don't invite female attention, you never lack it!"

"She's right," I told him.

"And how many girls'd love to be in your shoes!" Christian countered. "You're smart, pretty, you too, Ruthie! Everybody loves you guys!"

I couldn't answer to that. Everybody certainly didn't like me.

I happened to look at my watch when I picked up my coffee and saw it was four o'clock. "Oh, shoot!"

"What?" asked Christian.

"I have to pick up Anthony! I forgot all about it!"

They both looked confused. "Anthony?"

"Anthony Johnson, AJ's little brother. I tutor him. I'm supposed to be picking him up now."

Andrea looked at her watch. "Yeah, I need to get going, too."

Christian stood up. "I'll take you guys back to school."

He dropped us off at school, then I rushed to my car and drove to AJ's house. I was ten minutes late.

121

Anthony ran out to my car. "Where you been?"

"I was out with my friends. I'm sorry. Are you ready to go to the library?"

His big eyes lit up and he looked excited. "Yeah!" But then he looked perplexed. "Have you seen AJ around?"

"No. Why?"

Anthony shrugged nonchalantly. "He hasn't come home all week."

I thought for a moment. Come to think of it, I hadn't seen him since we'd talked a week ago. He hadn't been to school at all. I'd been too wrapped up in my own life to notice. "Do you know where he might be?"

Anthony shook his head, unaffected. "He probably at one of the fella's houses!"

I was silent. Was it because of me he left?

"Earth to Ruthie!"

I smiled at him. "Let's get going."

At the library, I couldn't concentrate on Anthony. I kept thinking about AJ, wondering where he could be. He'd told me some pretty personal things, things I know he wished he hadn't have told me. And if I had driven him off, then I needed to find him.

# AJ

I went straight to Ray's and slept off my hurts there. Then I headed over to Evergreen cemetary. All the while I didn't really know what I was doing, why I felt I had to go to the cemetary to talk to Mom.

I guess I should've been scared cuz I was in a dark place full of dead people but it didn't bother me. It didn't take me long to find Mom, even though the only other time I been there was when she was buried. She was in a corner under a tree. There was a small gray stone marking her.

Patricia Todd Johnson

1951-1987

I sat on the grass by the stone. It was weird to think Mom was under the ground, right beneath me. It was kinda scary, too. It took me a second to get up the nerve to actually touch the gravestone. Then I reached out to touch it and saw God wasn't gonna strike me down so I touched it again, running my hand over the engraving.

"Mom?" That word sounded strange coming out of my mouth. I hadn't said it in so long. Then I touched the grass, getting a good feeling inside of me. A peaceful feeling. Cuz I felt like she could be sitting right here next to me. And maybe if I closed my eyes and listened hard, I could hear her whispering to me. It used to be so hard for me to picture her. After she died I sort of blocked her out of my head. But now I could see her real clear, and maybe she could hear me if I talked to her. But I didn't speak out loud. I couldn't. Everything was so quiet, like everyone was asleep or something. So I just thought.

What should I do, Mom? Tell me what to do right for Anthony. I'm all he got, Mom. Don't let him mess up like I almost did. Don't let him be like Franco.

I must've fallen asleep there cuz when I sat up the sun was starting to come up over the horizon. And I felt real . . . peaceful. I left to go back to Ray's to eat and take a shower. I didn't feel like going to school so I went back to the cemetary. I did that every day, all week. I felt like I had a mom again, someone to talk to about stuff. Sometimes I'd just lay there on my back staring at the sky, not even thinking. I was sitting there like that on Thursday with my eyes closed when I heard a voice above me.

"I thought I might find you here."

I opened my eyes and saw Ruthie standing over me. "What you doing here?"

She shrugged. "Making sure you're alive, I guess. Am I disturbing you?"

I shook my head. "Nah—"

She looked around. "This is where you've been all week?"

"Here and at Ray's."

She nodded. "So it's helped, talking with your mother?" She said this real soft.

I just looked at her. Anyone else would think it was weird

for me to be talking to a dead person. But Ruthie, she understood.

She sat down next to me. "What was she like?"

"My mom?" I was kinda surprised. No one ever asked me that before. "Shoot, she was—" I stopped.

"She was?"

"A shitty mom. But she the only mom I got."

"Shitty? All the time?"

"Nah, not all the time. Sometimes. She was real sickly. Kinda mental, too. But she could sing, lord could she sing. She used to hold me and Franco in her lap and sing Revelation 19—"

"Revelation 19?"

"You know, hallelujah, salvation and glory—"

"Yeah, I just didn't know what it was called."

"She almost died havin Anthony. She didn't want him, neither. He was a mistake. She said she could barely keep up with me and Franco. And one day, after she and Dad was in a fight—"

"What happened?"

"They was fightin about Anthony. Somethin about how she didn't think she could take care of him. Too tired or somethin. She wanted her mother to take him in but Dad was callin her lazy and shit. And one day, shoot, Anthony must've been about three . . . she took Dad's shotgun and shot herself in the head."

Ruthie didn't say nothing.

"Franco just about went crazy. He was closest to her. That's why he so messed-up now. I was messed-up too for a while. I was down with the Compton Posse but I never went all the way in cuz of football. I was always high, in fights—"

I expected her to be shocked but she just nodded. Then for some reason, I got mad. "See, I'm just the type of guy

125

you hate. I don't RESPECT myself, I'm a thug, well, now a conceited asshole jock!''

But she just smiled. And it was such a pretty smile that for a second there I thought I was in love.

"You do have respect for yourself," she said softly. "More than you know."

I stared at Mom's gravestone. "I'll bet your closest friends don't know as much about you as you've told me right now."

I shrugged.

"I'm glad you can talk to me."

I was kinda embarrassed. "I guess you not such a bitch after all."

She just laughed.

I looked her in the eyes and saw her looking back at me. We looked at each other for a long time like that. For one crazy second I even thought about pulling her close and. . .but that thought faded real quick.

Now she smiled again, looking shy.

"You got dimples."

She shrugged and nodded.

"I never noticed before."

She shrugged again, but now she looked uncomfortable. Maybe she thought I was coming on to her or something. I shut up real quick cuz I didn't want her to think that. There was no way anyone like her could like anyone like me.

"Hey, I invited Anthony over for dinner and wondered if you wanted to come, too."

"Tonight?"

"Yeah, why not?"

I was surprised. "Uh. . .I guess so—"

She grinned. "Great! Come on, let's go." I got up and followed her to her car. "Why'd you invite Anthony over for dinner?"

She shrugged. "Why not? I've told my parents all about

126

him and they want to meet him. And I'm sure they'd love to meet you, too."

I shook my head.

"What?"

"That's just weird, hearin you talk about tellin your parents shit. That's stuff you hear on the *Cosby Show*."

"It happens."

I laughed. "Not at my house!"

We picked up Anthony at his friend's house. He came running out to the car and jumped in the front seat. He threw his arms around me when he saw me. "Where you been?"

"Around. You been keepin away from Franco like I told you to?"

"I stayed at Stevie's. Franco wasn't around at all!" Now Anthony turned to Ruthie. "What we havin for dinner?"

She laughed. "Whatever my mom fixed!"

"I remember your mom," I told her. "Real nice lady."

Ruthie nodded.

We got to her house and I just looked around. Her neighborhood was so quiet! There's always something going on in my neighborhood. It's weird to think how two neighborhoods ten minutes apart could be so different.

"Wow, this house is neat!" Anthony said as she let us into her house. Everything was still nice and neat, just like the last time I saw it. I could smell homemade food. I haven't smelled that lately. Usually Dad cooks when he's home, or I do, but neither of us has been home much lately.

"Does your mom cook like this all the time?" I asked Ruthie.

"No way! Who has time? But we have company tonight."

"Who?"

She laughed. "You and Anthony, idiot!"

We went up to the kitchen where her mom was standing over the stove. Ruthie introduced us. "Mom, this is Anthony

127

and AJ Johnson. You've met AJ before.''

Her mom looked up and grinned at us. She was young-looking. I'll bet she could pass for Ruthie's older sister. "Yes, I remember you," she said, then she looked down at Anthony. "Hi Anthony!"

He grinned back. "Hi! What's for dinner?"

"Spaghetti. Do you like spaghetti?"

"Yeah!"

This kid came into the kitchen and stopped and looked at us. He looked a lot like Ruthie, too.

"AJ, Anthony, this is my brother Derek. He's twelve."

"Hey," I said.

He looked at me. "Hey, don't you play football?"

I felt sorta self-conscious. "Yeah—"

"I read about you in the paper. So you're going to Florida State?"

"Yeah—"

"That's great!" said her mom. "On a four-year scholarship?"

I nodded again.

"I wish Ruthie'd get a four-year scholarship. Keep us out of the poorhouse!"

I laughed, deciding I liked her mom. She was pretty easygoing.

"Do you like Nintendo?" Derek asked Anthony.

Anthony's eyes lit up. "Yeah! Do you have Super Mario Brothers, three?"

"Yeah! Let's go!" Derek said and he and Anthony went upstairs.

I grinned at that.

"Ruthie, help me set the table," her mom said. Ruthie went to put dishes on the dining room table. I was feeling stupid so I asked if I could help.

"No, no!" her mom said. "Ruthie doesn't do enough

128

around the house as it is! Go sit down!''

I laughed and sat down at the table. The table was set all nice, as if they was expecting somebody important.

''Your mom didn't have to go through all this trouble just for us,'' I said to Ruthie.

She grinned. ''Mom always makes a fuss when we have guests.''

I heard a garage door opening. ''Who's that?''

''My dad.''

''What's he do?''

''He's an engineer.''

I whistled. ''He smart?''

''Very. I inherited my genes from him.''

''Figures.'' Her dad came up to the kitchen, dressed in a suit and wearing glasses. He looked smart.

''Dad, this is AJ Johnson,'' Ruthie said. ''AJ, this is my dad.''

Her dad shook my hand. ''Hi AJ.''

''Hi,'' I mumbled. I don't like dads too much. I met some dads of the white chicks I used to go out with and I could tell most of them didn't like me much. At least Erika don't got a dad to worry about.

I noticed that both of her parents talk black. Not as much as most black people but more than Ruthie. So I felt a little more relaxed toward them.

''Derek, come on!'' her mom yelled. Anthony and Derek came up to the kitchen and Anthony was talking away, as usual.

We all sat down to eat dinner. I sat between Ruthie and Anthony. ''So what are you doing next year, AJ?'' her dad asked.

''He has a scholarship to Florida State!'' her mom said, sounding proud.

Her dad looked impressed. ''So you were the one in the

129

papers, the one all the college scouts were looking at?"

I shrugged, feeling uncomfortable.

"I hope Derek can get a sports scholarship. That's an opportunity for a free education." He went on, talking about college and stuff and I just sat there for a moment, kinda amazed. I guess no one's really been that...impressed with me before. Yeah, people think it's great I'm a good ball player, but there was something different about how Ruthie's mom and dad were acting. They were more...genuine. I looked from Ruthie to her mom and dad and brother. I guess Ruthie was right, there is such a thing as a good family. You could tell her folks loved her and her brother. Erika and her mother was always saying crap to each other but I could tell Ruthie had respect for her parents. No wonder she was such a good kid.

After dinner, her dad went to watch TV while her mom and her brother cleaned up the kitchen. Anthony decided he wanted to help, too. Her mom seemed to really like Anthony. Well, how could anybody not like him?

Me and Ruthie went to sit in the living room by ourselves. Neither of us said anything for a minute. I was feeling kinda uncomfortable. I had too much on my mind.

"AJ?" Ruthie said, looking kinda uncomfortable.

I looked at her.

"Is something wrong?"

I shrugged, staring at the ground.

"Um...do you want to go for a walk?"

I shrugged again and stood up. Whatever. I followed her out the door and we walked down the block in silence.

I turned to watch the sun go down behind the mountains. "It's a nice night, huh."

She nodded.

"This whole neighborhood, it's nice. So quiet—" I laughed a little. "Y'know, I can see why you are the way

130

you are. So proper, y'know? Your folks're like that, too.''

She didn't say nothing.

"Anthony really like your brother."

She smiled. "Anthony's a friendly little boy."

I sucked in my breath.

Ruthie looked at me. "Is something wrong, AJ?"

I sighed and looked at the ground. "It's Anthony—"

"What about him?"

"Franco been puttin ideas in his head. He even let Anthony do a run for him—"

"A what?"

"Drug run. Paid him, too. And he so young, he don't know what's going on!"

She didn't say nothing.

I sighed again. "And he and his friends play gangster. That's how he see it. As a game."

She shook her head.

I took a deep breath, getting frustrated. "That night, after you dropped me off last week, Anthony told me what Franco been up to and I just about lost it."

"What'd you do?"

"Me and Franco started scrappin pretty hard. He was even tryin to kill me."

"And...you're frustrated because you don't know what to do to keep Anthony away from Franco."

I sighed again. "I mean, it wouldn't be a big deal if Anthony had a mom, or even a dad who was around a lot, to tell him what's right and what's wrong. But he don't! All he got is me and Franco, and Franco could really mess him up! I ain't gonna let Anthony mess up, he too sweet! You see how sweet a kid he is!"

She nodded. "He's pretty smart, too. Wise, I mean."

I chuckled. "I taught him to be like that. He don't take crap from nobody. He good at takin care of himself. He wear a key around his neck and he know how to microwave snacks for himself.''

"Is he alone a lot?"

"Not really. He spend a lot of time with his friends, stayin at their houses and stuff when I'm not around.''

"Don't their parents mind?"

"Mind? Nah, they don't care. In my neighborhood people's pretty open. His friends' moms watch him a lot cuz they know he really don't got no one else to watch him. Except me.''

"What about your father? Why doesn't he do anything?"

I shrugged. "He work, he pay the bills. But he never been one to pay attention to kids. He didn't pay much attention to me and Franco when we was little, either. He got himself to worry about.''

She nodded slowly. "I guess I can't understand what you go through but I can sympathize, AJ. It must be hard—''

I shrugged, not saying nothing. I looked at her and saw her shivering. "You cold?"

She shrugged.

I took off my jacket and gave it to her.

She looked kinda embarrassed. "No, I—''

"Go on—''

She took it from me and put it on, still looking uncomfortable. Then she looked at her watch. "We should probably be getting back. I don't know what time Anthony goes to bed.''

I nodded and we headed back to her house. "I'll wait in the car," I told her.

She nodded and I went to sit in the car, staring at the dashboard. Every time I thought about Anthony I got frustrated. How the hell was I gonna keep Franco away from him? And what was I gonna do about him next year? I was starting to think about that more and more, now that it was getting closer to graduation. Shoot, I'd be going to Florida in two weeks for a spring workout. I'd be gone the whole week of spring break. What would Anthony do then?

I guess he could stay at Stevie's, one of his little friend's houses while I'm gone. That's what he usually do. But with Franco coming around more and more, that wasn't too good an idea. Stevie lives a few houses away from me and I know his mom don't keep a close watch over the kids. And who knows what kinda shit Franco could put in his head while I'm gone?

I grinned when I saw Anthony come running out to the car. He jumped in the back seat. "Let's have dinner here again!"

I laughed. "We'll see, kid."

Ruthie drove to my house, then stopped the car and turned to look at me. "Will I see you at school tomorrow?"

I shrugged. "I guess. Thanks for dinner. Tell your folks thanks." Then me and Anthony went into the house.

The place was dark, no one was home. "Go get ready for bed," I told Anthony. He went to his room and I went to mine. I took off my shirt and lay on the bed, staring at the ceiling in the dark. Talking like that with Ruthie had really gotten me down.

A few minutes later my door opened and I heard Anthony walk in. "AJ?"

I looked and saw him standing in the doorway in his Snoopy pajamas. I could see his big eyes shining in the dark. "Hey—"

He climbed onto the bed and lay down next to me. "What'cha doing?"

"Same thing you are. Just layin here."

He sighed a little. "Oh—" He had a serious look on his face. He looked like he had a lot on his mind.

"Hey," I said. "Whassup, kid?"

"AJ, tell me about Mama."

I sucked in my breath. He hadn't asked me that in a long time, not since last year. And I used to sit him on my lap and tell him this fairy-tale story about a pretty and gentle woman who loved him very much. And he'd sit there with that same thoughtful look in them big owl eyes of his that he was wearing right now. But should I tell him the truth? Should I tell him Mom was sort of psycho and she wished he'd never been born? That the only one of us she might've loved was Franco?

"AJ?"

I made myself grin. "Aw, kid...I told you about her before. Don't you remember?"

"Yeah, I remember. Tell me again."

"All right." I took a deep breath. "She was real pretty, and nice—"

"Like a princess?"

"Yeah, like a princess. And she used to sing, too. Just like an angel." At least I wasn't lying about that.

Anthony sighed again, closing his eyes.

"She loved you lots. She used to hold you in her arms and rock you to sleep. Said you'd grow up to be a king someday."

Anthony opened his eyes and looked at me in a sad way. "Why'd she kill herself?"

He looked so sad I put my arms around him and held him close. "I think...God wanted her to be in heaven with him."

"But what about me? Don't God want her to be with me?"

I sighed. "I dunno, kiddo. Maybe someday we'll both know."

Anthony nodded slowly. "Was she like Ruthie's mom?"

"Uh yeah, yeah. Just like Ruthie's mom."

"I like Ruthie's mom. She nice. I like Ruthie, too."

"So do I, kid." And I had to grin cuz I never thought I'd

ever hear myself say that.

Anthony sighed again. "I wish I had a mama."

I patted his head. "You do, kid. You do."

Anthony put his head on my shoulder and closed his eyes. Soon I could hear his breathing light and regular. He was asleep. I grinned. He looked like an angel. An innocent little angel. I got even sadder. It ain't fair, when you think about it, how some kids got great parents while others don't got shit. Anthony deserved to have parents like Ruthie's, parents who'd really care about him and love him. But I'm all he got, really. And I ain't gonna let him down, whatever I do. No way.

I must've fallen asleep cuz when I sat up again, it was six thirty and the sun was rising. Anthony was lying there asleep next to me. I rubbed my eyes and stretched. My legs felt stiff cuz I'd fallen asleep in my jeans.

I got out of bed and went to take a shower, hearing Dad snoring in his room. I wondered what time he came in last night.

Anthony was awake and sitting up on my bed when I came back to my room. He had a big grin on his face. "Good morning!"

I grinned back. "Hey, kid. Go get ready for school."

He nodded and went running to the bathroom.

I was pretty slow getting dressed. I guess it was about time I went back to school even though I didn't feel like it. I'm sick of school in a big way.

Me and Anthony ate breakfast together as usual and Ray swung by at seven fifteen to get me.

"You gonna be home today?" Anthony asked me on my way out.

"Yeah, I'll be home. I'll see ya."

"Yeah. See ya!"

I went outside to Ray's truck. "Whassup?"

Ray shrugged. "Nothin. Comin back to school now?"

"Yeah. I had some shit going on, y'know—"

Ray nodded, not saying nothing.

I hung out with the fellas before school, slept through first hour, then went to chemistry. Ruthie was already there.

"I'm glad you're back," she said as I came in.

I shrugged. "It ain't great to be back!"

"No, it isn't," she said, then handed me my jacket. "I forgot to give you this last night."

"What? Oh." I'd forgotten about it. "Thanks."

"Don't worry, I didn't wear it this morning or anything—"

"Why would I care about that?"

She grinned in a weird way. "Erika'd have your head."

Erika. I'd almost forgotten about her. She was probably wondering where I was. Well, she better not give me any shit cuz I wasn't in no mood to be putting up with her!

Mrs. Fleener started lecturing but I didn't feel like listening. I could always get the notes from Ruthie. I tapped her on the shoulder. She turned to look at me.

"What'd I miss in here, anyway?"

"Two labs and a worksheet."

"And I suppose you ain't gonna give me the answers."

She grinned and shook her head.

I rolled my eyes. "Girl, you a trip!"

She didn't say nothing to that.

"Will you HELP me then?"

"Sure," she said. "When?"

"I dunno. You better check your APPOINTMENT book, see where you can pencil me in!"

She laughed at that. She's such a trip I had to laugh with her.

"Why don't we get together sometime this weekend?"

"I got a track meet Saturday."

"What about Sunday? Sunday evening. You could have

136

dinner at my house again. Bring Anthony if you want.''

I chuckled. ''Man, Anthony got a kick outta your folks!''

She grinned. ''They liked him, too. So will you and Anthony come over Sunday then?''

''Yeah, I guess—''

''Good. Come by around six. And Anthony can do something with Derek while we work on chemistry.''

''A whole night doing chemistry. What fun.''

She chuckled and turned around to face forward. I just sat there watching the back of her head. She's all right, really. Too proper, but all right. I don't know no one else like her and that's the truth!

I ran into Erika at my locker after class. Like I expected, she didn't look too happy. ''So where you been, AJ?'' she asked, standing there with her hands on her hips.

''Not here.'' I opened my locker, not paying her much attention. I didn't wanna be bothered by her.

''But where have you been, I been worried sick! You don't call, you don't—''

Now I turned to look at her. ''I'm back now, ain't I?'' I sounded a lot meaner than I meant to.

She rolled her eyes. ''Why you gotta be like this, AJ? Here I am, worried sick about you and you're being like this!''

''Then stop being such a goddamn nag!''

''I ain't naggin, I just—'' She closed her eyes and sucked in her breath. ''Forget it, just forget it!'' She turned and stormed away from me. I watched her leave, You know, she looked real cute from the back. Real cute.

# RUTHIE

Of course, Mom was excited when I told her AJ and Anthony would be eating dinner with us again on Sunday.

"He really is a handsome boy," Mom said as she put a roast in the oven late Sunday afternoon.

"Who, AJ?"

Mom smiled coyly. "Are you two an item now?"

I rolled my eyes. "Mom!"

"Well!" Mom protested. "Why not?"

"Why?" I countered. "He and I have to work on chemistry, and I figured he might as well bring Anthony along with him. Isn't he a great little boy?"

Mom smiled and nodded. "So talkative!"

I nodded. "I should be getting ready. They'll be here soon."

"Don't forget to vacuum the basement!"

I groaned as I went downstairs to my room. I put on a sweater and a pair of pants, then brushed my hair and fixed my make-up. I vacuumed the basement and went back upstairs to help set the table. AJ and Anthony were due any minute. But fifteen minutes passed and they hadn't arrived.

"What time did you tell them to come?" Mom asked me.

"Six," I said, looking at the clock.

By six thirty, they still hadn't showed and I was getting mad. He'd better not stand us up, especially after Mom went through so much trouble for dinner!

The doorbell rang at six forty-five and I went to answer it. AJ and Anthony were standing at the door.

Anthony had a big smile on his face. "Hi!"

"Hi," I said. "You can go upstairs to Derek's room if you'd like!"

"Okay!" Anthony ran upstairs.

Now I glared at AJ. "Did your clocks stop?"

He looked sheepish. "Sorry. I was helpin my dad do some stuff."

"What?"

"Move some stuff. He bought this new washer and dryer cuz ours broke."

I nodded.

"You look pissed off."

I shrugged. "You're here now, aren't you?"

AJ looked uncomfortable. I sighed. "Don't worry about it. Come on, let's eat!"

Mom called all of us to the table and we sat down to eat. Mom looked excited to see him again. So'd Dad. And Anthony and Derek were chattering away. I noticed AJ looking from Anthony to my parents in a strange way throughout dinner.

After dinner, Dad did the dishes and AJ and I went down to Dad's study to work. This time he remembered to bring his books. But as during dinner, he looked preoccupied.

"Is something wrong?" I asked.

139

He shrugged. "It's nothin—"

"If you don't want to tell me, I won't pry. I just thought I'd ask—"

Now he looked up and smiled at me.

I smiled back. He said nothing so I assumed he didn't want to say anymore. So I opened my chemistry notebook. "Okay, the first thing we have to do here is equations—"

AJ was staring into space.

"AJ?"

He looked at me. "Huh?"

"You're not paying attention to me."

"Oh. Sorry—"

I closed my book. "Have you seen your brother lately?"

"Franco? Nah—"

I nodded, not knowing what to say. I felt a little foolish. "Um—"

AJ chuckled. "That's okay. You don't gotta say nothin."

"What?"

"You look like you tryin to think of somethin to say."

I laughed nervously. "Yeah, I guess I was." I felt even more foolish. But AJ just smiled. I sucked in my breath, feeling a strange fluttering in my chest. I lowered my eyes. When I looked up again, he was staring at the table, silent and immobile.

"You know, you're a very distant person—" I said softly.

He didn't reply.

"It's funny, how you're so closed off and Anthony's so open—"

AJ smiled again, but like most of his smiles, this one lasted for a fleeting second, then vanished. He looked so...vulnerable.

"You're still worried about Anthony, aren't you."

"I don't ever stop worryin about him—"

"Um...is there something I could do?"

He shook his head. "I was just thinkin about spring break—"

"What about it?"

"I'm going to Florida for a recruit week."

I clapped my hands together excitedly. "Anthony can stay here that week!"

AJ looked at me like I was crazy.

"I mean it! I'm sure my parents wouldn't mind! We have plenty of room—"

AJ shook his head. "Nah—"

"AJ, where else can he stay?"

He said nothing and stared at the table.

"AJ, I want him to stay with us. I'm asking you, okay? So that should satisfy your pride, shouldn't it?"

"Satisfy my pride?"

I looked him in the eye. "Because I know you'd never ask me."

"Hey, you gotta see if it's okay with your folks—"

"Don't worry about that!" I said firmly. "In fact, I'll go talk to them right now. Promise me you won't get up and leave."

He laughed. "Why would I do that?"

"You have this knack for running away from things—"

"I won't leave!" he said and smiled.

I smiled back and went to the living room, where Mom and Dad were watching TV. I cleared my throat to get their attention. "Uh, Mom? Dad?"

They looked at me.

"I was wondering . . . first of all, what do you think of AJ and Anthony?"

"They're good kids," Dad said. Mom agreed.

"It's good to see that they're good kids," I spoke quickly and nervously. "Their mom died a few years ago. So AJ takes care of Anthony."

"What are you trying to say?" Dad asked.

I took a deep breath. "AJ has to go to Florida over spring break and I was wondering if Anthony could stay with us that week."

Mom and Dad looked at each other.

"The reason why I'm asking is that they have an older brother, too. He's in a gang and he's a drug dealer. And AJ's trying so hard to protect Anthony from that!"

"And staying here over spring break is going to fix everything?" Mom asked.

"When AJ's away, Anthony really won't have anyone to take care of him. And who knows what their brother will tell him or what he'll do? Even when AJ's here, he has track, he has his own life. It's too much to ask an eighteen year old guy to be a parent to a six year old boy! And you see what a great kid Anthony is!"

"I thought you were talking about the week of spring break," Dad said with a grin I couldn't place.

"I am!" I said quickly. "So can he?"

"And the older one, AJ, he asked you this?" Dad asked.

"No, he was too proud to ask. I offered."

Mom laughed. "You offered?"

"Anthony's a great kid! I've spent a lot of time with him. He can sleep in the guest room. He wouldn't be any trouble—"

"Ruthie, do you really think this is fair to Anthony?" Mom said gently.

"Fair?"

"Suppose he does stay here for the week and begins to really like us and become attached to us. Would it be fair to bring him here only to rip him away?"

"But it's only a week—"

"That's plenty of time for a young child to become attached to someone."

I sighed. "And what if he did stay longer? We have the room, don't we?"

"Ruthie—"

"I'm serious!" I insisted, surprising myself with my conviction. "You guys always talk about how a lot of black kids don't have enough parental influence. So this is your chance to do something! To maybe make a difference in someone's life! Don't tell me you didn't mean it when you said that!"

Dad grinned strangely. "You'll make a great lawyer someday, you know that?"

"Don't make fun of me now, I'm serious!"

"You can't save the world, Ruthie," Dad said.

"I'm not talking about the world, I'm talking about Anthony! Can he stay here at least for the week? Please?"

Mom looked at Dad. "Well—"

Dad sighed. "A week's no problem. Any longer than that, well, we'll see—"

I flew to hug them both. "Mom, Dad, you're the greatest!"

"Don't you and AJ have homework to do?" Dad said.

"Dad!" I said and hugged him again. I jumped up and ran to the study.

AJ was sitting there stoically. He looked up at me and I could see the anticipation in his face. "Anthony can stay here spring break," I told him.

He smiled rather uncertainly. "That's great!"

I smiled and nodded.

He sighed. "Hey Ruthie, I really appreciate this—"

"I know. You don't have to tell me."

He smiled in a surprised way.

I opened my chemistry notebook. "Come on, we have work to do."

He laughed at me and opened his book, too.

143

# ERIKA

I see AJ and Ruthie walk in together Monday mornin while me and the girls is standin in the cafeteria. "Somethin's gotta be up with them!" I tell Kelli and Monica.

Kelli shake her head. "Girl, I'd have kicked her ass a long time ago!"

"When've I had time with the musical?" I snap. I got rehearsals every day so AJ don't see me much anymore. Plus he got track. But now I'm startin to feel like I'm losin him. Before, whenever I saw him with another girl I'd first make her life hell, then I'd go flirt with some other guy to make him jealous. And it usually worked. But now AJ seem so different. He been actin real cold to me, plus I keep seein him with that chick Ruthie. But now I gotta put my foot down. Enough is enough. So I march over to them and stand between him and Ruthie.

I take him by the arm and pull him away from her. "AJ, I need to talk to you!"

AJ look mad. "What the hell—"

"I need to talk to you and this is the only way I can talk to you anymore!"

He cross his arms and roll his eyes.

"No, don't be rollin your eyes at me! I mean it!"

He shrugged. "Whassup?"

"That's what I wanna know! Whassup? What's with her?"

"With who?"

"Ruthie or whoever the hell she is! You and her got somethin going, don't you!"

"No!"

I just look at him. I know he lyin. "Then why you always WITH her?"

He shrug again. "She just a friend."

I roll my eyes. "Don't give me that shit, you and her got somethin going!"

"I don't got nothin going with Ruthie!"

"Yes you do and I'm gonna find out what! And when I do I'm gonna get you and I'm gonna get that Ruthie chick!" I turn and run away from him, mad as hell. He don't try to follow me or nothin. I go to my locker, feelin down. So he don't care about me no more. Never calls, never wants to talk to me. It's cuz of Ruthie, I know it! Friends, bullshit! What kind of fool do he think I am?

I'm so mad I don't go to first hour. I just sit by my locker, lookin over my script for the musical. I already got all my lines memorized but I stare at it cuz I don't got nothin else to do.

My life ain't too great right now. Mom's on my ass about college and shit. I don't even know if I wanna go to college. And now all this shit with AJ. Damnit, I need AJ! He can't just forget about me like this! I guess I do got the musical and that's going good. When Shanice ain't at my throat, that is. Sometimes I wish I could just go somewhere and sing,

145

get away from here, join a band or somethin. Come back when I'm rich and laugh in everyone's face.

This black cow bitch walk by and mumble "half-breed bitch" loud enough for me to hear. I'm on my feet real quick.

"What was that?" I step in front of her. She my height so we stand face to face.

"Nothin," she say.

"I heard you say half-breed bitch!"

She didn't say nothin.

"You better not let me catch you sayin shit about me again!" I shove her. I expect her to throw down her books and us to start scrappin but she don't do nothin. Wimp. And I'm feelin like a good fight, too. But the girl turn and run away.

I sit down, suddenly thinkin about Ruthie. What the hell do AJ see in her? She ain't even light-skinned! And I know all AJ like is light-skinned girls! Maybe she rich. She dress sharp and drive a nice car. She okay, she ain't that pretty. I get pissed off, picturin her with AJ. No dark-skinned chick is gonna take him away from me! I'm gonna have to let her know that, make it sink in real good. She gotta learn to leave AJ alone!

# RUTHIE

"Yo Ruthie!" I heard a loud voice calling me as I stood at my locker Friday morning after first hour. I turned around to see a very pretty light-skinned girl with long brown hair and blue eyes. Erika, AJ's girlfriend. I'd never spoken to her before. For a moment I just looked at her. She was a little shorter than me and curvier. "You better stay away from AJ!" she snapped.

I shrugged. "AJ and I are friends."

"Well I don't like it!"

I rolled my eyes. "Then talk to AJ." I walked away, leaving her standing there. I guess my annoyance showed on my face because AJ asked me about it in chemistry. "You look like someone pissed you off," he said.

"Someone has! Your girlfriend!"

He laughed. "Erika? What'd she do?"

"She came up to me telling me how I'd better stay away from you. I told her to talk to you if she has a problem!"

AJ whistled. "You got guts!"

"What do you mean?"

"Erika pretty vicious. You better watch out for her."

"No, you'd better talk to her. Because if she antagonizes me again, I'm holding you responsible!"

He laughed again.

I took my lab write-up sheet from my folder. "Is Anthony excited about staying with me?"

AJ grinned fondly. "Yeah. He kept me up half the night talkin about it. What time you gonna get him?"

"About three. We'll go get his things, then we'll come to your track meet."

"We?"

"Andrea's coming with me. So you can finally meet her."

"Oh, that white chick you hang with?"

"She's a nice girl," I said. "Are Anthony's things ready?"

"Yeah. I helped him pack his suitcase last night."

I smiled. "Are you excited about Florida?"

He shrugged and nodded. "Yeah—"

"What time do you leave tomorrow?"

"Early. About eight. Tell your folks thanks again, okay?"

"Sure. Now let's get started on this lab!"

He rolled his eyes. "Yes master!"

I met Andrea at my car after school.

"Are you excited about having Anthony stay with you?" she asked.

I smiled and nodded. "It'll be a lot of fun having him."

"How long is he staying?"

"A week, at least."

Andrea nodded. "You know, that's really great of you. That little boy's gonna benefit so much from staying with your family, even if it is for just a week. And you and AJ seem to be getting along, too—"

I smiled, thinking about him. "He really is a nice guy,

once you get to know him.''

She nodded. "He seems to act differently around you. Differently than how he acts around most people.''

"I know a lot about him. And he knows a lot about me, too.''

"Would you ever get together?''

That jolted me. "What makes you ask that?''

Andrea shrugged. "You're always together nowadays. Why not? I think you'd be good together.''

I shook my head quickly. "He has a girlfriend! Erika!''

"What's she to him besides someone to sleep with?''

"Andrea!''

"Really, what could she ever be to him? I never see them together anymore, anyway!''

"He's busy with track and she has the musical—''

Andrea laughed. "I'm sure she doesn't think too highly of you!''

"Did I tell you what she did today?''

"No, what?''

"She came up to me and told me I'd better stay away from AJ!''

Andrea's eyes lit up. "What'd you say to that?''

I shrugged. "I told her to talk to AJ if she has a problem.''

Andrea shook her head. "Some people can be so—''

"Petty? Yeah.'' Now I drove into AJ's neighborhood. From the corner of my eye I could see Andrea sitting rigidly in her seat. "What's wrong?'' I asked.

I could hear her clearing her throat. "Um, he lives...here?''

I shrugged and nodded. She said nothing else but I could tell she was nervous. I smiled wryly. Her reaction reminded me of my reaction the first time I saw his neighborhood. But there are places a lot worse than this.

That edgy look was still on her face when I parked the

car at AJ's house. She gulped. "Nothing's going to happen to us, right?"

I laughed wryly, feeling a mixture of annoyance and understanding toward her ignorance. "No. Come on!"

Anthony came running out of the house and threw his arms around me. "Hi Ruthie!"

I hugged him back. "Hi Anthony! Are you ready to go?"

"Yeah!" He turned to look at Andrea. "Who this?"

"This is my friend Andrea. Andrea, this is Anthony."

Andrea smiled at him. "Hi Anthony!"

"Hi!" Anthony held out his hand. Andrea laughed and shook it.

"Let's go get your stuff!" I said.

"Are we gonna see AJ at the track meet?"

"Yeah, if we hurry." I saw Andrea looking around in wonder as Anthony went to his room. "What?" I asked her.

She shrugged, her face coloring. "Um...it's nice, though, I mean, this house, even if it is small—"

I said nothing but I grew embarrassed. Is this how I looked when I first came to AJ's house? Now I could see why he was so cynical toward me.

"Come on, help me get his things," I said, leading her to Anthony's room.

Anthony was stuffing toys into a Garfield backpack.

"Ready?" I asked.

He looked up. "Yeah! Can you take my suitcase?"

"I'll get it!" Andrea offered, picking it up off the bed.

"Do you have everything?" I asked.

Anthony nodded. "Let's go!"

He picked up his backpack and we followed him outside. I hoisted the suitcase into the trunk and Anthony climbed into the back seat.

"Guess what, Ruthie!" he exclaimed. "I got a loose tooth!"

"Do you?"

"Yeah!" From my rearview mirror I could see him wiggling his tooth. Andrea laughed.

"Is the tooth fairy gonna leave me some money?"

"I don't know!" I told him. "Let's wait and see when the tooth comes out."

"The tooth fairy left me a dollar last time I lost a tooth!" Andrea laughed again. "He's so cute!"

"Cute!" Anthony exclaimed. From the rearview mirror I could see his face contort dramatically. Andrea laughed again and turned to look at him. "Do you like track meets?"

"Yeah, I go to all AJ's meets! Cuz he don't win if I don't go!"

"Who do you sit with?"

"The team," Anthony said seriously. "I sit with the fellas. Kevin and Wakeen and all them! I gotta cheer 'em on!"

"Oh yeah, Kevin. He runs track?"

"Hurdles. AJ do the 100."

"Does," I corrected.

He rolled his eyes. "Does!"

Denver Public School track meets are pretty big events so I had to park my car in the far corner of the stadium. "C'mon!" Anthony took us both by the hands and ran us up into the crowded stands where the Centennial boys were sitting in their red team uniforms. He led us over to AJ's friends.

"Well if it ain't the man Anthony!" Kevin shouted and slapped his hand.

"Hey Kevin!" Anthony said. "Where's AJ?"

"Down warming up. He runs first!"

Andrea sat down and looked around. "You know, I've never been to a track meet before."

"That's cuz you're Miss Student Council!" Kevin told her. Andrea gave him the finger.

"Uh-oh, obscene gesture!"

Andrea laughed. "Shut up! Oh look, AJ's gonna race!"

We saw AJ get into his starting blocks along with five other runners.

Anthony stood on the bleachers. "Go AJ! Go AJ!"

The gun sounded and all six lean racers sprang from their starting blocks. AJ took off like thunder, his face set in concentration, legs pumping like machine pistons. The muscles in his arms and legs rippled as they sliced through the air.

"He's beautiful, isn't he," Andrea said softly.

I couldn't reply.

Eleven seconds later, the race was over as AJ crossed the finish line one length in front of the others. We all cheered.

"All right AJ!" Anthony yelled.

Andrea grinned. "This is kinda neat!"

Anthony turned to her. "You never been to a track meet before?"

Andrea shook her head sheepishly.

Anthony looked authoritative. "Then I better explain everything to you!"

I chuckled as he sat next to her and began to explain all of the events to her. Then to my surprise, Kevin came to sit next to me. We watched the second heat race in silence, but stood up to cheer when Wakeen crossed the finish line in ten point five seconds.

"He's gonna win state, you know," Kevin told me as we sat down.

"Wakeen? He's good."

"Man, that brother is fast!"

I nodded.

"So Anthony's gonna stay with you next week?"

Again, I nodded.

"AJ wouldn't say nothin but it's cuz of Franco, right?"

I shrugged.

Kevin nodded. "Yeah, I figured. He's changin."

"AJ? In what way?"

Kevin scratched his head. "I dunno. I mean, he still hangs out with all of us and we go to parties and stuff but I dunno... sometimes he acts like an adult or something. I mean, I know cuz we're so tight, y'know? Other people wouldn't notice."

"I'm glad you're observant."

He shook his head at me. "You're one smart-assed chick!" Then he smiled. "But it's okay, I guess. You're good for him. Just don't turn him too straight, okay?"

I laughed. "I haven't done anything to him!"

"You've done somethin!" He stood up. "Well I gotta get going. My race is next."

"Break a leg."

He glared at me. "Well you have a nice day, too!"

I laughed. "That's just an expression, you idiot! It means good luck!"

He smiled. "In that case I'll break two legs!"

AJ came up into the stands with a towel around his neck. He smiled when his eyes caught mine and came to sit next to me.

"Good job," I told him.

"Yeah, I guess—"

"So you're in the finals now?"

"Yeah. They don't start till six." He stretched out his legs in front of him and winced. "Man, my shoulders is tight!"

"Need a backrub?"

He nodded. So I went to sit behind him and began kneading his shoulders. I was surprised at how hard his muscles were. But soon I felt his shoulders relaxing and I felt a strange sensation in my chest as I ran my hands over his warm, slightly moist skin. I closed my eyes. Stop being foolish,

Ruthie . . .

Now Anthony came running over to AJ. "Hi AJ!" he said, giving him a high five. "See, I cheered for you and you won!"

"You're right, little guy!" AJ said fondly.

"Have you met Andrea before?"

"No, not really—"

Andrea smiled at him. "I know who you are. I'm Andrea. Ruthie's best friend."

AJ smiled back. "Yeah, I know who you are, too. I'm AJ."

"You were good," she said. "You've got a great little brother. He just explained all of the events to me."

AJ looked at Anthony. "Really?"

"Yeah! She didn't know nothing!"

Andrea laughed. "Well I do now!"

Doug and Wakeen came to join us, slapping hands and exchanging "good going, man" with AJ. Then Doug turned to Andrea, looking surprised. "I didn't think I'd see you here!"

Andrea smiled. "Why not?"

"Miss Student Council Smart Person," Wakeen said, "you should be at the tennis club. Or better yet, at a library or somethin!"

"I hate tennis!" Andrea protested.

Wakeen put on a snooty air. "Oh, did you tire of the country club?"

She swatted him with his towel. "Oh right! I don't belong to any country club!" She and Doug and Wakeen and Anthony began some animated discussion. AJ and I turned to watch the meet and I continued to massage his neck.

He sighed. "You gonna put me to sleep, girl—"

"You need to relax."

He nodded, then leaned against me. "That girl's nice."

154

"Andrea?" I looked to see her laughing with Doug and Wakeen.

"I always thought she was stuck-up—"

I shrugged. He looked up at me and I brushed a piece of grass from his face. My fingers were trembling slightly.

He smiled at me and I took a deep breath, trying not to let my sudden nervousness show.

"I gotta go," AJ said, then got up to return to the field. I watched him leave, feeling my skin tingle from where he'd touched me. I closed my eyes, feeling my face flush for thinking what I was thinking. Be rational, I told myself. Keep your feelings in control...

But wait. Denying my feelings wouldn't solve anything, would it? I mean, I could feel whatever I wanted to toward AJ, as long as I didn't let it show. And how hard would that be?

# AJ

I went straight to Ruthie's when I got in from the airport Sunday night. Anthony was waiting for me at the door. "AJ!" he yelled, throwing his arms around me.

I hugged him back. "Hey kiddo! Have you been good?"

"Yeah! Ruthie and Andrea took me to the zoo and to the movies and Derek took me fishin and we all went out to dinner and—"

I grinned. "Did ya miss me?"

He nodded, then put on a big grin. "Did you get me anything?"

I laughed. "Yeah, but you'll get it later."

"What'd you get me?"

"I said I'll give it to you later!" Then I looked up and saw Ruthie standing there.

She was grinning. "How was Florida?"

"All right. Hot. I met up with some of the other recruits, we did a little workin out—"

She nodded. "Looking forward to college?"

"Yeah, I like the football program there."

She shook her head. "Football!"

I rolled my eyes. "I forgot to check out the library and shit—"

She grinned. "I'm not surprised!"

"But I ain't lookin forward to startin up with school."

"Who is?"

I looked around and didn't see Anthony. "Where'd he go?"

Ruthie shrugged. "Probably up to Derek's room to play Nintendo. We could hardly drag him away from it."

I laughed. "So how was he?"

"Great."

"And your folks, they didn't mind?"

Ruthie shook her head. "They really liked having him. Especially my mom. He helped her make cookies yesterday and Dad took him along when he and Derek went to practice baseball."

I grinned.

"Have you been home yet?"

"Nah. I came here right from the airport—" I got uncomfortable standing there.

"Um, is Anthony's stuff ready?"

She shook her head and took a deep breath. "So...can you watch Anthony now? With track and all?"

I looked at her strangely, not knowing what she was trying to say. "Why you ask that?"

"Because—" She took another deep breath. "While you were gone I had a long talk with my parents. Two days ago, actually. And they were wondering what you were going to do."

"What do you mean?"

"Well, my dad says you have your own life and you

shouldn't have to be worrying about raising a growing boy. They said that if you want, and if it's okay with your dad, Anthony can stay here, at least for a little while."

I felt like someone'd taken the breath right out of me. Anthony stay here?

I must've looked as frozen as I felt cuz Ruthie looked at me all concerned and said, "AJ, are you okay?"

I tried to laugh but my laugh sounded weird, like my voice'd dried out. "Yeah I'm okay, it's just—"

"If you don't want him to stay here, I can tell him to start packing his things—"

"Nah, I didn't say that, I'm just. . .your parents? They said this?"

She nodded. "We talked about it for a long time. My parents really didn't see much of an alternative, at least not for now."

I was still in disbelief. Anthony, stay here and have the kind of family I wished I had? To stay away from Franco for good? How could I let him pass that up? "I, uh, don't know what to say—"

Ruthie grinned and I knew she understood.

"Um, it wouldn't be for long or nothin, just till I make sure Franco stay away from him for good—" I spoke fast and I sounded nervous. "It won't be for long—"

Ruthie laughed. "AJ, don't worry about it!"

I sighed. "You don't know what this mean to me—"

Ruthie just grinned and I grinned back.

Right then, her mom came downstairs and smiled at me. "Oh, hi AJ! How was your trip?"

"Good," I said. "I really like the school."

"That's great! Well come up to the kitchen! Don't stand in the doorway!"

I laughed and followed Ruthie up to the kitchen.

"Did Ruthie tell you Anthony's welcome to stay here?"

I nodded, feeling uncomfortable and emotional at the same time. "Yeah, thanks. Thanks a lot. It'll be really good for him—"

Her mom smiled again. "It's nice to see you care so much for your little brother."

"I have to. I'm all he got. I was just tellin Ruthie it won't be long, just till I can get some stuff straightened out—"

"Don't worry about it, AJ," her mom said.

I nodded and grinned at Ruthie again. Her folks was great. "Um-does Anthony know yet?"

Ruthie shook her head, still smiling. "Why don't you tell him? He's upstairs."

I nodded and headed up the stairs, a thousand things running through my head. If Anthony stayed here, who would I roughhouse with at home? Who'd listen to me when I was in a pissed-off mood? But man, Anthony in a place like this...I know Ruthie's folks'd take good care of him. But I couldn't help feeling sad.

Anthony was up in Ruthie's brother's room playing Nintendo. He stopped when I came in and looked up at me. "Whassup, bro?"

"Let's go to your room, kid. I gotta talk to you." He jumped up and we went down the hall to the room he was staying in. I sat on the bed and sat him on my lap.

"Whassup?" he asked.

I grinned. "First let me show you what I got ya!"

Anthony's owl eyes lit up. "Okay!" I laughed and reached into my bag for a FSU baseball bap and sweatshirt.

"Oh wow!" Anthony jumped down from my lap and pulled on the sweatshirt. It came down to his knees.

I laughed. "Shoot, I forgot to check the size."

Anthony sat in my lap again.

"So do you like it here?"

He nodded.

"Hey, would you like to stay here a while? With Ruthie and her folks?"

Anthony looked confused. "Stay here?"

"Yeah, just for a little while. Isn't it nice here?"

"Yeah, but—" Anthony looked scared. "What about you? Are you gonna stay here too?"

"Nah—"

Anthony looked like he was gonna cry. "No, I wanna stay with you!"

I took a deep breath and hugged him close. "Hey, you'll still see me! I'll come by every day! I just want you to stay here cuz it's so nice here. Ruthie and her folks are nice people. They want you to stay here with them!"

Anthony wiped his eyes. "They do?"

I grinned and nodded. "And I'll see you every day!"

"Promise?"

I hugged him again. "Promise! Now let's go downstairs and tell Ruthie and her folks, okay?"

Anthony nodded with resignation. "Okay!" He took my hand and we went downstairs to the kitchen, where Ruthie and her mom were sitting at the table.

"Hi Anthony!" her mom said and smiled at him.

Anthony looked nervous. "You want me to stay here with you?"

Her mom kept smiling. "If you want to, Anthony."

Anthony looked from me to Ruthie to her mom, looking like he was deep in thought. "Okay. I'll stay here a while!" I chuckled. That kid was something else.

"I'm gonna go play Nintendo!" he said ran upstairs.

I tried to look okay but inside I felt like crying. He already seemed like he was a part of their family. Where did that leave me?

I cleared my throat. "Uh . . . I guess I should be gettin his stuff—"

"Need some help?" Ruthie asked.

I shrugged. She followed me outside.

"How'd you get here?" she asked.

"Took a cab."

"We'll take my car," she said. I followed her out to her car, not saying nothing. She turned to look at me when she parked in front of my house. "Are you okay, AJ?"

I shrugged.

"It must hurt pretty bad. I know how close you two are—"

I still didn't say nothing.

"If there's anything I can do for you, let me know. I mean that."

Now I grinned at her. "Thanks, Ruthie."

She grinned back and we went into the house to get his stuff. She sat on his bed while I gathered up his toys and clothes and stuffed animals and school stuff. She helped me take it out to her car and we drove back to her house. Both of us was quiet. I guess there wasn't nothing to say. After we finished putting his stuff away, I said goodbye to Anthony and she took me back home.

I was surprised to see both Franco and Dad sitting in front of the TV set when I came back.

"Well well well, if it ain't the Golden Boy himself," said Franco. "How was Florida?"

"All right," I muttered, dropping my bag on the floor.

"Hey, where's Anthony?" asked Dad. "I ain't seen him around all week!"

"He been stayin with a friend of mine. He gonna stay there a while."

"What for?" Franco asked with a weird grin.

"I ain't around much and neither are you, Dad. He need someone to look after him."

Dad nodded. "Yeah, I guess he do."

I didn't have no more to say so I went to my room to start

161

unpacking my stuff. Franco came to stand in the doorway. I didn't pay him no attention.

"So you're keepin him away from me, right?"

I didn't say nothing.

Franco laughed and walked into the room. "Yeah, I get it. I'm a bad influence and shit."

I still didn't say nothing.

"So where is he? With that half-breed chick you date?"

Erika! I'd forgotten all about Erika. I guess I'd better call her. I went to the phone and dialed her number.

She answered the phone. "Hello?"

"Hey, it's me."

"Nice of you to call!"

"I just got in tonight!"

"I don't mean that! I mean you haven't called me in two weeks! Havin fun with that chick Ruthie?"

"No, don't start up with that shit—"

"I will start up with that shit! Cuz I been puttin up with it for too long!"

I sighed. "Can't you be my girlfriend, for once?"

"What are you—"

"Without bitchin about this and that! Can't you just be my girl? Huh?"

She got quiet. So'd I. After a long time she spoke again. "You know, I just get worried, that's all. I don't mean to bitch, but—" She sighed. "Yeah, I'll be your girl."

I didn't say nothing.

"How was Florida?" Her voice got soft.

"All right."

"Why don't you come over?"

"I got stuff to do—"

"You comin to see me in the musical, ain't you?"

Musical? Oh yeah, she had the musical. That's what'd kept her off my back for the last month. "Yeah. Just tell me

162

when."

"We going to prom too, right? I gotta get busy buyin a dress—"

"Yeah, I guess—" I don't know why I said that. I hate prom. I went last year and it sucked. I got dressed up in this pain in the ass tux and my date was this stupid white chick. The only fun part was getting hammered with the fellas afterward. "I gotta go, okay?"

"Okay. I love you."

I hung up and finished folding my clothes. Franco had gone to sleep on the floor. But I couldn't sleep. All I could do was think about Anthony, how he wasn't gonna be around no more. What was I gonna do when I didn't see him after school? I didn't know.

I slept late Monday and woke up in time to make it to chemistry. I was in a shitty mood cuz I hadn't got much sleep. Ruthie was there as usual. I don't think she's ever missed a day of class. As usual, she had on a nice outfit. Man, what I wouldn't do to see her in a miniskirt, or even in a t-shirt and jeans. Mrs. Fleener was yapping about something but no one was listening. How could anyone listen? School was gonna be over in two months and nobody gave a shit anymore. Even Ruthie didn't look like she was listening. She turned around and looked at me. "Did you just get here?"

"Yeah."

"Is something wrong?"

I shrugged, not knowing what to say.

"What is it?"

"How come you always know when somethin ain't right with me?"

She shrugged. "Call it intuition. What is it?"

Mrs. Fleener glared at us.

"I'll tell ya later," I mumbled. She nodded.

After class, I walked out the room with her. "I been thinkin

163

about next year—"

"It's unrealistic to think that you can take Anthony to college with you."

"But I'm all he got! Shoot, maybe I won't go. Maybe I'll just stay here and get a job or somethin—"

She stopped and stared at me in a weird way. "You'd do that?"

I shrugged, not knowing what she was getting at. "Yeah, he's my brother!"

She smiled a real pretty smile. "But you have your own life to live."

"That was great of your folks, offerin to keep him. But he can't stay forever! I feel like he's a freeloader or somethin—"

She smiled again. "AJ, he's a little boy!"

"But I can't ask you to keep him while I'm two thousand miles away at college. It just ain't right! You ain't relations!"

"What about extended family. Do you have any extended family?"

I chuckled. Extended family. "All my relations's in Dallas. But they got their own problems, they can't be takin in a kid!"

"I honestly don't know what you can do—"

"Give up my scholarship," I muttered.

"No, you can't do that!"

"But what about Anthony?"

Ruthie took a deep breath. "I don't know. But you don't have to worry about it right now."

I sighed and she stopped.

"This is my class."

I nodded. We stood there looking at each other.

"I'll see you later."

"Yeah. Later—"

She grinned at me one more time and went into the room.

I didn't feel like going to third hour so I went to the cafeteria.

Erika and all her friends was sitting in a corner. I guess they was ditching too. Erika came running to me and threw her arms around me. "Hey baby!" she said and kissed me. "I missed you!"

"Yeah?" was all I could think of to say.

"You wasn't lookin at any of them Florida chicks, was you?"

"Nah—"

She looked at me. "Whassup?"

I shrugged. "I just got stuff on my mind—"

"So tell me!"

"It's nothin, really—"

"I know somethin's up, AJ! I want you to talk to me! I'm here for you!"

I grinned at that. It sounded like something Ruthie'd say. But Erika wasn't Ruthie. She started yapping about some fight she'd been in, but I could hardly listen. Then some of the fellas came running into the cafeteria. I guess they was ditching, too. "It's the Dream!" yelled Wakeen, giving me a high five. "How was FSU?"

"All right."

Erika grinned at me. "What we gonna do next year, anyway?"

I shrugged. I hadn't thought about that. The fellas started joking around but I didn't feel like joining in. For some reason they seemed stupid to me.

"I think I'm gonna head on home," I told them. As I left I could hear them talking about me.

"What the hell's up with him?"

"It's that Ruthie chick. He been hangin with her too much—"

"Do they got somethin going?"

"Man, they got to!"

165

I laughed. They'd never believe me and Ruthie was just friends. But I don't know what's wrong with me, why I was feeling so weird. Maybe it was just a phase or something. But to tell the truth, it was kinda scary.

# ERIKA

I'm gonna be great tonight, I know it. I never thought this day would finally come, when all the rehearsin was through and I could finally take center stage. The musical opened last night and of course, Shanice got to play Bess. It was hard watchin her in the audience, listenin to folks clappin for her. I feel like Bess is my role and mine alone. It was almost like watchin someone else play me. There was a big old article in the paper this morning with Shanice's picture. Like I said, Centennial musicals is big deals. But it pissed me off to see her in the spotlight, black cow bitch. I don't care how good she do sing, I know what a bitch she is.

But tonight is my night. I'm gonna go out there and bring down the house. And AJ gonna be there and Mom and all the fellas and all the girls. I'm gonna be great.

I sit in the dressing room fifteen minutes before curtain, finishin my makeup. Imani sittin with me. "You gonna do it, huh!" Imani say, excited. "You gonna tear the place up!"

I smile but I'm so nervous I can hardly talk. I close my eyes and take a deep breath. Please God, let me sing my best tonight...

"Erika, you okay?"

My eyes open and Imani is starin at me. "Yeah, c'mon," I say. We head on up to the stage and get in our places. Mr. Pauly is runnin around makin sure everything is set up straight.

Ronell come up to me, lookin ridiculous in his costume and make-up. He put an arm around me. "Ready for your big night?"

I smile back. "You know it!"

Ronell shake his head. "We gotta be good as we was last night. Man, we tore the place up!"

I roll my eyes.

He hug me again. "But hey, I like kissin you better than kissin Shanice!"

Now I laugh and smack him.

"Five minutes, everybody!" say Mr. Pauly. We all take our places on the stage.

The lights go out and I hold my place in the darkness, listenin to the overture, my heart racin. This is my night. I'm gonna do it.

*Porgy And Bess* is about a girl named Bess who fall in love with a cripple named Porgy in Charleston, South Carolina. Bess's old boyfriend Crown had killed this other guy Robbins in a craps game and has to leave town. While he's gone she fall in love with Porgy, who love her so much he end up killin Crown for her. But then he's taken to jail for the murder and one of his friends tricks Bess into goin up to New York with him. It's a sad story, really, but it's real romantic and got some pretty songs.

When me and Ronell sing *Bess, You Is My Woman Now* in the second act, the audience goes wild. I smile at Ronell and he smile back but I'm really thinkin about AJ. Cuz every song I sing is to AJ. That's how much I really love him.

When the final curtain fall, I run onto stage to hug Ronell. The tears is pourin down my face. "We did it! We did it!"

He pick me up and swing me around. "Yeah, we did!"

We run out in front of the curtain to take our bow and everyone is on their feet clappin. I can hear some of the fellas hollerin. The band teacher, who was conductin the orchestra, come up to give me flowers. Me and Ronell bow one more time, then run backstage. The whole backstage area is filled with bouquets of flowers, all for me.

Now Imani hug me. "Girl, you was the best!"

I laugh and hug her back. "Can you believe all these flowers?"

"Who they all from?"

"Let's see—" I pull out some of the cards. "Here's some from Mr. Pauly, Mom, AJ—"

I cradle the bouquet of roses AJ sent me and smile. He really do love me. He hasn't forgotten me.

Now Mom run to me and hug me. "Erika, you were wonderful!"

I hug her back. "Thanks, mom."

She dab at her eyes. "I can't get over how wonderful you were, how beautiful—"

I'm so happy I start cryin, too. "Mom—" I say, huggin her again.

Imani laugh. "Look! Here some flowers from Ronell!"

I laugh with her. "Ronell!"

Now Ronell come over and hug me again. "Yeah! Flowers for my favorite leadin lady!"

"Ronell, you is too much!"

Now I see Shanice glarin at me and I wanna laugh. I'm just as good as she is and she know it. But I'm too happy to be payin attention to her.

"What time will you be home?" Mom ask.

"I dunno—" I say. "Imani havin a party for the cast. I might just stay over there."

Mom nod. "Don't come in too late if you decide to come home."

"Okay. Bye Mom," I say and smile at her.

Mom smile back and take my hand. "You're a beautiful singer, Erika."

I smile again. As soon as Mom leave AJ come runnin.

"Hey baby!" he say and pick me up off my feet. I laugh and throw my arms around him.

"Man, you was somethin!" he say then kiss me.

"Mmm—" I sigh. "Haven't been gettin enough of that lately—"

He laugh. "You got my flowers?"

"Right here," I say and hold them close, smellin their perfume. "They're beautiful—"

He pull away and and that's when I see that Ruthie girl right behind him. I cross my arms and stare at her. What the hell is she doing here?

"You were really good, Erika," she say in that proper voice of hers.

I shrug, not sayin nothin. I look at her, then I look at AJ. Did he come alone with her? Why the hell'd he come with her?

AJ start to look uncomfortable. "So what you doing tonight, Erika?"

"Imani havin a celebration party. I guess I'll be there." I glare at Ruthie. She startin to look real uncomfortable.

"Um...I'll be in the car—" she say and leave real quick. I watch her go. Good. She got the message.

Now AJ start to look mad. "Whassup, Erika?"

"That's what I should be askin you! You came with her, huh!"

He sigh. "What's wrong with her comin with me to see the show?"

"What do you mean, what's wrong with it?" I snap. "You bring another girl to come see my show, no, I don't like it!"

He roll his eyes.

"AJ, I ain't gonna stand for you going out with other girls!"

"Stop trippin, girl!"

"I ain't trippin, you the one who trippin! I mean it, I ain't gonna stand for it!"

He shake his head, lookin mad. "Forget it. Maybe I'll see you at Imani's tonight."

And he turn and storm away. I watch him leave, gettin madder. Who the hell's he to ruin my night? Well shoot, I wasn't gonna let him! I shake my head. He can be such an ass sometime!

# RUTHIE

I had just finished my homework Wednesday night at eleven thirty when I heard a knock on my window. I put down my pencil, perking my ears for noises. Again, I heard a knock and sucked in my breath in both curiosity and fear. Who was at my window? I certainly wasn't expecting anybody. I moved cautiously to the window, peeking through the curtains.

AJ was sitting on the ground next to my window, motioning for me to open it. I smiled when I saw him. He's been a regular visitor at my house for the past few weeks. He was even here to congratulate me the day I received my acceptance letter from Stanford. I sighed with relief and let him in.

He jumped inside, bringing a wave of cold air with him. I shut my window behind him. "Why didn't you come sooner?" he asked, rubbing his arms. "It's cold out there!"

"I didn't know who it was. You could've been a burgular

or something!''

He smiled. "I didn't wanna ring the doorbell. Your parents are upstairs, right?''

I nodded. "They're asleep.''

He sat on my bed and I grew strangely uncomfortable. I clapped my hands together. "Um, what brings you by?''

He shrugged. "Just felt like talkin, I guess.''

I nodded, confused. "Okay—''

"Is it all right? Cuz I'll leave if it's not. I know your folks wouldn't want me in your room—''

"They're two stories up and like I said, they're asleep.''

"Plus it's late and all—''

"As you can see, I'm still up—''

He looked me up and down and grinned. "Is that what you sleep in?''

I felt self-conscious. I always wore a t-shirt and boxer shorts to bed. I must've been looking pretty awful; my hair was back in a ponytail and I'd already removed my make-up. "Yeah, why?''

He was still smiling. "I never seen you dressed sloppy before.''

I laughed nervously. "Well, this is what I sleep in!''

"It's good to see you in somethin sloppy.''

"That sounds strange, but I'll take it as a compliment.''

He leaned against the headboard and looked around my room.

"So...is Erika still mad at you?''

He looked annoyed. "God knows—''

I nodded, remembering how angry she was to see me with AJ Friday night. It was no big deal, the glory was all hers. (Except I was the one who told AJ to buy her flowers) I have to admit, I couldn't help feeling jealous as I watched AJ put his arms around her and kiss her. But I didn't show it. "She's so talented.'' That was the truth. She had a beautiful voice.

It was too bad her personality didn't match it.

AJ shrugged. "I didn't come here to talk about Erika."

I sat down next to him. "So...what made you want to come over?"

He shrugged. "I dunno. I was just sittin in my house and I couldn't sleep. No one else was there. I got kinda lonely."

"Really?"

"Yeah. Usually I just head over to Ray's or bring Anthony to my room, but Anthony's here now and the guys, I dunno—"

"They're seeing a change in you," I said softly. "Kevin told me. They think it's because of me."

AJ chuckled. "They think you and me got somethin going."

"Well, we don't—"

He shook his head. "I dunno. I do feel different though—"

"Better or worse?"

"I dunno. What is it? This feelin?"

"I'm not sure. Some people call it a coming of age."

"What?"

"You know, growing up."

"But I'm eighteen, I'm grown—"

"I don't mean that. I mean you're becoming more...mature. I've noticed it, too. And it's not necessarily because you spend so much time with me."

"But I like spending time with you."

I smiled, getting a jittery feeling.

"You understand me," AJ went on. "I been hangin with the fellas a long time now and I think you understand me better than they do—"

I shrugged.

"And I know I'm pissin them off—"

I sighed. "Change is hard for anybody to take."

"Huh?"

"Everybody wants things to stay the same. Like you and the guys going out partying every weekend—"

"We still do that—"

"But there's a difference. You don't spend as much time with them now."

"Yeah—"

"And a lot of people at our age think that life'll stay this way forever. But it doesn't. It can't."

AJ swung his legs onto the bed, then turned to smile at me. "See, you understand everything!"

"Not everything."

"What don't you understand?"

"A lot of things."

"Like what?"

I took a deep breath. "Well. . .there're a lot of things about myself I don't understand."

"Yeah, I guess I can see that. You're the most different person I know. And it ain't cuz you act white or nothin. It's just. . .you."

"Really?"

"You're so smart. Not just book-smart, but life-smart. That's kinda scary for a guy, you know. You can make a guy feel like he ain't good enough for you."

I was surprised. "How do I do that?"

"It's nothin you do. It's everything about you. You know how some people say everyone's equal? Well I don't think that at all. Some people're just better than other people. And you're just that. Better than other people."

"But it shouldn't be like that!" I exclaimed. I lowered my eyes and sighed. "Maybe that's why I don't date much."

AJ chuckled. "Guys see you and they think man, she gotta have a boyfriend!"

"But I don't!"

"Or they see you with white dudes like Christian—"

"Christian's my friend."

"Yeah, I know that. That was hard for me to see, how a black chick and a white dude could be such good friends. But I guess I can see it now. You and him's a lot alike. He better than other people, too. That's why so many guys wanna kick his ass!"

I laughed at that.

He laughed with me. "And I never thought I could get this close to a girl and have it be so—"

"Platonic?"

He laughed. "Yeah, Miss Dictionary. Platonic!"

I smiled, then got serious. "But I don't think I'm better than other people. I just have my head on straight, I guess."

"That's what makes you better. Like when you walk into a room, everybody knows you're there. They give you respect."

"Ha! You're one to talk!"

AJ shook his head. "Nah, it ain't the same for me. Yeah kids like me, but to adults I'm just another nigger. I know Mr. Ferris don't think I'm nothin more than a thug—"

"He doesn't know you the way I do," I said softly. "You're a hard person to get to know."

He shrugged. "Maybe. But I know you gonna make it big somewhere. You'll get a good job, marry a good guy—"

"How can you be so sure?"

"Just by lookin at you," AJ said, looking me in the eyes with a soft expression I'd never seen before. I blushed, feeling a shiver go up my spine.

His eyes lowered to the bedspread. "Even Erika. She's nothin compared to you."

"That's not true—"

"It is true. Y'know, I don't even know if I like her."

"Really?"

"Yeah. She's convenient, I guess—" His eyes met mine

176

once again. "I'll bet you think I'm awful for sayin that!"

"No, because you're probably just as convenient to her."

He laughed. "Yeah, maybe. And then there's prom. I really don't wanna go to prom with her. I don't even like prom."

I didn't answer.

"Who you going to prom with?"

"Christian. As friends."

He turned away, his jaw rigid.

I placed a tentative hand on his arm. "What's wrong?"

"Christian, huh," he muttered. Then he sighed. "Yeah, I guess he the only guy really good enough for you."

I smiled. "Like I said, we're going as friends. We decided to go together because I didn't have a date and he didn't want to go with somebody who'd spend the whole night drooling over him. We'd never be anything more than friends, anyway."

"Yeah—" he said, then sighed again. "Man, it'd be nice if—" He stopped abruptly.

"What?"

He shook his head quickly. "Nothin—"

I looked him in the eye. "AJ—"

He blushed. "Like me. I could never be good enough for you."

I was at a loss for words, my heart pounding wildly in my chest. How could I tell him how wrong he was?

I closed my eyes and sighed, trying to regain my composure. "You know, it's really ironic that a guy who could have his pick from both the white and black girls at school would think he wasn't good enough for me."

AJ shrugged. "I'm not."

"AJ—" was all I could say. I looked into his eyes, hoping he could see in mine that that wasn't true, that he was good enough for me, maybe the best thing for me.

I think he saw it because he was looking back into my eyes with a gentle expression. He brought a hand to my face, lightly touching my cheek. I sat immobile, my eyes locked with his. And before I knew it, I felt his lips on mine with a softness I never thought he'd have. I lost myself in that kiss, trying to hold on forever to that moment by wrapping my arms around him, our bodies touching, and covering his face with small kisses. All of the longings I'd held in for so long were spilling out of me with complete unrestraint.

He pulled away and looked at me in surprise. I turned away, fiercely embarrassed. Now he knew how I felt toward him and I didn't know what to do or say.

"Ruthie—" I heard him say. But I couldn't look at him. I stared at my bedspread, seeing even my hands trembling. I was finding it harder and harder to breathe.

Then I felt his arm circle my waist and I was pulled toward him. We both lay down and faced the ceiling.

My first thought was no...this shouldn't be happening, but that thought was never completed. I forgot everything as I turned to look into his eyes. We lay there, arms intwined and eyes locked together. There was no need to say anything. I sighed, closing my eyes and resting my head on his chest. I could feel his heart beating and his hands slowly rubbing my back, relaxing me even further. I could feel the warmth of his body through his shirt.

"Hold on a sec." He sat up to kick off his shoes and pull off his shirt. I now leaned against his bare chest, feeling his smooth, warm skin.

"Are you more comfortable now?" I asked.

He nodded and kissed me again, lightly and tentatively. I responded with more intensity and his arms circled me tightly, as if he were trying to press our bodies into one. His hands ran lightly down my back, over my stomach, my thighs and my face. I touched his face, feeling a light sweat

178

breaking out over his brow, then ran my hands over his shoulders, feeling the lean, compact muscles. It was as if it were all a part of some beautiful dream...

Then my eyes flew open and I realized the position we were in. I gently pulled away.

His eye opened also. "What's wrong?"

I looked at him with longing, wanting every part of him, but I heard myself say, "It'd be better if we stopped."

His eyes traveled downward and he sighed. I wanted to tell him no, I didn't mean it, but my voice seemed to be acting independently of my thoughts. So I placed my head on his chest, his heartbeat a lullaby.

"Okay," he said softly. I closed my eyes, drifting to sleep.

When I woke up again it was four thirty in the morning. AJ was asleep next to me. I rubbed my eyes, quickly remembering what'd happened between us. I shook him gently. "AJ?"

His eyes opened slowly and he smiled at me. "What time is it?"

"Four thirty."

He sat up and stretched. "I better get going. Your parents wouldn't be too happy if they knew I was here—"

"Will you be at school today?" I asked, not wanting to see him go.

He sighed. "Yeah, I guess—"

We walked to the window. The sky was still dark and the moon was setting. I opened the window while he retrieved his shoes and put on his shirt.

Then he turned to me. Without a word, he gave me a light kiss, then turned to leave.

I strangely felt like crying.

# ANDREA

Ruthie came into first hour looking disturbed and withdrawn. Instead of coming over to talk with Christian and me as she usually did, she sat in a desk and put her head down.

Christian noticed her strange behavior, too. "Is something wrong with Ruthie?"

I shrugged. "There must be something wrong for her to be acting like this—"

Christian looked worried. "Try talking to her. Use the workroom if you have to."

I nodded and walked over to Ruthie. I touched her arm. "Ruthie, it's me."

"I know," she said without looking up.

"Are you okay?"

"Yes—"

"Ruthie—"

"No, I don't know—"

"Would you like to go to the workroom to talk?"

Now she looked up. Her eyes bore deep circles and she looked tired. She stood up and I led her into the workroom, then shut the door behind us. Ruthie sat at a table and put her head in her hands.

"You look like you didn't get much sleep last night—"

She sighed. "I didn't. AJ came over at about eleven and didn't leave until four thirty."

"What happened?"

She sighed again. "It was great! We sat and talked for two hours and everything was great—"

"Ruthie, what happened?"

She burst into tears.

"Oh Ruthie—" I went to hug her, letting her cry into my shoulder. Now I was really worried, because it took a lot to make Ruthie cry. "What is it?"

She wiped her eyes. "I don't remember exactly how it happened, but all of a sudden, he was kissing me—"

"Ruthie, that's wonderful! I've always thought you guys should get together!"

"But that's it!" she said. "We were talking so comfortably, and then we were kissing...for a while I even thought we'd end up—"

"But you didn't?"

She shook her head listlessly. "I wanted to, but for some reason I said no. Just being with him last night made me feel things I never thought were possible—"

"So what's wrong?"

"Everything! He has a girlfriend, what about her?"

I shook my head. "Ruthie, it's not like they're married. If everything was so great between you and AJ, then maybe that's what's meant to be!"

She didn't answer.

I hugged her again. "If there's anything I can do for you,

let me know!"

She smiled. "Thanks Andrea."

"I'm your best friend," I told her. "I'm here for you."

Now Christian poked his head in the door. "Sorry. Am I interrupting anything?"

"No, come on in," said Ruthie.

Christian went to hug her. "Are you okay?"

She sighed. "No, not really—"

"It's AJ, right?"

She nodded, then got up to get a Kleenex. "He came over last night."

Christian nodded slowly. "Well, he's here now."

Both Ruthie and I turned to look at him in surprise. "What?"

"He wants to talk to you. He's waiting in the hall. I told him I'd get you. Do you not want to talk to him?"

"No, I'll talk to him," she said and left the room.

Now Christian and I looked at each other.

"What's going on?" he asked.

I smiled excitedly. "I think they might be finally getting together! Come on, I'll tell you later."

We went back to the classroom and saw Ruthie leaving the room. She'd left the door open. Out of curiosity, I went to stand by the door. So'd Christian.

I saw AJ and Ruthie standing in the hall with their arms around each other, as if they'd never let go.

"—didn't want you to think I was just comin on to you last night—" AJ was saying to her. "Everything that happened, it's cuz I really like you, and—"

"I know, you don't have to say that—" said Ruthie.

He closed his eyes. "What other girl'd understand that, huh?"

Christian and I looked at each other and smiled.

"But what about Erika?" Ruthie asked. "And what about

182

me? You know how I feel toward you—"

"And I feel the same way about you—"

"But it isn't fair to me or Erika—"

Now Kevin came to stand by the door. He looked at AJ and Ruthie and shook his head. "Oh man—" he mumbled.

"Want me to break up with Erika, is that it? Cuz I will if you want me to—"

The two of them walked away together.

"It looks like I'd better find another prom date," Christian said mildly.

I sighed. "But they'll be so happy together—"

Kevin was still shaking his head. "But Erika, man, she's gonna be pissed!"

"Who cares!" I sang. "AJ and Ruthie are in love!"

# RUTHIE

Thoughts weighed heavily on my mind as AJ and I left the building.

"No one's home at my house," AJ said. "Wanna go to my house to talk?"

I nodded without a word. He smiled at me and took my hand. I smiled back, getting that same shivery feeling I'd had last night.

"I'll drive if you want," he said.

I nodded and handed him my car keys. We were silent as he drove to his house. We went straight to his room and AJ shut the door behind us. He sat on the bed while I paced the room.

"Why you so nervous?" asked AJ.

I shook my head. "I don't know—"

AJ just smiled.

"I talked to Andrea this morning and she said I shouldn't feel guilty but I do! And I think about Erika—"

AJ shrugged. "So you worried about Erika—"

I sighed deeply. "It's not only that. I'm trying to figure out exactly what's going on between you and me, too!"

AJ chuckled. "You know what your problem is?"

"What?"

"You always want an answer for everything."

I bit my lip. "I guess you're right—"

He held out his arms. "Come here—"

I went to sit beside him. He pulled me close, stroking my hair. I felt myself relaxing. Then he kissed me and just like last night, I closed my eyes, losing myself in that kiss.

But I sat up as reality surfaced.

"Whassup?" asked AJ, stretching languidly on the bed.

I smiled at him, then shook my head. "I just have to wonder what's to come of this. Of you and me—"

"Hey, I ain't takin advantage of you or nothin—"

I looked into his eyes. "I believe that. I really do."

He smiled and sat up to kiss me again.

I pulled away. "But you haven't answered my question."

AJ took a deep breath, looking as if he was searching his head for an answer. Then he shrugged and put his arms around my waist.

"AJ—"

"Will you relax?" he said softly. "I said I'll break it off with Erika if you want me to!"

I was at a loss for words. "AJ, I'm not asking you to do anything!"

He laughed then faced me, looking into my eyes. "Okay, Miss Questioning! I'm gonna break it off with Erika cuz I don't like her no more and I do like you! And I want you to be my girl cuz—" He stopped.

"Because—" I said softly.

He smiled shyly. "Cuz I love you."

I sucked in my breath, my heart racing. When I was finally

able to speak, my voice was barely audible. "You, you do?"

He shrugged and nodded. "Remember how I asked you about love? Now I think I know what it feels like. Love with a girl, I mean."

I felt tears come to my eyes.

He took my hands. "Hey, you don't gotta cry!"

I wiped my eyes quickly and smiled. "I've never had a guy tell me he loves me before."

He smiled and we lay down together. "So did I answer all your questions?"

I had to laugh. "I guess so. I'll let you know when any more come up!"

He laughed and kissed me again.

# ERIKA

I wait for AJ after his third hour class cuz I wanna tell him about the prom dress I bought yesterday. It's got a short skirt and it's made of this shiny gold material. It's real sexy. It cost me over two hundred bucks but it's pretty so it's worth it.

"Wait'll AJ see it!" I tell Monica. "He won't be able to keep his hands off me!"

"Ain't that the idea?" Monica say and we laugh.

"You got it. Now that the musical's over I gotta start spendin more time with him. Keep that Ruthie chick away from him!"

Monica roll her eyes. "Yeah, his FRIEND!" The bell ring and all the guys start comin out the locker room. Kevin and Wakeen and Jamil and Doug come out together but AJ ain't with them.

"Whassup Erika, hey Monica!" they all say and Kevin put his arms around Monica. "Where's AJ?" I ask. The guys look at each other with guilty looks on their faces. I narrow my eyes at them, wondering what's up. Finally Wakeen say, "He ain't here." I cross my arms and glare at him. "So where is he?"

Kevin move away from Monica and put his arm around me. "Erika, there's somethin I gotta tell ya—"

I push him away from me. "What the hell's going on! Where's AJ?"

"That's . . . what he gotta tell you," say Wakeen, still lookin guilty. I glare at all them. "You better tell me what the hell's up and tell me right now!" Kevin swallowed hard. "I think AJ and Ruthie—"

"What?" I scream. "No way! No fucking way!"

"I saw them this morning together!" say Kevin. "I don't know if I should be tellin you this—"

I grab him by the collar. "You better tell me if you wanna live!" He shake away from me. "Okay, okay! I heard Ruthie's friends Andrea and Christian talkin and I guess he spent the night at her house last night. And in first hour this morning, she and AJ had their arms all around each other and they left together!"

I close my eyes, takin deep breaths. No way. AJ's mine! I ain't gonna lose him to some dark-skinned bitch or anyone for that matter! "I'm gonna kill her! I'm gonna find her and I'm gonna kill her!"

"You should," say Monica. "I hope that bitch had fun with AJ cuz it's all the fun she ever gonna have! Cuz she's dead! I'm gonna kill her!" I turn and run out the building.

I know the guys are starin after me. "Shoot, I feel sorry for that Ruthie chick!" I hear Wakeen say.

Yeah, he better be sorry! Cuz that bitch is dead!

# PART IV

# ERIKA

That bitch is dead and I mean it! I went lookin for her Friday but I didn't see her. AJ neither. I kept callin his house but he wasn't there. I know they was together somewhere! But Ruthie can't hide from me forever. I'm gonna find her and I'm gonna kill her!

"I haven't seen that bitch anywhere," say Kelli at lunch on Monday. "She must be real scared."

"She better be," I say.

"You shoulda kicked her ass a long time ago," say Imani. "Cuz she just got in closer and closer with AJ right under your nose!"

"Well she dead now!" I tell them. I'm so pissed off I can't eat. All this weekend I was so pissed off I couldn't do nothin. The more I thought about it, the madder I got. I'm prettier than Ruthie, lighter than her, plus I known him longer! And the second I see her, her white-wannabe assed self is dead!

"There's her friend!" Monica point to a redhead white

chick. "Her name's Andrea somethin."

I narrow my eyes at the girl. She sittin by herself doing homework. It'd be fun to kick her ass, scare her straight-laced self up a little. I get up and walk over to her. All the girls follow me. I slam my fist on the table and she look up, scared. I wanna laugh but instead I say, "You the bitch that hang with Ruthie!"

She roll her eyes and I wanna knock that stuck-up attitude right outta her. "What do you want?" she ask.

"She wanna know where your bitch friend Ruthie is!" say Imani. "And why she hidin!"

"Ruthie isn't hiding!" say the girl. "The truth is, I don't know where she is."

The girl is lyin. I get mad. "Bullshit! You better tell me before I get your ass, too!"

"I haven't seen Ruthie since she left Friday with—" She stop and blush.

I slam my fist on the table. "You know where they's at!"

The girl sigh. "So you know about her and AJ. Well, I don't know where they are. Your guess is as good as mine."

I just look at her. She look right back at me. I get madder. She don't look scared no more and I want her good and scared. I'm about to talk more shit to her when I hear someone say, "What the hell's going on?" I turn around and see that straight-assed Christian guy. The one all the white chicks giggle over.

The girl grit her teeth. "Will you get out of here!"

Michella point a finger in her face. "You better watch what you say, bitch! Cuz we'll be comin for you next!"

Christian sit down next to the girl and look at all of us like dirt. "Just get out of here!"

I back away from the table, keeping my eye on both of them. "You tell Ruthie she can't hide forever! Cuz I'm gonna find her! And when I find her, she's dead!"

We go outside to the smokin area.

"You told her good, girl!" Imani say. I ignore her and light up a cigarette. But I'm too mad to smoke so I put it out and punch my fist into my hand, wishin it was Ruthie's face I was hittin.

"We gonna get her tomorrow," I say. "She'll be here tomorrow."

"How do you know?" ask Kelli.

"I just do! A studious bitch like her don't stay away from school too long. And I ain't gonna wait no more!"

"Tomorrow," say Imani, grinning. I gotta grin, too. Cuz it's gonna be fun, smashin her up, messin up those nice clothes of hers, bruisin her up real bad. I'll mess her up so bad she won't never go near AJ again!

I can hardly sleep tonight. I hang out at Imani's till eleven, then go home and lay in bed, thinkin about what I'm gonna do to Ruthie.

Tuesday I get up extra early and get dressed in jeans and a sweatshirt. I ain't gonna get none of my nice clothes messed up. Then I put on all my rings, rings ex-boyfriends gave me. One's real sharp, I cut up a girl with it two weeks ago. Then I hurry over to the school. All the girls is there, dressed like I am.

I smile. "Ready for some action?"

"You know it!" say Imani, showin me her set of brass knuckles. One of her ex-boyfriends gave them to her.

"That girl ain't going near your man ever again after we're done with her!" say Kelli.

I laugh. There's nothin better than revenge. Nothin. We all go inside the building. I know she here cuz I saw her car in the parking lot. "Where her locker at?" ask Imani.

"Downstairs by the science rooms," I say. "Let's get movin!" she say eagerly.

"Chill out, girl!" I tell her, headin upstairs to my own

193

locker. I throw my purse in there, then look in the mirror and brush my hair. I still look good, even though I'm dressed like a slob.

Monica come runnin to my locker.

"Hey girl, where you been?" I ask.

"With Kevin," she say, out of breath. "AJ's here today."

I suck in my breath, feelin myself shake a little. "Did you talk to him?"

She shake her head.

I slam my locker shut. "Let's get that bitch now!" The girls all follow me downstairs. Everyone is lookin at us as we go by. We look tough and we know it. Nobody mess with us!

I see Ruthie standin at her locker at the end of the hall. She by herself. Perfect. I start clenchin my fists. I can't wait to rough her up. But I keep calm and walk over to her locker with all the girls behind me.

She don't see us. She lookin through some book. I look her up and down and laugh. She wearin nice pants and a nice shirt with a matchin scarf. It's gonna be fun messin up those fancy clothes and that fancy hair. That girl gonna be beggin for my mercy. I'll bet she can't fight, neither. I picture her and AJ together and get real mad. I slam her locker door shut as hard as I can.

Now she look up, startled. I glare at her, tryin to keep myself from knockin her cold right there. When she see me she get this real cool look on her face.

"Go on, Erika," Kelli say. "Kill the bitch."

"Y'know, I can't have that," I say, my voice quick. "I can't have you on my guy. I told you to stay away from him!"

She take a deep breath. I can tell she gettin some smart answer ready and I don't wanna hear it. So I haul off and knock her one in the eye. She fall back against the locker, her hands going up to her face. Now I hold her shoulders up against the locker.

"You think you can take him away from me, bitch?" I scream and slam her head against the locker. The locker make a loud clangin sound. Her eyes are wide and she look surprised and scared. Now she break away from me with more force than I expected her to have. She back up, her chest heavin up and down, keepin her eyes on me. Me and the girls take a few steps toward her. She hasn't said nothin.

"You can't run from me, bitch," I tell her. "Cuz I'm gonna mess up that face so bad AJ won't never look at you again!"

"I don't know what to say—" Her voice sound squeaky and scared. "AJ and I, well—"

"AJ and you, nothin!" I scream. I notice the crowd around us growin bigger and bigger. Ruthie's breathin faster and faster, her eyes big and scared. I'm lovin every minute of it.

"Dark-skinned bitch! I'll make you stay away from AJ!" I hiss. Then I hear a loud "What the hell—" I look away from Ruthie and see AJ runnin toward us, pushin through the crowd. Ruthie run to him and throw her arms around him. That sight make my blood boil and I go runnin to break them apart.

"I'll kill you!" I scream. He let go of Ruthie and grab my arms so tight I can't move. "Let me go!" I scream but he stronger than I am. He pull me through the crowd and out the door just as a teacher start to break up the crowd. I look around. Ruthie is gone.

"Where is she?" I yell, still tryin to break loose. But AJ hold me tight and won't let go. I try clawin at him but he start shakin me. I start seein spots in front of my eyes and my head is poundin. But I keep wrestlin with him and finally I break away from him, breathin heavy. I glare at him and he look back at me with an expression I never seen on him before.

"You son of a bitch!" I scream. "What the hell you doing with her, huh?"

Now he sigh, leanin against the building. "That's what I gotta talk to you about."

I cross my arms and glare at him.

"Me and Ruthie, well, we got together—"

"What about me, huh? You're my boyfriend, AJ! What about prom?"

He sigh again, still lookin me in the eye. "That's what I gotta say. I gotta break it off with you."

I stare at him.

He go on, lookin uncomfortable and nervous. "Ruthie, well, she's gotten to be real special to me."

I shake my head, like I'm tryin to get rid of a bad dream. "What about me? Don't you love me?"

"I love Ruthie. I don't know what to say cuz nothin I have to say gonna sound too good. It just happened, I guess. I know it's a pretty shitty deal for you but I don't know what to tell you. There ain't nothin else I can tell you."

"That fucking bitch!" I scream and burst into tears. "How can you do this to me when I love you, AJ?"

He keep lookin at me. "Why you love me, Erika? What do we ever do besides fight?"

I don't say nothin. I can't. I just keep lookin at him, not wantin to believe what he sayin.

"And Ruthie, she understand me. I need that. I know you don't get it. I dunno, maybe you'll get it when you find the right guy—"

I back away from him. "No, you don't get it! No dark-skinned bitch can take you away from me!"

"I want you to stay away from Ruthie—"

That push me over the edge. "No, you better do your best to keep her away from me! Cuz when I find her, that bitch is dead! You hear me?'' And I turn and run away from him, runnin across the street to City Park. I collapse on the ground and bawl my eyes out.

# RUTHIE

I went straight to the bathroom to inspect my eye. My face felt hot and flushed and my left eye was throbbing as if it had a pulse of its own. The skin around it was starting to bruise.

Both Christian and Andrea came running into the bathroom. Andrea looked horrified. "Omigod Ruthie, are you okay?" She threw her arms around me. "Kevin told us about the fight—"

I sighed. "There was no fight. Erika punched me. She and her friends were about to annihilate me when AJ showed up and took her outside."

Christian wet some paper towels and pressed them to my eye. I winced from the pain. "That's a nasty bruise," he said.

"It doesn't feel too good, either. Pretty vicious enemy I've made, huh!"

Andrea looked frightened. "She's going to be out for you now. She came up to me yesterday, telling me how she and her friends were going to kill you. I thought they'd get me, too!"

Christian's mouth tightened. "Someone'll have to keep an eye on both of you for a while."

I turned to him and laughed. "People're going to be shocked to see you coming out of the girl's bathroom!"

He grinned and shrugged. "What's been going on with you and AJ?"

I smiled, getting a warm feeling. "We're together."

Andrea's face lit up. "That's so wonderful!" But she sighed. "And now he's telling Erika the bad news—"

I nodded.

"I guess you won't be needing me for a prom date anymore—" Christian said.

I smiled at him. "Actually, I'd still love to go to prom with you."

"But what about AJ?"

"AJ doesn't like prom. And he knows we're going as friends."

Christian's eyes twinkled. "Are you sure it's okay? I'm not going to get beat up or anything, am I?"

I chuckled. "No!"

He smiled. "Now let's get out of here before someone sees me and throws a fit!"

The three of us left the bathroom. Second hour had long since started and the halls were clear and quiet.

"My attendance record hasn't been too good this quarter," I declared.

"So what?" Christian said. "It's your senior year, you're going to Stanford. Who cares about school now?"

I spotted AJ coming down the stairs. My heart raced as it did every time I saw him now. I suppose it was the jitters of a much-belated first love. "I'll see you guys later," I told Christian and Andrea and went to meet him.

AJ looked irritated, but he smiled when he saw me. "I was just lookin for you," he said. He must've noticed my eye because he mumbled something under his breath.

"Don't worry about my eye," I told him. "It's fine. I assume you've told Erika about us."

His face was grim. "Yeah, I told her."

"And she didn't take it too well—"

He shook his head.

I sighed. "Look, if you're reconsidering—"

He looked me in the eye and smiled. "No, I'm not reconsidering! I love you, remember?"

I smiled back. "I remember."

But his face became grim once again. "But I don't know what Erika's gonna do."

"She said she wants to kill me," I said. "Should I be worried?"

He looked at me in a strange way and nodded slightly.

I sucked in my breath.

"What?"

It took me a moment to regain my composure. "She really hates me this much?"

Again, he nodded.

I shook my head. "I guess I've never had anyone...dislike me so much. I mean, I can't believe it's possible for anyone to feel that much hate—"

"Believe me, it's possible."

"But why?"

He shrugged.

I took a deep breath. AJ hugged and kissed me. "Don't worry about it. I'll keep watch over you. So will the fellas. You and your friend Andrea. Cuz there's no telling what Erika might try to do."

"Okay—"

"I'll show you who her friends are, too. They'll probably

start followin you around, tryin to find out where you live and shit.''

"I know who they are,'' I said. I shook my head, still stunned by the days events.

AJ hugged me again. "Like I said, don't worry about it!''

"I'm just not used to violence and murder!'' I exclaimed. "She'll really try to kill me?''

He laughed. "Not kill you. Just hurt you real bad.''

"I feel better already,'' I mumbled.

He laughed again.

# ERIKA

I sit there in the park cryin for God knows how long. I feel so empty, like somebody done ripped my heart right out my chest. AJ just dropped the news on me, no warnin or nothin. How could he do this to me? I thought he loved me! Sure we fought but all couples fight! And what do Ruthie got that I ain't got? I just don't get it. I don't get it all.

I can't handle school so I just go home. Mom's here, I can hear her with some guy in the bedroom. I sigh and make myself a drink. I want to cry some more but I done cried myself out. So I go to my room and curl up on my bed. Oh God, AJ. . .I need you!

And that chick Ruthie, she don't need him! She got good folks and good grades and lots of money, what do she need with AJ? And she hang out with all them white snob types. AJ don't like those kind of people! What's he seein in her that he don't see in me? They'll never last, I know it! AJ'll leave her and come crawlin back to me. I shouldn't take him back, just to piss him off. But I would. Of course I would.

I sit up and go to my closet, takin out my prom dress. For a second I just stare at it. Then I laugh. I won't be needin this no more! And AJ'll never see how pretty I look in it.

"AJ YOU SONOFABITCH!" I scream and tear the dress in half. It rip easily cuz it's delicate. I throw the dress on the floor as hard as I can. That's what I'm gonna do to Ruthie! Stay away from Ruthie my ass, I'm still gonna kill her! And AJ ain't gonna stop me!

Now I take the picture of me and AJ at Homecoming off my dresser. I look at the two of us, arms around each other and smilin. Then I throw that across the room and it crash against the wall. The frame break in two.

"Shut up in there!" yell Mom from her room.

"DON'T TELL ME TO SHUT UP!" I scream. "I'M GONNA KILL HER!" I throw myself onto my bed and cover my face with my hands. I'm so mad I can feel my whole body shakin. I feel like I can rip that girl apart, just like I did that dress.

I hear my door open. "What the hell's going on in here!" It's Mom and she sound sober.

I sit up and look at her. "AJ broke up with me. We ain't going to prom—"

Mom bend over to pick up the dress. "So this is what you do with your dress? You paid good money for this!"

I don't say nothin.

Mom throw the dress on the floor and wipe her forehead. "Anyway, you're better off without him. He was nothing but scum—"

I start to cry again. "He dumped me for some dark-skinned bitch who act like she's white!"

Mom shrug. "Come on, forget about him!"

"But I can't!" I sob. "I can't!"

To my surprise, Mom sit down next to me and put her

arms around me. I lean against her and cry and cry and cry.

"Oh honey—" she sigh. "I know men are scum. All men are scum, black and white and everything else! You just have to learn that it doesn't matter!" She sound like she about to cry, too. "Forget about him."

"But I. . .don't want to. . .forget. . .about him—"

"You'll find someone else. You're a pretty girl and there are a lot of men out there. But you just remember, men are only good for two things. Sex and money. You remember that and you'll be fine—"

I wipe my eyes and sit up. "Thanks Mom—"

Mom hug me again. "You don't have to thank me—"

I sniffle. "I mean for not fightin with me."

Mom sigh again. "I know there're a lot of times when we don't get along, but I'm still your mother."

"I'm glad," I say, not wantin her to leave. I feel protected, sittin there in her arms.

But she pull away and stand up. "I have to go now, I have a friend over. Will you promise me you'll be quiet?"

I nod. She leave and go back to her room.

I lay on my bed and stare at the ceilin, feelin empty all over again. Thinkin about seein AJ and not being able to go up to him and put my arms around him, that hurt so bad. And havin to see him with another girl. . .that thought make my blood boil. I'd have to kill the bitch. And I will! And I'm gonna make AJ suffer, too! I'll go out with other guys to get him good and jealous. After that and after I kill Ruthie, then I'll take him back!

I sigh. My eyelids are startin to feel heavy. I'm exhausted. All that cryin wore me out. Maybe I just need to get away from here for a few days, get away from Denver and everything that got to do with Ruthie or AJ. Maybe I'll go see my dad in Phoenix. Yeah.

I pick up the phone and call him. His wife Juanita answer

the phone.

"Hi, is my dad, um, Omar Whitman home?"

"No, he at work."

I sigh. "This is Erika. Where can I call him?"

She don't say nothin for a minute. I know she don't like me at all. And I don't like her neither. "Call him at work. Same area code, 555-7712." And she hang up.

"Bitch," I say then dial the number.

It take a while to get through to Dad. He a computer programmer at a big company.

"Daddy, it's Erika."

"Hi baby. Did you get my check?"

"Yeah, I got it. I want to know if I can come down to Phoenix."

Dad don't say nothin.

"Daddy?"

"How long, baby?"

"Just a few days. I got a lotta troubles here."

"Boy troubles?"

"Nah, I ain't pregnant or nothin like that. I just got a lotta troubles and I need to get away."

"Well you know how Juanita feels about you—"

"I'll stay outta her way. Please Daddy?"

He sigh. "We got relatives comin this weekend. You can come the weekend after this one."

"Yeah good, that's prom weekend."

"Ain't you going?"

"No...my boyfriend broke up with me."

"Oh Erika—"

"Yeah, I had my dress and everything. He dumped me for another girl. I gotta kick her ass before I leave, the sleazy bitch!"

"Yeah, get her good! Don't let her mess you over like that!"

"I won't. So I'll see you in a week and a half?"

"Sure thing."

"Bye Daddy."

I hang up the phone and think about Ruthie. How'm I gonna get her? I know AJ'll be lookin out for her. Same with all her whitey friends. But she can't stay protected forever! And I'll drop her a few hints to let her know I mean business! If she so smart she'll leave AJ alone all together! I call up Imani to tell her.

"So what you gonna do?" she ask.

"I'll think of somethin. Bring your blade to school tomorrow. Ruthie in for a warning!"

Kelli and Imani meet me out in the parking lot during first hour the next morning.

"So what we gonna do?" ask Imani.

I lead them over to a certain blue Ford Escort.

"Her cute little car," Kelli roll her eyes and say.

"Gimme your blade, Imani," I say. Imani hand me her switchblade. The thing is six inches long and sharp!

"Oh man!" Kelli giggle as I slash each one of Ruthie's tires.

I watch the air go out of them. "That a good warning?"

"Leave her a note," say Imani.

I rip a piece of paper from my notebook and scrawl, "This is what I'm gonna do to your face!" I put the note under her windshield wiper and we go runnin back to the school.

"Think that'll give her the message?" giggle Imani.

I shrug. "We'll see."

Kelli stop in her tracks. "Oh shit," she say, narrowin her eyes. I see three of them Black Cows comin our way. Shanice and her friends.

Shanice is grinnin. "I hear AJ dumped you for that Ruthie chick!"

That make me so mad I haul off and punch her in the face.

Shanice hit me back. "Bitch! Half-breed bitch can't keep a hold of your man—"

I remember I'm still holdin Imani's blade and flip it open. Kelli has to pin my arms back to keep me from cuttin her open. I struggle with her but she don't let me go.

Shanice just look at me. "Forget it, Erika. You better pray your half-breed ass don't meet up with me!" And she and her friends go across the street.

"Bitch!" I yell after her, still strugglin with Kelli.

Imani look after them. "Damn. Why'd you stop her, girl? Erika shoulda sliced the bitch."

Kelli let go of me but she don't say nothin. I throw Imani her blade. I guess it's good Kelli did hold me back cuz in the mood I'm in, I might've sliced her.

We go inside and I go to class. But I can't concentrate on nothin nobody say. All I can think about is AJ.

# MONICA

Me and Kevin and Doug and Kelli got to prom at ten because we all shared a bottle of champagne before we went inside. Prom was at the Regency, a ritzy hotel downtown. But prom night's never any fun without getting drunk first. Well, at least a little buzzed.

"So Erika ain't comin?" asked Kevin as we went inside.

I shook my head. "She's seein her dad in Phoenix. She was so pissed off, she ripped up her prom dress."

Kelli shook her head too. "AJ really did her wrong."

Neither of the guys said anything to that but they both got these uncomfortable looks on their faces.

We all sat at a table and the guys took off their tux jackets and threw them in a chair. "Man, I hate this thing!" Kevin grumbled, loosening his bow tie.

Doug shook his head. "What I don't get is if AJ's seein Ruthie now, why ain't they at prom together?"

"I guess Ruthie'd been plannin on going with Christian

as friends," said Kevin. "At least that's what she told me."

Kelli's eyes narrowed and I saw Christian and Ruthie sitting at a table across the room. I gotta say, Christian's pretty hot, especially in that gray tux he was wearing. But what he was doing with that bitch Ruthie I don't know.

"Man, that bitch is dead!" Kelli said. "I say we go talk some shit to her!"

Kevin grabbed my arm.

"What's up?" I asked him.

He cleared his throat, looking nervous. "Leave her alone."

I just looked at him. "What do you mean, leave her alone?"

He cleared his throat again. "What I said."

I glared at him. "What, you protectin Little Girl Ruthie?"

He sighed. "C'mon, it's prom!"

"So?" said Kelli.

Doug grabbed her arm, too. "C'mon, don't you think you can be nice one day out of the year?"

I rolled my eyes. "Well I don't care if you guys are protectin her or not cuz when Erika gets back, that bitch is dead!"

Kevin shook his head and got up to go sit by himself at an empty table. I followed him, starting to get mad. He was acting weird.

"What's up your ass?" I exclaimed.

He shrugged. There was a weird look on his face. A look I've never seen before. "I'm startin to see why AJ broke up with Erika."

"What?"

"At first I thought he was crazy cuz Erika's so cute and all. But now I see it. Ruthie, she's sweet and nice and stuff like that—"

"Kevin!"

"Erika, all of you really, all you guys ever do is fight and bitch this and bitch that and she's dead and all that shit. I get tired of hearin it. So does AJ.''

"So that's it? You gonna dump me now for some straight-assed Honor Society bitch?''

"See what I mean? You're always so angry. What's up?''

"C'mon Kevin, you get in more fights than I do! I don't get this, this is bullshit!''

"But I don't hate anybody! You do. All of you do.''

I stared at the table. "So what're you tryin to say, huh?''

He shrugged. "I dunno. Just leave Ruthie alone. She never done nothin to you.''

I glared at him. "She took away my best friend's boyfriend!''

"She didn't take him away, can't you see that? AJ's the one who broke up with Erika!''

I didn't say anything.

"Well I don't know what Erika's gonna do but I don't want you havin nothin to do with it.''

That made me really mad. "Who the hell do you think you are, tryin to tell me what to do?''

"I love you Monica, but I won't put up with that shit. If I find out Erika does somethin and if you have anything to do with it, you and me, that's it.''

I stared at him in disbelief. Kevin was never like this. Never. He was always joking around and acting silly. This serious guy sitting here wasn't my Kevin. "I don't know what kind of shit Ruthie filled your head with!''

"Not for Ruthie. For AJ. AJ's my buddy, and no one's gonna mess with his girl. No one.''

I was so mad I got up and walked away from him. I ran into Wakeen and Imani and Jamil and Michella and went to talk to them. "Whassup, Mon!" Michella said when she saw me.

"Kevin's being an asshole. Stickin up for that Ruthie

bitch!''

"There she is," Imani said, narrowing her eyes at her. Ruthie and Christian were out on the dance floor.

I rolled my eyes. "You won't believe what Kevin said to me. He says he sees why AJ broke up with Erika!"

"You serious?"

"Damn straight! Sayin how nice Ruthie is and shit."

"She is nice," Wakeen said.

Imani glared at him.

"Nice! Man, she's stuck-up!" said Jamil. "One day I asked her for her phone number and she gave me this smart-ass answer!"

"Kevin said he'll break up with me if I do anything to her!"

Michella shook her head. "No way!"

I sighed. "I don't know what's up his ass."

Wakeen shrugged. "He didn't mean it, I know he didn't. He just don't want you messin with Ruthie. And you girls shouldn't be."

I glared at him. "Now you too? Shit, I've had enough of this!"

I left them and sat at another table. I lit up a cigarette, pissed off. Imani and Michella and Kelli came to sit with me and I guess Wakeen and Jamil went to sit with Kevin and Doug.

"Something's screwed here," said Imani. "That bitch Ruthie's screwin everyone up!"

I shook my head and put out my cigarette. "I don't get it."

"They just wanna jump on her," Imani said. "But why they'd wanna jump on a dark is beyond me!"

I rolled my eyes. Imani's so stupid sometimes! "No, she's too straight for that. She's a good little girl!"

Imani shook her head. "Man, Erika's gotta hear about this!"

211

I sighed. "This is one messed-up prom!"

Michella nodded. "Tell me about it. Look, the fellas are over talkin with Ruthie now!"

Imani slammed her fist on the table and stood up. "That's it!"

I pulled her down by her dress. "Sit down! All her bodyguards won't let you near her. But don't worry, we'll get her."

"Yeah, she better have her fun tonight cuz she won't be havin much fun when Erika gets back!"

"When does Erika get back, anyway?" asked Kelli.

"Tommorrow afternoon," I said. "Well shoot, she hasn't missed anything. Prom sucks."

"So we'll get Ruthie Monday, once and for all!"

I nodded. And I was gonna get my share. Screw Kevin. Maybe he didn't think we had anything against Ruthie but we do! And she was gonna get it!

# ERIKA

I leave town Friday cuz I don't wanna be around for prom. I been hangin low all week, going to a few classes at school, stayin in my room. It still hurt too much to see AJ. I'll bet Ruthie think I forgot about her but I haven't. She gonna get it when I get back and I mean that!

But Friday I didn't wanna think about her or AJ. I just think about gettin away.

Dad meet me at the airport when my plane land in Phoenix. I run to hug him. "Hi Daddy!"

Dad hug me back. "Hi sweetheart! It's good to see you!"

"Yeah, it's good seein you, too," I say as we go to get my suitcase. Dad look the way he always do. He a goodlooking man, I think. Tall and slim. His hair startin to go a little gray but he still look good. "So how you been?"

"I'm fine, the kids are fine," say Dad. "What about you?"

I shrug. "I been hangin low. I haven't kicked that Ruthie chick's ass yet."

Dad nod. "Make sure you do. Don't let that girl mess you over like that. How's your mom?"

"Mom? She don't change—"

"Have you talked to your boyfriend?"

"Nah. Haven't seen him around."

We go out to his car. He got a new car, a Honda Accord. We don't say nothin as he drive to his house. I guess Dad and me never had much to say to each other. We was always fightin when I lived with him. It was mostly cuz of his wife Juanita. She think I'm a whore and stuff. We used to get in some pretty nasty fights. Dad still live in the same house he lived in when I used to live there. "Evita's got your old room now so you'll have to sleep on the couch," Dad say as we go inside. I shrug. I don't really care.

Juanita don't work so when we come in, she come runnin out of the kitchen to give Dad a kiss. But she don't even smile at me. She just say "Hi Erika" real coldly.

"Dinner's almost ready," she tell Dad. Then she look at me. "You hungry, Erika?"

I shrug. I'm not.

She call the kids downstairs. The kids, Evita, Saul and Shelifa, all come running downstairs and we all sit at the kitchen table. They all look surprised to see me. "What you doing here, Erika?" say Evita, the oldest. I think she twelve.

I shrug. "Just visitin."

Shelifa, the youngest, looks confused. "Why?"

I shrug again. "I wanna see my dad. That's all."

Juanita fixed steak and rice and everybody starts eatin. Evita tell everyone about some school play she in. I sit at the table feelin uncomfortable just like I used to. Juanita's dark-skinned, so's Dad and the kids. So I always feel like an outsider. And they never really try to make me feel like I'm welcome. But Dad do sometimes. Like tonight. He turn to me and say, "Erika, wasn't you in a school play this

214

year?"

"Yeah, we did *Porgy And Bess*," I say. "I had the lead."

Evita laugh. "You! How could you have the lead?"

"Hey, she can sing!" say Saul, defendin me.

Evita keep laughin. "But she ain't black enough!"

That piss me off but I finish my dinner without sayin nothin else. I can never get away from that shit.

After dinner I go down to the living room and curl up on the sofa. Why the hell can't it ever end? I get so damn tired of tryin to prove I'm black. The white people sure as hell don't want me, I'm too dark for them. But I'm too light for the black people. So where do I fit in? Even Imani and Michella piss me off sometimes. Both of them's half-breeds but Imani's so stupid about it, talkin about how much better she is cuz she light. Same with Michella. And I know I say that kind of shit too, but I don't think it. Not deep down I don't. But I act that way cuz it's a safe way to act and it's how I'm expected to act. But I don't feel it.

Shoot, why does my life have to be so messed up? Ruthie, her life's perfect! She got two black parents still married, good grades, plus she got AJ too! I'll bet everything been handed to her on a silver platter. Well, I'm gonna make her suffer. Cuz she took away the only good thing in my life!

I hear the kids upstairs yellin about somethin and decide I had enough of this house. I get up and walk out the door. It's been a while since I been here but I know nobody's moved. This place is sort of like the hood where AJ live. No one come, no one go. Everyone sort of stay put.

I remember Dane Franklin, this half-black half-Mexican guy I used to go out with. He live three houses down from Dad. I figure I'll go see him. I know he'll remember me. He live with his grandma, this slow old lady who go to church but don't really give a shit what Dane do. It take her a while to get to the door after I ring the bell. Just as I'm startin to

215

get pissed off she open the door, wearin a bathrobe. "What you want?"

"I wanna see Dane. He here?"

The old lady grunt, "He in his room" and let me in the house. Dane's room's in the basement so I go down there, hearin loud rap music from the stairway. I knock on his door.

"Come in!" I hear him yell so I open the door and walk in.

He sittin on the floor with two of his homeboys and the three of them's sharin a bowl. He look about the same as he did last time I saw him; tall, good-looking, light-skinned, except I can tell he's high. He lost some weight, too. He look good, but not as good as AJ. Nobody look as good as AJ.

Now Dane look up at me and squint. "Who the hell're you?"

"Erika Whitman, remember me? I used to be your girl."

His boys look me up and down and whistle. I roll my eyes. Both of them look high, too.

"Erika." Dane get up and come over to give me a hug. He smell like weed. "Yeah, how could I forget you, baby?"

I hug him back, gettin a warm feelin inside. It's nice to feel a guy's arms around me again.

"Oh yeah, this is that light-skinned chick you always talked about," say one of his boys.

Dane sit me down next to him on the bed and smile. He take my hands, still lookin me up and down. "So what you doing in Phoenix?"

"Stayin with my dad a few days."

"I thought you and your old man didn't get along."

I sigh. "We don't, it's just that—" Now I look down at the floor, bitin my lip. That awful achy feelin is comin back to me. I feel Dane put his arms around me and pull me closer. "C'mon, you can talk to ole Dane. Whassup?"

I sigh again. "My guy, he started seein this other chick."

216

Dane look surprised. "Over you? Who is she, LaToya Jackson?"

"No, some dark-skinned bitch," I muttered. "As soon as I get back, I'm gonna kick her ass!"

He laugh and take a hit off the pipe. Then he hold it out to me. "Go on, take a hit." I take a hit off it. I usually don't get high but today I don't care. I need to forget about AJ and this is a way I can do it.

"That's a girl," Dane say, pattin my shoulder.

I take two more hits, feelin myself relaxin. I turn to him and smile. "So what you been up to?"

"Nothin—" Then he take another hit. "This—" And he laugh. He finish the bowl and light up another one.

"Guys get outta here," he say, then smile at me.

His boys laugh. "Yeah, go Dane!" They get up and leave, then Dane turn to smile at me again. I start laughin not only cuz I'm high but cuz I know what Dane's gonna try to get from me. Some people don't change.

He run his fingers through my hair, then over my face. "You is somethin, you know that?"

I don't say nothin but I stop laughin.

"You know, you should stay down here in Phoenix. Maybe you and me could get somethin going again. Cuz I never forgot you, y'know—"

I start laughin again. Yeah, right. A few minutes ago he didn't remember my name. But I let him kiss me, run his hands up and down my sides, pull me down on the bed close to him. All the while I'm not noticin much of nothin cuz I'm high and I feel good and I don't care.

He kiss me all over, unbuttonin my shirt, tryin to get his hands down my pants. The shirt I don't mind but in my semi-consciousness I push his hand away from my jeans. I can feel myself comin down as he gets more and more turned on. And I'm beginnin to realize I'm makin a mistake. I don't

217

want to sleep with this guy. I'm becomin more miserable as I come down off my high and being with a guy ain't gonna help me any. Cuz the only guy I wanna be with is AJ.

I sit up and Dane look at me with glazy eyes. "Whassup?"

I button my shirt. "I gotta get going."

I expect him to pull me back down and start kissin me again to shut me up but he don't. He just lay there. And I feel even shittier cuz I know he really don't care if I stay or if I go.

But I don't want to stay so I get up and go. On my way out I look at a clock and see it's after midnight. But I don't want to go back to Dad's yet.

I walk out on the street, my hands in my pockets. It's completely dark out except for the streetlights and a little piece of moon in the sky. I walk by some guys sittin on a front stoop and hear them callin at me as I walk by.

"Hey baby—"

"Man, she look like Vanessa Williams!"

"How about my place tonight!"

Usually when guys I don't know talk to me like that I don't pay them no mind and keep going. But today I turn to look at them and say, "You serious?"

They all look at each other and laugh. Nothin but thugs, I can tell. About five of them, high school age. I go up to the stoop.

"Who're you?" say one of them who look about eighteen. In the dark I can see his eyes glowin and bloodshot.

"Bridget," I say.

"Bridget! What you doing out here, Bridget?"

I shrug. "Lookin for some action, I guess—"

"Action!" They all look at each other. Then one of them say, "Baby, I can give you action like you never seen!"

I suddenly get disgusted. What the hell'm I doing talkin to these guys? "Yeah, right," I say and walk away.

"Bitch!" one of them yell after me. "You ain't that cute!"

I don't give a shit. Now, walkin alone in the night, I don't know what I want to do with myself. I don't wanna go back to Dad's, I don't wanna go back to Denver, I don't want to stay out on the streets.

So I say to hell with it and go back to Dane's. His grandma answer the door and bitch at me for comin by so late. But I ignore her and go downstairs to Dane's room.

He asleep on his bed or passed out, really. There's an empty bottle of Old English on the floor. I look around his room. The light from the moon shine in, makin everything glow in the night. The cigarette butts, pipes, bottles, even the centerfolds on the wall. All the girls in the pictures is white but they look blue in the moonlight, like ghosts.

I kick off my shoes and get in bed next to Dane. I cuddle up next to him and try to sleep, but I can't. I feel like shit. I keep thinkin about AJ, and the nights we used to lie together. I use to watch him sleep all the time. I loved to do that. Cuz in his sleep he looked so innocent and loving. I know he love me. He do. He has to! He can't just forget about everything we been through together!

We was going to be together again, I know it. Once I got Ruthie out of the way, AJ and me would be together...

# AJ

I was sorta pissed off when Ruthie went to prom with that Christian dude but it was okay, I guess. He was just friends with her. I saw her at the After Prom party and we came back to my house afterward to go to sleep.

We both got up late Sunday morning. I woke up first to see her head lying on my chest. For a second I just watched her, sort of amazed. I never knew I could feel this way for a girl, to really be in love and know she loves me back. I never felt like that with Erika, not in the whole time we went out.

Ruthie sat up and grinned when she saw me. "Hi—"

I hugged her. "Hey—"

"What time is it?"

"Eleven."

She stretched. "We should be getting up—"

I took her hands and grinned. "We don't gotta be getting up yet."

She grinned back. "Yes, we do. Anthony has a game today and you told him you'd be there."

I groaned. "Yeah—"

"You haven't been to his last two games. He was pretty sad about it."

I stretched. Anthony plays Little League t-ball. Ruthie's dad got him into it. He's got games every week and I make it to most of them, but I've had track meets the last two weeks.

"I'm going to take a shower." She leaned over to kiss me, then left the room. I got out of bed and went to open the drapes. Yeah, it was gonna be nice out today. I pulled some shorts from my drawer.

Franco came walking into the room and I just looked at him, wondering what he was doing here. He was grinning in a weird way. "So that straight little chick spent the night here. I always knew you'd be stickin it to her one of these days."

"Get outta here!" I hissed. I wasn't gonna listen to him talk that way about Ruthie.

Franco just laughed. I decided to ignore him. I didn't have to listen to his shit.

Ruthie came back a few minutes later, wrapped in a towel, hair dripping wet. She stopped when she saw Franco. Franco looked her up and down with that same strange grin on his face. She stood there staring him right back in the eye until he shook his head and left.

I frowned. "Asshole—"

She shrugged. "What'd he say to you?"

"Just talkin shit—"

She grinned. "Forget about it."

I grinned back. "Hurry up, we have to get going!"

I went to take a shower and when I came back, she was dressed and ready to go. "Come on," she said. "We'll pick up something to eat on the way.''

''So how's my brother been?'' I asked as we drove to McDonalds. I haven't seen him in a few days cuz we had late practices. We was training for the state meet.

She shrugged. ''Fine. He's doing great in school—''

We headed for Anthony's t-ball game. T-ball's like baseball, except the kids hit the ball off a tee, then run around the bases. It's pretty stupid but the kids are cute cuz they're so little and they don't know what they're doing.

Ruthie's folks and her brother was there when we got there. Seeing them all there cheering for Anthony made me feel something weird. It was like Anthony was part of their family now. I could tell when I went to see him and take him out that he was starting to think of Ruthie's folks as his folks. I guess that was great for him, but it made me feel a little out of it.

Ruthie squeezed my hand. ''Are you okay?''

I grinned at her. ''Yeah—''

She smiled back like she understood. She always understood.

Anthony went up to bat. ''Go Anthony!'' we all shouted. His face was all screwed up, like he was concentrating hard. He hit the ball off the tee pretty hard for a six year old kid, but I know the bat he used was pretty light. He'd shown it to me when Ruthie's dad first bought it for him. He was so proud of it, he took it practically everywhere. And he practically lived in his little team jersey. I chuckled, thinking about it.

The ball flew all the way out to left field, where some klutzy kid fumbled with it while Anthony ran all the way to third base. I was on my feet cheering for him with all the rest of the spectators.

Anthony's team, the Dodgers, won the game after a couple of innings. The games don't last long, I guess they think the kids'll get tired or something. When the final gun sounded, all the little kids went running off the field to their parents.

"Anthony!" I yelled. But his eyes were on Ruthie's folks. He went running straight to them and threw his arms around Ruthie's mom. Her mom and dad hugged him, telling him how great he was and how proud they were and all that. Then Derek picked him up and swung him around.

I stood there, feeling like someone had punched me.

Then I felt Ruthie tugging on my hand. "Come on—"

I shook my head, unable to speak. I walked away from Ruthie and stood by myself, watching Ruthie's parents fuss over Anthony. Anthony was yapping away with them, not even looking in my direction. I swallowed down a lump in my throat. What about me? Had he forgotten about me?

I couldn't help but get mad as I watched Ruthie's folks with Anthony. He wasn't their kid! Then again, I'd be a fool to be mad at them, after all they'd done for him. But I couldn't help but feel like shit. I felt like somebody'd ripped my heart right out of my chest. I stared at the ground and sighed.

"Hey bro!"

Now I looked to see Anthony tugging on my shirt. He threw his arms around me. I tried to grin and not let on to what I was feeling. "How's it going, kiddo?"

"Did you see me? I had a triple and a double!"

"Yeah, I saw you!" I said, grinning at him. "So when you going to the pros?"

Anthony grinned back. "In a coupla years! Then you can play pro football and I can play pro baseball and we'll be in sports together!"

I grinned at that.

"And now we're all going out to dinner!" Anthony said, sounding excited. "You're comin too, aren't you?"

"I dunno—"

"Yes, he's coming!" Ruthie said. I had to grin at her. I know she was trying hard to help me fit in with her family.

"We'll meet you there," she told her folks. Anthony went running back to Derek to talk to him and me and Ruthie went to her car. "No ducking out!" she said to me.

I grinned wryly. "Well you took care of that!" Then I stared at the dashboard.

I heard her sigh. "It hurts, doesn't it."

I looked at her. "How come you always know what I'm thinkin?"

"Because I know you. But Anthony hasn't forgotten you. He still thinks you're the greatest thing on earth—"

"It's just weird seein him with a family—"

"I guess it would be. Especially since he's gotten so close to us."

I nodded, saying no more.

Ruthie's folks was already sitting at the Black Angus when we got there and Anthony was still yapping away about his game. "Hi Ruthie, AJ," her mom said. I grinned at her folks.

Her dad turned to me. "So when do you leave for school, AJ?"

"I gotta go down sometime in July for trainin."

Her dad nodded.

Her mom turned to look at Ruthie. "By the way, did you ever find out who ruined your tires?"

Ruthie shrugged, not saying nothing. Both of us knew who did it cuz there was a note on her car saying something like "this is what I'm gonna do to your face." I felt bad cuz I knew all this had to do with me, so I helped Ruthie pay for new tires. She didn't want me to but I did anyway.

"That's a shame," her mom said, shaking her head, "how some people have to be so destructive—"

Ruthie didn't say nothing.

224

We finished dinner, then got up to leave.

"I'll stop by tonight to see you," I told Anthony as me and Ruthie got up from the table.

"Okay. See ya!" he said and went off with Ruthie's folks.

Ruthie and me went back to my house. We went to my room and I pulled her close to me.

"I can't stay very long," she said softly. "I have to get up early for that dumb field trip tomorrow."

I nodded. "I guess I'll be seein you. Call me tomorrow."

"Okay," she said and kissed me. "I love you."

"I love you, too," I said and just held her in my arms for a second. I really like this love stuff. There's nothing in the world like it.

# RUTHIE

"How was your trip yesterday?" Andrea asked me Tuesday morning when she met me at my locker.

I shrugged. "Boring. But I went over to AJ's last night and didn't get home until eleven, so I'm pretty tired."

Andrea smiled. "It's good to see you guys together."

I smiled, thinking about him. "I never knew he could be so sweet!"

"Well, I'm happy for you. What'd he think about you and Christian going to prom together?"

"He wasn't exactly thrilled, but he didn't say much about it."

"That's good," Andrea said, leaning against the locker. "Three weeks until we're out of here. Can you believe it?"

"I can't wait! You know, it's hard to get up the will power to even come to school now—"

Andrea sighed. "Tell me about it!"

"And with Erika still after me—" I shook my head. "I

don't understand how a person can carry so much hate!"

Andrea's eyes widened and she whistled slowly.

"What?"

She nodded her head in the direction of the door. "Speak of the devil!"

I looked and saw Erika coming our way, surrounded by her friends. I rolled my eyes. "I'm not in the mood to deal with her!"

Andrea bit her lip, looking frightened. "Oh, where are guys when you need them!"

"You can leave if you want," I told her.

"No way! They'll mutilate you!"

"They'll mutilate you too if you stay. Come on, you don't have anything to do with this!"

Andrea sighed with resignation. "Yeah, but you're my best friend and I'm not going to desert you."

I gulped as Erika and her friends came closer. They were looking straight at me so I know they were looking for me. To be honest, I was scared half to death, but I put on a brave face. Maybe she'd back down if she thought she couldn't get to me.

"Well, I was bound to have to face her again," I told Andrea, hearing my voice wavering slightly. The two of us fell silent as Erika and about four of her friends approached us, eyes smoldering. Erika looked like she was ready for a fight, dressed in tight pants and a tight top, a ring on every finger. For a moment I stared at her, awed by her beauty. Then I shook my head. It was a shame all that beauty had to go to waste. I knew she was trying to intimidate me and to be honest, it was working. But I was too proud to let it show on my face. And in my pride, I spoke first. "I figured I'd have to face you again."

"Listen, she smart!" laughed one of her friends.

I rolled my eyes.

"No, don't be rollin your eyes!" Erika snapped. "I got some stuff to say to you!"

I returned her gaze, eye for eye. "Then say it."

"No, I think I wanna tell you outside!" Erika now turned her glare to Andrea. "Without your white bitch friend!"

Andrea's mouth tightened.

"What type of fool do you think I am?" I exclaimed. "I'm not going out there so you and all of your friends can jump on me!"

"You don't get it, bitch!" hissed another of her friends, a beautiful brunette I recognized as Kevin's girlfriend Monica. "You're not gettin away from us this time!"

I sighed. This was pointless. "Listen, it's pretty obvious you have a problem with me, so let's solve it."

Erika glared at me. "Right on!"

"Your friends have nothing to do with this," I went on. "So let's take this outside, just you and me. That is, if you're not too chicken to risk a one-to-one confrontation—"

Erika looked me up and down and laughed. "All right! Just you and me!"

Her friends stared at her, surprised. Andrea was looking at me with wide eyes.

I turned to her. "Andrea, tell Christian I'll be late to first hour."

She nodded and hurried away.

Now I took a deep breath and turned to walk outside. I could hear Erika's footsteps behind me. My heart raced as I tried to think of what I'd do next. Okay Ruthie, I told myself, you got yourself out of a five-to-one fight. What are you going to do now? I honestly didn't know. I was making this up as I went along and every move I made was crucial. I knew Erika was expecting a fight, but I had no intention of getting into a fist fight with her or with anybody for that matter. Once we stepped out onto the lawn I turned to face her, standing a safe distance from her.

Erika clenched her fists, eyes narrowed to evil slits. "You better be ready cuz I'm gonna kill you, bitch!"

"And what good would that do?" I exclaimed.

She laughed harshly. "Mess you up real bad!"

She began circling me, fists clenched. I kept my eyes on her, careful to stay out of her range, careful not to make any sudden movements that would send her flying over to knock the sense out of me. My mind raced as I attempted to think of a way to get out of this fight. I attempted diplomacy. "I know you came out here for a fight, but you won't be getting one out of me."

"No, cuz I'm gonna kill you!" Erika took a swing at me but I jumped out of her way, keeping my eyes on her. Again, she circled me and I danced in and out of her path.

Finally, she stopped and laughed. "What kinda chickenshit are you?"

I said nothing. From the corners of my eye I could see students stopping to watch us curiously.

"I know you hate me and for all I know you probably always will," I said, attempting once again to reason with her. "But what will beating me up accomplish for you? Do you honestly think AJ will take you back if you beat me up?"

"AJ'S MY BOYFRIEND!" she screamed and sprang at me like a cat. I barely avoided being hit be jumping quickly to my right.

"Why don't you wake up?" I hissed. "AJ's not your boyfriend anymore!"

"I don't know what the hell he doing with an ugly dark-skin bitch like you—" She sprang at me again but once more, I avoided her fists.

Erika stopped again and laughed. "Yeah, just like I thought. You is chicken! You a wannabe wimp! And AJ don't like wannabes or wimps!"

While before I was thinking only of survival, now I grew angry. I felt anger like I'd never felt before, rising from the pit of my stomach to the top of my head and sending my mind spinning in black fury. "YOU ARE SO STUPID!" I yelled. "ANYTIME SOMEONE MAKES YOU MAD, YOU THINK BY SWINGING YOUR FISTS YOU'LL GET YOUR WAY? THAT JUST BECAUSE YOU CAN FIGHT YOU'RE SOME SORT OF GOD? WAKE UP!"

Now she managed to shove me and it took all the strength I had to keep from staggering. For one maddening, blinding second I wanted to shove her back. But then a calm haze filled my mind as I caught my breath and took a step away from her. And I felt strength like I'd never felt before.

"You know, you're so pretty and you are such a wonderful singer," I said, my voice ringing loudly clear and steady. "But for what? What the hell are you ever going to do with yourself?"

"COME ON, BITCH!" Erika screamed and lunged for me again but I managed to shove her off with enough force to send her flying backward.

She steadied herself and looked at me with surprised eyes. My voice grew louder and more forceful. "I don't give a shit if you do think I'm a wimp for not fighting you, because I'd rather be a wimp than what you are!"

She crossed her arms, her face filled with hate, her eyes challenging mine. "Oh, and what am I?"

"A nobody! A nothing! You never meant anything to AJ! All you ever were to him was a nice body for him to use at his disposal!"

"FUCKING BITCH!" She ran for me, fists clenched. But I danced around her, provoking her, challenging her to hit me but refusing to let her, frustrating her. She was swinging wildly but her fists didn't connect with anything but the air. I smiled, feeling all of the maliciousness in me boiling over,

230

and in a sadistic way, enjoying myself.

"It's the truth and you know it! That's why you're mad, right? And it's too bad because he really screwed you over! But you're dreaming if you think you and AJ ever had anything special! And you're a real fool if you think he's going to come back to you!"

Now I smiled, knowing I was getting to her, getting under her skin. Her brow was furrowed deeply and her eyes blazed. Her chest heaved in deep breaths and she was so angry I could see her shaking.

"You're dead, bitch—" she hissed.

"Is that all you can say? I'm dead?" I exclaimed. "Well I'm not feeling so dead right now! In fact, I'm feeling pretty good! What about you, Erika? How are you feeling right now?"

She swung again and again, I danced out of her way.

"And so what if you beat me up?" I went on, provoking her. "What good would it do? Who'll be on your side? Nobody, and you know it! Not AJ, not his friends, not this school! Who do you have, Erika? Or better yet, what do you have—"

"Oh, so you're a goddamn God now?" she shrieked.

I tasted this. "I'm telling the truth. Who would be on your side? Who at this school gives a shit if you live or die besides your little pack of followers? I'm going to Stanford in the fall, I have a future! And I have AJ!"

"Bitch—"

"And most importantly, I have my dignity and seft-respect! Do you have that Erika? Do you?"

Again, she circled me, crouched low. "You're dead, girl! And all this bullshit you talkin—"

"It's not bullshit and you know it!" I lowered my voice, noticing the crowd around us multiplying rapidly. "That's why you have to fight, right Erika? Can't risk talking things out? I don't think you can! What kind of life is that, Erika? You may be beautiful and you can sing, but I wouldn't want to be you for anything in the world. Because you're nothing. Absolutely nothing!''

My words were stinging her, I knew it. Her fists were slowly loosening and her face showed more hate than I ever thought imaginable. But it was a different sort of hate. It was the frustrating hate you feel when you begin to realize something about yourself that you don't want to know, something you've tried to repress.

Everything went silent. The crowd was silent, seemingly entraced. I was silent, taking deep, gulping breaths, watching her closely.

Erika was silent, her chest still heaving, eyes narrowed.

Then one of her friends shouted, "Kill the bitch, Erika! Go on, kill her!''

And another shout. "Go on, tell her Ruthie! Tell her good!''

And from that arose a chant. "RUTH-IE RUTH-IE RUTH-IE!''

I ignored all of this, keeping my eyes on Erika. She now reached up to put her hands to her face, her face contorting.

I took a deep breath, sensing this conflict was near its end, once and for all. "AJ and I have figured each other out, and ourselves. That's why we're together now. I know you'll probably always hate me for that.''

"Bitch—'' she muttered, her voice low.

I raised my voice. "You think I'm wrong?''

She looked up at me quickly.

I shrugged. "Well, that's your opinion. You do what you have to do. You want to kill me? Okay. Kill me.''

She stared at me, openmouthed.

"What?'' I heard several cries from the crowd.

I returned Erika's gaze, my jaw firm. I wasn't afraid. I'd

already won this fight, regardless of what she did.

"Go ahead," I went on. "Beat me up. Mutilate me. Do whatever you said you were going to do. Go ahead, if I'm wrong and you're right."

She stood motionless, the surprised expression frozen on her face.

"Is she crazy?" exclaimed someone in the crowd.

"Kill the bitch, Erika!" came a lone cry from one of her friends. But it gained no others, and fizzled out.

I stared at Erika and she stared right back at me. The crowd was silent. All eyes were on Erika now. The entire conflict was in her hands, just as I'd wanted it to be.

"Go ahead," I said softly, crossing my arms.

Her eyes grew defiant and she drew a deep breath, clenching her fists. "YOU FUCKING BITCH!" she screamed, flying toward me.

My muscles tensed but I didn't move. The crowd sucked in its breath, but remained silent.

Erika stopped a few feet in front of me, her expression changing to something I couldn't read. Her face contorted several times, expression changing from surprise to anger to frustration to hurt at record speeds. Her eyes turned to her fists and they loosened, slowly, painfully. Her chest heaved in and out at a racing pace and her chin quivered.

Her mouth opened, then closed, her eyes wide almost to the point of exaggeration. And she turned and ran away from the school.

A roar of victory rang up over the crowd but I stood where I was, stunned, frozen.

I was immediately surrounded by throngs of people.

"Man, it's about time someone told that bitch off—"

"All right, girl—"

But I couldn't acknowledge the comments. They raced in one ear and out the other, unregistered. I stared after Erika long after she disappeared, taking deep breaths, trying to regain the composure I'd so suddenly lost.

Suddenly Andrea was throwing her arms around me. "I was so afraid for you—" she said shrilly. "But I didn't have to be, did I—"

I smiled weakly.

Now Christian hugged me close. "You're one amazing girl, Ruthie!"

I couldn't answer. I looked up to see all of Erika's friends glaring at me. One of them looked like she was about to come beat me up herself, but there was no way she could get through to me.

Now Wakeen and Kevin and Doug broke through the crowd. "Man, you are one brave chick!" exclaimed Kevin, slapping me on the back.

Wakeen shook his head and smiled. "Tellin off Erika like that . . . AJ's a lucky guy, you know that?"

I smiled at him but said nothing.

I felt one more surge in the crowd and saw AJ standing in front of me. I ran to him and threw my arms around him, suddenly feeling safe in the protection of his arms.

"I got here late—" he said, holding me tightly. "You okay?"

I nodded quickly, breathing in the masculine scent of his aftershave, feeling myself relax.

"Man, you shoulda seen her!" exclaimed Doug. "The way she told off Erika!"

AJ smiled at me. "I ain't surprised." He kissed my cheek and I put my head in his shoulder, contented.

"Okay, back to class everybody!" I heard Mr. Ferris's booming voice as he and about five other teachers and administrators herded all of the kids up and moved them into the building. But AJ and I stood where we were, arms around each other.

234

AJ chuckled and I could feel his muscles spasm lightly. "I feel sorry for anyone who try to mess with you!"

I didn't answer, still relishing the security of his arms.

Once the lawn was clear, Mr. Ferris approached us, his face wearing a strange expression. I stepped away from AJ and we turned to face him.

For a moment he just looked from me to AJ, his eyes stopping on AJ for a moment, then lingering back to me. I looked at AJ and saw him staring back, wearing an expression I couldn't read.

I took a deep breath and spoke. "I caused quite a disturbance, didn't I."

He smiled but his eyes still wore that strange expression. "I don't think Erika Whitman will be bothering you for a while." He turned to walk toward the building.

AJ and I looked at each other, confused.

But then he smiled and I threw my arms around him once more.

"I love you," he said. "I love you, too."

# ERIKA

*"You're a nobody, a nothing—"* I run as fast as I can away from that school.

*"All you can do is swing your fists—"* Goddamnit, that's what I had to do all my life!

*"You never meant anything to AJ—"* Shit, I never meant nothin to nobody!

*"No one at this school gives a shit if you live or die—"* I don't give a shit, neither!

"What do you have, Erika?"

"I DON'T HAVE NOTHING!" I stop and scream at the sky. "I AM NOTHING!" I run all the way home and lean against the building. I can't take it anymore, I can't I don't know what to do. I hate everybody Ruthie AJ everybody they're right they're always right and I'm wrong...

"Oh God—" I clutch my throat and sink down against the building. "God help me please help me—" I put my head in my hands and cry and cry and cry.

# SHANICE

I start jumpin up and down and laughin when Erika run off like that. That half-breed bitch finally got hers! I wish I knew that Ruthie chick so I could go tell her right on. Man, that was somethin! First she take Erika's fine boyfriend and then she tell her off! Even when she ask Erika to beat her up if she so bad, what do Erika do? Run off and probably cry somewhere. Shoot, if someone ask me to beat them up I'll be all up in their face! But Erika, that bitch is nothin but a wimp. Everybody's talkin about it inside the building. I run up with Ronell, who shakin his head. "Man, I ain't never seen Erika back down from a scrap before!" he say. "She shoulda put that bitch in her place!"

"What the hell do you know Ronell?" I say. "The bitch deserved it!"

"But AJ was cheatin on her with that girl Ruthie!"

I laugh. "She deserve it, the whore bitch!" I can't feel sorry for Erika, cuz Erika's done too much shit to me.

237

# IMANI

Everybody go jostlin inside. I'm so mad I'm shakin. "I can't believe this!" I say to the girls as we go inside. "Erika shoulda killed that bitch! Especially when she was standin up there sayin beat me up! Shoot, I woulda kicked her ass—"

"Shut up!" say Michella.

I'm so mad, I shove her. "Don't start up with me, girl!"

Michella shove me back, lookin just as mad. "Cool it, Imani!"

Some teacher is shovin everyone inside and we all go up to Monica's locker. "I don't get it, what's with her?" ask Kelli.

"I dunno," say Monica.

"We should go after her, y'know—" say Michella.

Monica shake her head. "Nah. Let her be alone."

I don't know what's up with her. She been actin funny ever since she got back from Phoenix. And today, man, that was messed up! Erika shoulda kicked the girl's ass!

Everyone's gonna be lookin down on her after this! Her reputation's shot!

I see Jamil and Wakeen and go over to them.

"Man, that Ruthie is somethin!" Wakeen is sayin.

"Somethin dead!" I snap.

He just look at me, then turn back to Jamil. "Man, I don't know if I could do what she did!"

"Man, she knocked Erika so low that girl ain't never gonna get back up!" Jamil say.

"Erika shoulda kicked her ass!" I say.

"Erika ain't going no where near her now!" declare Wakeen.

"Y'know, I use to think she was stuck up, but man, she really is somethin," Jamil say.

I say forget it and go on up to my locker. I don't get it. Why is everybody trippin like this, actin all sweet on Ruthie? The girl's a bitch! And I don't care what no one say, she still gonna get her ass kicked!

I go to first hour, then meet up with Kelli afterward.

"Man, Erika ain't never gonna live this down," she say, shakin her head. "Nobody's gonna forget this! She made an ass of herself in front of the whole school!"

Monica and Michella join us and we go down to the cafeteria.

"Yeah, that's why she gotta kick Ruthie's ass now more than ever!" I say. "She gotta save her face!"

"I say we go find her," Kelli say. "Knock some sense into her if we have to!"

Monica shake her head. "Nah, let her be alone today. Alone and embarrassed. Then we'll knock some sense into her tomorrow!"

"Somethin's gotta be done about that Ruthie," Michella say.

"Yeah, if I hear that name one more time I'm crackin

skulls!'' Monica hiss. "Even Kevin's sweet on her now."

"Same with Wakeen and Jamil!" I say.

"Shit—"

Some dark chick walk by and mumble "Light bitches."

I turn around in a hurry. "What was that?"

The girl keep walkin.

"Yeah, you better keep walkin, you jig bitch!" I holler. "Cuz I ain't Erika, we'll scrap in a minute!"

"Screw this, let's go to my house," say Michella. "All these people is trippin."

Right then I see Ruthie and AJ walk by holdin hands.

"I don't care what nobody say, that girl is dead!" I hiss. "Cuz if Erika don't kill her, I will!"

"C'mon, let's go!" say Michella, grabbin my arm. She don't live too far from the school so we just walk over there. Kelli got some weed so we all sit around gettin high.

Erika ain't at her house Wednesday or Thursday. By Friday we all start gettin worried cuz none of us has heard anything from her.

"I think she hidin," I tell the girls Friday night. "She too embarrassed to see us. We need to slap her around so she can get her shit together!"

"All right, let's go," say Monica and we all head over to her place for the third day in a row.

This time Erika answer the door herself, wearin sweats and holdin a glass of somethin. Her hair a mess, lookin like she hasn't combed it in days, and her nail polish chipped.

"Hey girls," she say, soundin tired.

We all go into the apartment and Erika sit on the couch.

"So where you been?" ask Michella.

Erika shrug. "Around. What do y'all want."

"Man, you still gotta kick Ruthie's ass," I tell her. "It's the only way to save your face!"

Erika sigh. "You guys—" she say, her voice all soft.

240

That's weird cuz her voice is never soft.

"Really girl, you gotta do it!" say Kelli. "Everyone's talkin about it and makin out that Ruthie bitch like some hero. And I heard Shanice call you a wimp!"

"I don't give a shit," she say and close her eyes.

I get mad. "What's with you, Erika! What's with the wimp act? Shit girl, you makin all of us look bad!"

She don't answer.

I shake my head and stand up. "This is messed up. C'mon, let's get outta here. But girl, you better get your shit together, cuz none of us is gonna stand for this shit!"

She still don't say nothin and we all leave in a huff.

Kelli shake her head. "That girl is messed up!"

"She'll come around," I mumble. "Or I'll kick her ass and make her come around!"

# ERIKA

I don't open my eyes until after all of them leave. I didn't wanna see them cuz I knew they'd bitch at me. Especially Imani. I get tired of hearin her shit.

I finish my glass of vodka and pour myself another one. I'm drinkin it straight and am on my way to being drunk but I don't care. It's easier this way. I lay on the couch and stare at the ceiling. I don't feel like doing nothin. Haven't been to school all week. But I don't give a shit, I'll graduate. I only need one credit, anyway. Shoot, maybe I won't go back at all. Cuz I don't wanna see AJ or Ruthie or anyone for that matter.

What would I do if I saw Ruthie now? I laugh, thinkin about it. I wouldn't do nothin. I hate the girl, I really do, but I can't do nothin to her. She's untouchable. She was right, she's everything and I'm nothin. That's why I hate her now and I'll always hate her.

I think back to Tuesday, when all that shit happened. After

I stopped cryin I went to 7-11 to buy some cigarettes and I saw Franco there. Seein him reminded me of AJ and I broke down again, right there. Franco was real nice to me. He took me back to his place and lay me out in his little brother's room. I stayed there two days, lettin him take care of me. He really is a nice guy when he sober and as far as I knew he stayed sober the whole time. He didn't ask me nothin. Just took care of me and treated me nice. I didn't know what I'd do if AJ showed up but he never did come. Shoot, he was probably stayin over with that Ruthie chick! God, I hate her! Nah, them straight-assed folks of hers'd never go for that. He was probably at one of the fella's.

Now I sit up slowly, feelin like shit and knowin I don't look no better. I get up to take a shower and get dressed and fix up my nails. I gotta get outta this house. I'm afraid Mom'll come home and give me shit. But I really don't know where to go. The girls is trippin, I don't wanna see them. Maybe I'll go see Franco. I wait till I sober up some and walk over to his crib. I don't even know if he'll be there cuz I know he don't stay there a lot. He live about two miles from me so it take me a while to get over there. Plus it's gettin dark out.

Ronell come to the door and look at me. "Erika! What you doing here?"

I walk in. "Franco here?"

"Yeah, he here. Where you been?"

I don't say nothin. I don't got nothin to say to Ronell.

Franco sittin at the table with some of his boys, countin money. But he look up and smile when he see me. "Hey baby, whassup?"

"I just wanted to see you so I walked over here—"

He smile again. "I'll be back," he tell his boys, then take my arm and lead me back to his little brother's room. Franco sit on the bed. "So you wanted to see me."

243

"I got bored at my place and there's no one else I wann▒
see."

"Ronell told me what happened Tuesday."

I shrug. "I made an ass of myself, didn't I."

Franco shrug, too. "You did all you could do. Cuz if yo▒
wore out the girl you woulda looked even more the fool.▒

"I hate her!"

Franco laugh. "That was cold, what AJ did to you."

I sigh and sit down next to him. "Yeah, it was. But I can'▒
get him back or nothin. Ruthie was right."

"Ruthie's a smart girl."

"She a bitch!"

Franco laugh again. "Well you know you can come to m▒
when the shit get rough."

I look around the room, decorated with Muppets posters▒
"I haven't seen your little brother around. Where is he?▒

Franco smile in a strange way. "AJ keepin him away fron▒
me and my bad influence and shit."

"Do you know where he at?"

"I think he stayin with Ruthie. In fact, I know he is.▒

"You know where she live?"

He shake his head. "I could find out if I wanted to. Bu▒
AJ, he smart to keep him away from me."

"Why you say that?"

Franco just laugh.

"I wouldn't let him do that—"

"That's the difference. AJ care, I don't give a shit."

I don't say nothin else. I lay down on the bed and cur▒
myself up into a ball. I wish I could shut off the world and
protect myself from gettin hurt like this. Even my inside▒
ache. I never felt to bad in my life. So empty.

Franco pat my shoulder sort of indifferently. I sorta wish
he'd lay down next to me so I'd have someone to hold m▒
and make me feel good but he don't. He light up and start▒

244

smokin some base. I roll my eyes, watchin him. That shit's dangerous. Any cocaine's dangerous but especially base. I shut my eyes to ignore the fumes but I start gettin a headache.

"Can you go somewhere with that?" I say.

He look at me, then goes on smokin, sittin at the edge of the bed. I turn away from him and squeeze my eyes shut. I can hear him exhalin smoke but that's the only sound I hear.

I must've fallen asleep cuz when I sit up again, Franco gone and the house is quiet. I can't hear nobody. I check the clock and see it's two in the morning. I wonder where Franco is. I just shrug and go back to his little brother's room and go to sleep.

When I wake up again sunlight is streamin into the room and I know it's morning. Plus I can smell bacon fryin so I know someone's there. My stomach growls and I'm feelin pretty hungry so I get up and go to the kitchen.

My heart do a back flip when I see AJ standin over the stove. He the only one in the kitchen. I suck in my breath and turn away real quick. I don't want him to see me. But then I turn to look at him again and my heart ache. I still love him. I do.

Now he see me and his eyes widen. But then he look real cold. "What you doing here?"

"I was over with Franco last night. He musta left—" I say and swallow hard to keep myself from cryin. All sorts of emotions is runnin through my head. I want to slap him, hug him, kiss him, shake him, yell at him, I want him. I want him to hold me and kiss me and need me like I need him.

AJ shrug. "I don't know where he is."

I nod quickly. I gotta get outta here before I break down. I can't take it, seein him and havin him act so cold to me. It's like we strangers.

I turn and run out to his front porch where I put my head

in my lap and cry harder than I ever cried in my life. M
chest is heavin so hard it feel like it's about to explode, an
the tears is rushin down my face in rivers. Seein AJ just no
made me see that I've lost him, and that I'm never gonn
get him back.

"Hey, whassup?"

I wipe my face real quick and look up to see Franco standi
over me. Then I look down again, starin at the ground
"Why'd you leave me last night?" My voice sound cold an
harsh.

"Had stuff to do. Wanna come with me?"

I sigh, my breath shaking. Then I think, what the hell
I don't got nothin better to do. So I follow him out to hi
car, a red IROC.
The car got some jumpin bass and the sound vibrates throug
my body, makin my head ache worse than it already do
"Can you turn that off?" He shrug and turn it off.

"Where we going, anyway?" I mutter.

"Gotta see my boy Paul."

Paul stay over in Five Points, which ain't the nicest par
of town. He stay in a house covered with black graffitti an
busted-out windows. A crack house.

There's three boys inside smokin some base. Franco si
down with them and start smokin. I don't wanna do any bas
but somebody light up a joint and I hit on that. I gotta d
somethin so I don't go crazy.

I stay with Franco the next coupla days, sometimes at hi
house and sometimes with some of his boys. And he don'
try nothin with me at all. I'm surprised cuz I don't think he
got a girl. But I don't care much one way or the other. I
smoke a lot of weed to shut out all my bad feelins. I can
feel good again. Or at least calm.

We over at somebody's house Monday and I am sittin up
in this boy's room doing nothin when I look out the window

and see a dark blue Ford Escort parked in front of the house next door. All the breath go out of me and I realize I'm in the house next door to Wakeen's and that's Ruthie's car. So AJ there, next door, not far away from me. For a while I stand there, starin at her car. A little while later, Ruthie and AJ come out the house, holdin hands and walkin real slow. I can't take my eyes off them. They lookin in each others eyes and smilin. The pain slice through me like a knife. He love her, it show in his eyes. Did he ever love me like he love her?

They walk over to her car and she unlock his door. He pull her close and kiss her real sweetly. Now I bite my fist to keep from cryin. My stomach is doing somersaults and my heart is achin.

They drive away and I stare after them in a trance. I can't move or do nothin. All I can do is think, AJ love her now. He don't love me. He never loved me.

I hear footsteps come into the room and Franco's voice. "Anything interestin out the window?"

I can't say nothin. I know I'll cry if I open my mouth.

I feel Franco's hands on my shoulders. "Whassup?"

I can't take this loneliness any longer. I turn around and throw my arms around him. Franco hold me but he don't say nothin. I hug him tighter, buryin my face in his shoulder, feelin his muscles through his shirt, smellin the base on him but I don't care about that. Then I kiss him, over and over until he start kissin me back. I kiss him harder, feelin the tears roll down my face and smudgin his cheeks, tightin my arms around him, not wantin to let go. I keep kissin him, feelin the needs in me grow until I lead him over to the bed and we lie down together.

He don't make any objections so I start tearin at his clothes, my hands shakin so bad I can't pull off his shirt. So he help me pull off his shirt and jeans and my shirt and jeans so that we are lyin in our underclothes. Again I kiss him, tryin to satisfy my loneliness with his kisses, runnin my hands over his chest, feelin his muscles hard and tight. My tears have stopped but I don't feel no better. I need more than kisses. I need to feel like somebody love me. So I pull off my bra and panties and then his jockeys and roll on top of him, flattin my chest against his.

I close my eyes as he make love to me, tryin to lose myself in his steady rythm. But all I can do is picture AJ...and I start to cry again.

He collapse against me as I feel his warmth in me and hold him tightly, not wantin to release him from me, wantin to hold on to that little bit of emotion I feel. But I'm tired...so tired...

I wake up again some time later and Franco is gone. I sit up and look for him, even call him, but he nowhere to be found. The room is cold and I start to shiver so I get under the covers, tryin to get warm. But I can't get warm. I close my eyes and wrap my arms around my body, shiverin, naked and alone.

# PART V

# RUTHIE

Saturday morning, June 2. Graduation Day. I was sitting in my red cap and gown between LaTricia Baker and Marc Baynes, two kids I'd always seen around but never took the time to speak to. I had thought that they, along with the rest of the black kids at Centennial, were only out to judge me. But I had learned some far different at graduation practice three days ago.

I had been sitting somewhat uncomfortably between the slight, dark-complected girl with braided hair and a taller, light-complected and pleasant-looking boy. The girl, LaTricia, turned to smile at me during the middle of the opening address and I had smiled back.

"That was really brave, what you did to Erika Whitman. Erika's always such a bitch to anyone who isn't light-skinned."

"Or doesn't play football," put in Marc. He shook his head, his face wearing a look of disgust. "That's why I'm

251

so glad I'm getting out of this school. If you're black and aren't in a gang or play football or basketball or run track nobody knows who you are!"

I looked at him with surprise, then felt my face flush with embarrassment because I realized I had always grouped all of the black guys at Centennial precisely that way. "And what do you do?" He shrugged. "Marching band. But who gives a shit about that?"

I nodded slowly, growing more ashamed of myself. How could I have been so blind? So high on my righteous horse? And to think if I had opened my eyes and let down my guard I could have made so many more genuine friends. "It's really too bad you guys didn't get more recognition," I said earnestly.

He said nothing.

"What are you doing next year?".

"Going to Colorado State."

"That's great!"

Marc looked sullen. "It ain't Stanford."

"I've been wanting to go there ever since I was a freshman," I told him. "I worked my butt off for it."

Now the sullen expression melted from his face and he looked friendly. "Well if anyone deserve to go, it's you!"

"Yeah," LaTricia put in. "I remember seeing you around, how me and all my friends always thought you were such a wannabe because you're so smart and you always hung out with the white kids."

I shrugged. "I haven't been the friendliest person, either."

"But now I see that hanging out with white kids doesn't mean you're a wannabe."

I smiled at her.

Now I sat between them, waiting for the ceremony to begin. I watched Christian approach the podium to give his opening address. I smiled as I watched him, my heart aching proudly to see him walk up to the front of the gym, so dignified and handsome. Would I ever find such a wonderful friend next year? Now Marc leaned over to me and whispered, "Did you and him have something going before you got together with AJ Johnson?"

I shook my head. "Christian's been one of my best friends since I moved here."

He nodded and turned to face forward.

Christian's address was short, followed by a wave of applause and whistles from all of the girls who never succeeded in getting close to him but never stopped trying. He caught my eye as he returned to his chair and winked at me. I then noticed him sit next to Erika, who looked forlorn and small in her cap and gown. She looked up and her eyes caught mine, but she didn't look at me with hate as I'd expected her to. Her eyes showed a weariness that made me feel sorry for her. AJ had casually mentioned he'd seen her with Franco and I sincerely hoped she wasn't going to throw her life away with him. I wouldn't wish that on anybody.

I turned to watch the ceremony, clutching my notecards nervously, awaiting my turn to speak. Mr. Ferris was standing at the podium, delivering a winded rhetoric, sounding much like a preacher giving a sermon. About halfway through his speech a beach ball flew up over the middle senior section. I laughed and my laughter rang with the five hundred other seniors, many of whom were hitting the ball around in an attempt to keep it in the air. Even Mr. Ferris grinned as he continued his speech, but the ball was removed promptly by a disapproving teacher. I think AJ and Kevin had something to do with the prank.

Once Mr. Ferris finished his speech, he introduced me as the next speaker. There was a wild applause as I stood and made my way to the podium, and in that applause I felt a respect from the students I never thought I had. I swallowed down my nervousness, cleared my throat, and began.

"I was asked to stand before you and reflect on our experiences these past four years at Centennial. I've only been with you for two years, but in these two years this school has affected my life more than any other school I've attended.

"These weren't the best years of our lives, though we had many good times. These were not careless, carefree days, for we had much to be conscious about. Attending a socially and racially diverse school like Centennial taught us the lessons we needed to learn about tolerance, and also the pain we incur from being intolerant. This diversity taught sometimes taught us lessons we didn't want to learn, because they were lessons about ourselves, who we are, and how we reacted to everything around us. It's always easiest to close your eyes and pretend you can't see, rather than to open your heart and mind to others different from you. We were forced to do this at Centennial, and though this often brought pain, it also helped us grow. And if after this day we are together no more, we will always carry the lessons we taught each other in our hearts, for they have become a part of us."

I stopped momentarily to catch my breath, noticing my classmates staring at me wordlessly.

"Thank you," I finished, stepping down from the podium. This time the applause was more subdued. More . . . thoughtful. I caught AJ's eye and he smiled at me.

LaTricia took my hand and squeezed it when I took my seat. I smiled back.

I turned to listen to the junior choir sing, now starting to hear occasional sentimental sniffles coming randomly over the senior section. We really were leaving, and I'd never see most of these kids ever again. When I thought about it, there were so many people I hadn't gotten to know, so much I hadn't done. If I had to do it all over again, I would have done it differently. But I can't, and I have to learn from the mistakes I've made and move on.

I listened to Andrea give her address as valedictorian, then Mr. Ferris stood up to announce our names, one by one, to give us our diplomas. Another senior officer gave a closing speech and we began our recessional.

Once we left the stage I looked for AJ and found him amid his friends. I ran to him and threw my arms around him.

He held me close and buried his face in my neck. "It's about time, huh!"

"Yes, it's about time."

After stopping at my house to change clothes and receive congratulations from my family, AJ and I headed to Christian's.

"Why he givin a senior party?" AJ asked.

I shrugged. "He wants to. Why do you ask?"

His jaw tightened. "I know he don't invite folks over unless they rich like him!"

"He's not a snob, really," I said. "You just have to get to know him."

AJ didn't reply. I drove into the Hilltop area and AJ was all eyes. "Yeah, I guess it is true what they say about him, how rich he is and shit—"

I didn't reply.

Christian's house, mansion really, stood on the corner of a dignified-looking street with cars already lined up and down the sidewalk. AJ was looking around, his face wearing an expression I couldn't read. I led him up to the front door.

Christian answered it himself, smiling. "Hey Ruthie! Hi AJ!" He held out his hand but AJ didn't respond. He only stared at Christian suspiciously. Christian blushed, dropping his hand to his side. I gave him a look of apology.

Christian cleared his throat. "Everyone's out back," he said, leading us through the house to the backyard. "I'll need to take your keys."

"That's okay, I don't plan on drinking," I said.

AJ looked at me, surprised. "C'mon, it's graduation!"

"Somebody has to drive!"

He smiled and put an arm around me.

Christian's backyard was filled with seniors, dancing around the pool, drinking beer or champagne, and sitting around on lawnchairs, talking and laughing.

AJ led me over to his circle of friends, standing by the pool. Kevin was spraying a squealing Monica with a bottle of champagne.

"The Dream shows!" shouted Wakeen, well on his way to being drunk. "Where you two been?"

AJ laughed. "Shut up, man!"

Jamil threw AJ a beer, then turned to me. "Want one?"

I shook my head. "No thanks."

Now all the guys looked at me, surprised. "You don't drink?"

I said nothing.

Kevin shook his head. "Man AJ, you really do got a prissy one!"

I laughed. "Prissy!"

"No offense," he said, then laughed. "Man—"

AJ put an arm around me and led me away from them. "Listen, I know you don't drink and stuff—"

"But you do," I finished. "Go have fun with your friends."

He looked surprised.

"I'm serious! This is graduation! But make sure you let me drive you home."

He smiled at me. "I'll see you later then."

I kissed him goodbye, then went to find Andrea and Christian, exchanging hellos with Marc and LaTricia on the way.

I found them at the door collecting keys.

"Isn't it a pain, being responsible?" I said wryly.

Andrea laughed. "Somebody has to be! Where's AJ?"

"Getting drunk with his friends."

Christian laughed and set the bowl of keys on the table. "I think that's all who'll be coming." He went to the bar and took out a bottle of champagne and some glasses, then led us to the den and shut the door behind us.

"Aren't you afraid the kids'll tear down your house?" I asked.

He shrugged. "That's why they're outside."

He poured us each a glass of champagne. "To our friendship," he said, holding up his glass. Andrea and I toasted him.

"I'm gonna miss you guys next year," Andrea said softly.

Christian smiled. "We'll keep in touch. Shoot, Ruthie'll be at Stanford, I'll be at Yale and you'll be at Duke... We couldn't have picked places any farther away from each other, could we."

Andrea and I laughed. I drained my glass and Christian filled it again. I drank that one and again, Christian filled my glass.

I laughed. "No—"

"C'mon, one more glass won't kill you!"

"Are you trying to get me drunk?"

He laughed. "No, not you. Andrea, either." She was still sipping her first glass.

Christian drank right from the bottle, then stared at the floor.

"Are you okay?" Andrea asked and we both went to sit by him.

He looked up at us and smiled. "I love you guys."

Both Andrea and I burst into tears and we all hugged.

# ERIKA·

Well I did it. I graduated. And now I don't know what the hell I wanna do with myself. Me and AJ's over, well, Ruthie made that sink in real good. So I said screw it. Screw AJ, screw the world. And I got myself a job workin as a receptionist in this hair weave studio. All I do is answer phones and I get paid pretty decent. So now I just work all day long, then stay with either Monica or Franco. Sometimes I go home but I don't like dealin with home much. Me and Mom's been fightin.

I'm also sick of the girls. I was over at Imani's one day and all she did was bitch. "Man, this summer's weak! Shit, we ain't been in a good fight since, God—"

Kelli laughed. "Know anybody we can start up with?"

"Let's go find somebody," Imani said. "Some stupid dark bitch—"

I tuned them out. I haven't seen them in about a week and I don't want to. But I'm suprised when Kelli call me up one morning real early. "Girl, you know what time it is?" I grumble.

"Erika, I gotta talk to you!"

"Can't it wait?"

"No!" Kelli sound like she cryin, and it take a lot to make her cry.

I sigh. "Okay, come on over." I hang up the phone, then I go take a shower and fix myself up.

Kelli come over around seven, lookin like she didn't get much sleep. We go to the kitchen and I fix coffee for both of us. "So what's up?" I ask.

"Erika, I'm pregnant."

"What?"

Kelli stare at the table. "I took one of them tests yesterday and I am. I'm pregnant."

I shake my head in shock. "But...don't you use stuff?"

She shrug. "Sometimes. But you know how it is...you get into it and you don't wanna stop—"

I guess I know how that is, but I went on the pill last year so I wouldn't have to worry about it. "So...who's the father?"

She shrug again. "I dunno. It might be Doug's but I don't think so. It might be Nathanial's, y'know, that Compton guy. But it might be that college guy's too. I dunno. I don't even know how far along I am. I mean, I've been sick in the mornings for a while now."

"Why didn't you say nothin?"

"Shoot, you had your own problems with AJ. And I don't wanna hear the girls' shit. That's why I'm tellin you and not them."

"What you gonna do?"

"Have it, I think. It'll be kinda fun havin a baby."

"You wanna have a baby now?"

"Shoot, why not? I don't got nothin else going on in my

259

life.''

I shake my head. I can't see her havin a baby! She too messed up to be havin a baby!

She finish her coffee. "I just wanted to tell you, you know?''

"But what if you can't handle it? What'll you do?''

"Give it up, I guess." She look at me with sad eyes. "But I wanna try. Hey, you won't tell the others, will you?''

"No—''

"Cuz they'll think I'm crazy." Kelli chuckle. "Shoot, maybe I am. But I really want this baby. I—'' She stop.

"You what?''

"I want somebody to need me.''

I just nod cuz I don't know what to say.

Kelli stand up. "I should be going. You probably have to get to work and shit—''

"Yeah—''

"You and Franco still talkin?''

I shrug.

"Anything gonna come of it?''

I laugh. "Franco? He don't care about nobody but himself!''

"And what about AJ?'' she say in a soft voice.

I sigh. "I guess he and Ruthie's pretty tight.''

Kelli nod. "Well I'll see you. You'll be at some of the parties, won't you?''

I sigh. "Probably. I guess I'll see you.''

"Yeah—'' Kelli say and leave.

I stand there lookin after her. How she gonna have a baby when she don't even know who the father is? And how she gonna support it? She never know how messed-up she is till it's too late.

And I don't wanna be like that. No way.

# AJ

Me and the fellas was sitting in my room drinking one day near the end of summer. Well, not the end of summer, it was only the middle of July, but I was leaving for school in a week. Doug and Wakeen was leaving in about a week, too. And Kevin was leaving in two days. We was all sitting around pretty quiet.

"I can't believe it's almost all over man," said Wakeen, lying on the floor half-drunk.

Kevin took a swig from his bottle of Old English. "Y'know, it's gonna be great. I mean, college, the parties, the girls—"

"Shoot," I said, staring at the floor. "I don't wanna even think about girls!"

Doug shut his eyes, leaning against the wall. "Yeah, you're gonna be leavin Ruthie. Man, that's rough."

I nodded.

"Where's she going? Somewhere out in California,

right?''

"Stanford."

Jamil whistled. "Well you two couldn't be any further apart!"

"Yeah, that is rough," said Kevin. "I'm not too sorry about leavin Monica. She's been fun, but you gotta move on, you know?"

I shrugged. It wasn't like that with me and Ruthie.

Doug finished his beer and reached for another one. "That's one thing I don't gotta worry about. I hear Kelli's pregnant, anyway."

"No way!" said Wakeen. "Little Kelli?"

"Yeah!"

I chuckled. "Whose is it?"

"She don't know. Long as she don't try to pass it off on me—"

"Who told you, man?" asked Ray.

"Imani found out somehow. And I guess Kelli got mad and kicked her ass. The only person she told was Erika."

"Erika—" Wakeen said slowly. "You seen much of her lately?"

I shook my head.

"I guess she been hangin low," said Jamil. He chuckled. "Shoot, I would too if Ruthie crucified me like that!"

I chuckled too, thinking about Ruthie. Kevin sighed and finished off his bottle. "I dunno, man. It all scares me."

"What does?" asked Ray.

"Everything! I get on that plane in two days and I'm outta here! Everything, hangin out with you all, sittin around drinkin like this, it's over!"

Nobody said nothing.

Kevin looked like he was gonna cry. "I'm gonna miss you guys!"

"Oh hell Kev, you just drunk!" said Wakeen. "Man, I'm

sick of hearin us babble like a bunch of girls!'' He tried to sit up but he was so drunk he just fell over. We all laughed at him.

"So no more talk about college and leavin," said Jamil. "We'll just talk about old times."

Doug was grinning. "Like the time that Mexican dude was startin up shit with you AJ, over that girl Marisa!"

I grinned, too. "Yeah. I whipped his ass good, too."

"And got the girl!" said Jamil and gave me a high five. "That's why they call you the Dream!"

I laughed.

"And the time we all showed up drunk to football practice and Coach threw us out!" Kevin laughed. "We was suspended three days and sat around drinkin all three days! What a trip!"

"Yeah," Doug said, laughing. "What about all those videotapes we made of ourselves. AJ, you got any of those around?"

"I got one of 'em. It should be by the TV," I said. We got up and went to the living room. "How old was we when we made those?"

"Shoot, we musta been about fifteen—" We all sat on the couch and I found the dusty tape and put it in the VCR.

The tape was kinda blurry; Jamil was filming and he was drunk. All of us was sitting in Ray's basement, flipping off the camera and laughing about something. Then Kevin got up and started dancing.

"Man, you still haven't learned how to dance!" said Wakeen. Kevin just laughed.

Then I saw myself on the tape, bragging about some girl or something. I sat there comparing myself then to myself now. I looked the same, really. I'm a little taller now. I grinned, listening to myself talk. "Man, that fuckin—" I was saying. I wanted to laugh cuz I never talk like that no more.

Shoot, every other word that came out of my mouth then was obscene. I was still upset over Mom, but I never talked about it. It showed in my eyes. I can see it now.

The camera turned back to Wakeen, who had gotten up and started dancing, too.

Jamil shook his head. "Man, we was obnoxious!"

"That hasn't changed!" said Kevin. "Well, except for AJ cuz he's been hangin around Miss Prissy too long!"

"Hey—"

Kevin laughed. "I'm just messin with you, man. Ruthie's a good person. She's good for you."

I grinned.

"I know somebody havin a party tonight!" said Wakeen. "I say we get drunker, pick up some girls and have ourselves a good time!"

"Nah, not tonight," I said.

"What you doing tonight?"

"Ruthie's comin over. Shoot, I better get sobered up before she gets here!"

Doug stood up. "We should get going then."

He and the fellas went to the door. "Later, man!" I said.

"Yeah, later—"

I went over to Kevin. "So when you leavin, man?"

"My plane gets outta here two o'clock Wednesday."

"Try to come by tomorrow."

"I'll try."

"Well if I don't see you again, good luck, call, write, all that—"

Kevin grinned. "You've been great AJ. I'm gonna miss you."

"I'm gonna miss you too." I gave him a big bear hug. "Find yourself a girl like Ruthie."

Kevin laughed. "Yeah, there's gotta be one in Texas!"

"Yeah, see ya—"

"See ya—"

I watched him jump off the front porch and run out to his truck. Man, I was gonna miss him, miss all of this. Why does stuff have to change? Why is it that once you finally get your shit together, you gotta move on? I went to lay down on the couch, feeling pretty low. And Ruthie, man, I didn't wanna think about leaving Ruthie. What was I gonna do without her?

I was half-asleep when I heard Franco come in. He stood over me. "So the Golden Boy's home. Where's your female sidekick?"

I yawned. "Ruthie'll be here in an hour or so." Usually he makes a crack about her and keeps on going but today he sat on the arm of the couch.

"What's she doing next year? I know she ain't going to Florida."

"Stanford."

Franco chuckled. "Stanford. Yeah, I can see her at Stanford. So what you gonna do with her three thousand miles away?"

I didn't say nothing. I wanted him to leave so I could sleep.

"And what's Anthony gonna do with her at college next year? Cuz that's who he stayin with, right."

I still didn't say nothing.

"Is he comin back here?"

"Nah. He stayin with her folks. They gonna keep him."

Franco nodded slowly. "Her parents are saints. Takin in an extra kid like that. Shit—"

"So he don't end up like you!"

Franco laughed. "I guess I wouldn't want him endin up like me."

I didn't say nothing. I don't know what's up with Franco half the time. Then the doorbell rang. Franco got up and answered it. "Guess who, AJ?" I opened my eyes and saw

Ruthie. I was surprised. I wasn't expecting her for a while.

"I know I'm early," she said. "Is that a problem?"

I sat up slowly. "Nah—"

She sat down next to me and looked at me closely. "You've been drinking."

Franco laughed.

I shrugged, kind of embarrassed. "The fellas was over. Kevin's leavin in two days—"

She nodded. "It's going to be sad seeing them go, isn't it."

I didn't say nothing.

Franco sat on the arm of the couch. Ruthie just looked at him. I laughed cuz I know she don't think much of him at all.

"So you been keepin AJ in line," he said.

She rolled her eyes. "I'm no babysitter!"

Franco grinned. "But your folks don't mind babysittin Anthony!"

She didn't say nothing but she looked mad.

"That's great though. That kid's gonna have opportunities me and AJ never had. That's real good."

"What's it to you?"

"What's it to me!" Franco repeated. "Well shit—"

"I'm sorry, but I don't know why you're talking to me. I can't tell if you're mocking me or what—"

Now I laughed. Ruthie's a mess!

"Just havin friendly conversation," Franco said. "So I guess you don't think too highly of me—"

"Truthfully, I have no respect for you whatsoever!"

Franco laughed again. "No, I guess you wouldn't."

Ruthie just looked at him.

Franco pulled out roll of money and peeled off a couple hundred dollar bills. "Here. Give this to your folks for Anthony."

She took the money, looking from it to Franco in surprise.

Then she handed it back to him.

Franco grinned. "Oh, so you don't want it?"

"I...wouldn't feel right taking it. Neither would my parents."

"Oh, cuz it ain't honest money?" Franco said. I honestly didn't know what he was driving at. He didn't look mad or nothing but I could tell he was serious.

"Well you can't deny that, can you?" said Ruthie.

Franco chuckled. "Go on. Take it anyway."

"What am I supposed to do with it?"

He shrugged. "Figure out a way to get it to Anthony."

She hesitated, then shook her head. "It's nice of you, but—"

"Nah, it ain't nice," Franco said. "I ain't nice. But that's all right, I get it." He put the money back in his pocket. Ruthie looked uncomfortable.

I stood up. "Let's get going." Ruthie nodded and hurried out of the house. I started to follow her but Franco held my arm.

"What?" I said.

"And you only got one more week with her?"

I didn't say nothing.

"Use it wise, man. Cuz you ain't gonna find another one like her." He let go of my arm and I left the house.

I had her drive me to the minibank before we went to her house. I've been working all summer at Safeway, bagging groceries. I make okay money, four-fifty and hour, and I've been saving up all of it to give to Ruthie's parents for Anthony. To show I wasn't gonna let him be a freeloader.

When we got to her house I asked her where her parents were.

"Probably in the den," she replied. "Why?"

I shrugged and grinned. "I got somethin I wanna give them."

She looked confused, but she led me to the den, where both her mom and dad were sitting watching TV.

"Hi AJ," they said when they saw me.

"Uh, hi," I said, feeling uncomfortable. I'll always feel kinda uncomfortable around her parents just cuz they're parents, y'know?

"What have you been doing?" asked her dad.

"Workin." I handed her dad the envelope of money.

He looked confused. "What's this?"

I was kinda embarrassed. "My paychecks. All of them. There's about seven hundred dollars there. Now that I've been workin, I wanna start contributin, you know, so Anthony's not freeloadin."

Her dad grinned and handed me back the money.

I was confused. "Don't you want it?"

"You keep it. You'll need it for college."

"But what about Anthony?"

"Let us worry about Anthony. You worry about college!"

I shook my head quickly. "No, I can't let you guys take care of him without helpin out—"

Her dad looked me in the eye. "AJ, the best help you can give us is doing well in college. If you do that I promise you, you'll never have to worry about Anthony."

"But—"

"Do we have a deal here?"

I didn't know what to say. I looked at Ruthie and she grinned back. So I swallowed down my pride and said, "Deal."

Her dad grinned. "Good."

I was even more embarrassed. "I don't know what to say—"

Her mom grinned, too. "Doing well in school is thanks enough."

I nodded, a good feeling rising in my stomach. For that

I might even get A's or something!

Me and Ruthie went downstairs to her room and I sat on her bed. "Y'know, you got some great parents. Takin in another kid like that who ain't any relation—"

She grinned and took my hands. "Believe me, they have their moments! But now you won't have to worry about Anthony next year."

I grinned, thinking about him. "Man, I'm gonna miss him next year—"

"Have you thought about what you might want to do in college?"

"Shoot, I don't got no idea."

"Whatever you do, don't major in PE!"

I grinned. "Nah, I won't do that. But kinesiology sounds kinda interesting—"

"You should try it."

"I might." I leaned up against the headboard and pulled her to me. "I'm gonna miss you next year."

"I'm going to miss you, too."

I got sad. Or scared. I don't know. "I think about next year, college and all that, and it don't seem real. It's like a dream, y'know? But come next week I'm gonna be gone—"

She nodded.

I sighed. "And I'll be in Florida and you'll be way off in California...we just got one more week together!"

Ruthie didn't say nothing.

"What happens next year, with us?"

She didn't say nothing for a long time. Then she sighed. "I don't know. My logical side tells me it's impossible for us to stay together so far apart. But—"

"But what?"

I saw tears in her eyes. "My sentimental side can't picture me with anyone but you."

I hugged her. "I can't see myself with anyone but you, either. Maybe you should transfer to Florida State."

She laughed.

"I mean it! I'll go into the pros and make millions, then I'll take care of you! I'll even pay your folks back for keepin Anthony!"

She kept laughing.

I got kinda mad. "I mean it!"

She hugged me. "Oh AJ, it'd be nice if real life worked out like that—"

I stared at her. "You don't think I'll make the pros?"

"AJ, only one in a thousand college players make the pros...you know that—"

"But all them recruiters tell me if I keep playin the way I'm playin I'll make the pros easy!"

She grinned. "AJ, that's their job to tell you stuff like that. They were selling their school to you."

I pulled away from her. "Thanks for havin so much faith in me!"

She hugged me again. "I wish you the best of luck in making the pros, I do! But you still need something to fall back on in case you don't make it, or in case you get hurt."

"So what you say we do then?"

She grinned. "I go to Stanford, you go to Florida State. You make the pros and put me through law school, then I can take care of you when I'm a famous lawyer and you can take up golf or something. It's safer."

I laughed. "Right! But yeah, I can see you as some big-shot lawyer."

She sighed. "I hope—"

"You gonna make it, I know it!"

"How do you know?"

"I just do," I said and kissed her.

"I wish I did," she said and sighed again.

# ERIKA

Ruthie and AJ's at Michella's party Thursday night. I know
cuz Imani come runnin to me and say, "Guess who just
walked in?"

I shrug. "Girl, most of northeast Denver's here!"

"So's AJ and Ruthie!" say Imani. "Michella, you should
throw them out! Shoot, this is your house—"

"Cool it, Imani," I say.

"But—"

I look at her good and hard. "I said cool it!"

Imani glare back at me, then turn to Michella. "So when
you comin downstairs?" Me and Michella is sittin up in her
room. Everybody else is downstairs near the keg.

"Why don't you go downstairs and see how everything
is," Michella say. Imani run out and me and Michella roll
our eyes. "I'm gettin tired of her."

I sigh. "So'm I. I'm gettin tired of everyone!"

Michella nod. "I'm worried about Kelli."

"She here?"

"Yeah. Downstairs gettin trashed. Ain't that bad for her baby?"

I shake my head. "Kelli too messed up to be havin a baby." I laugh and my laugh sound harsh. "And I thought I was messed up!"

"You and Franco still together?"

I shake my head. "Nah. It wasn't going nowhere. I dunno, maybe I should pack up and move out."

"Where'd you go?"

I sigh. "I dunno. Atlanta's supposed to be a happenin place right now. Or DC. I got relatives in DC. I could get an apartment somewhere, get a job, look for a man—"

"I'd like to get outta this town, too. I been here too long."

I laugh. "Maybe we should go out together. Get an apartment—"

Michella smile. "You know, I'll bet we could—"

"Tell everyone out here to go to hell and get out. Start over. This town got too many bad memories. And so do Phoenix."

Michella stand up. "Yeah, let's talk some more about it. But I need to be headin downstairs. Make sure no one tear up my house."

I nod and follow her downstairs. One thing I like about Michella is that when she talk, she got somethin important to say. Not like Imani, who always shootin off at the mouth.

The living room is filled with kids from our graduating class. Kids I'm sick to death of.

"Hey girl!" say Monica. I see her sittin over with Doug and Wakeen and go to join her.

"Whassup?"

She shrug. "I'm hangin in there, I guess—"

I nod. Kevin left for college a few days ago and I know she takin it pretty hard.

"What about you, Erika? What you been up to?" ask Wakeen.

I shrug. "Workin. Keepin busy. So when do you all leave?"

"Friday," say Doug. "But shoot, we'll just be up in Boulder—"

"But you'll be too busy to be comin around here much—" say Monica.

I look around and see everyone's sort of subdued. Nobody's being obnoxious and dancin all over the furniture like people usually do at parties. Nobody even dancin. Everybody just sittin around drinkin and talkin. Everybody's changed. Nobody'll ever be the same. That's good though. High school's over, and you gotta move on.

Monica start talkin about some secretary's course she enrolled in and I leave to go talk to some other people.

"Yo Erika!"

I turn around and see Ronell standin there holdin a beer. "Whassup, girl?"

"Nothin—"

"Yo check this out. That Ruthie chick, she here! This is a perfect chance to kick her ass—"

"Ronell!"

"What?"

"Cut it out!" Ronell the only person I know who hasn't changed. He'll always be the same old Ronell.

I'm on my way to the keg when I bump into somebody. "Hey, watch where you're—" I begin, then look up to see AJ. My pulse stop.

"Uh, hi—" I say and swallow. He smile but he look uncomfortable. All my old feelings go rushing to my head and for a second I feel like I'm gonna faint. My heart is pounding and I can hardly breath. But I pull myself together and say, "How's it going?"

273

"It's going all right—"

"So you probably gettin ready to leave—"

"Tomorrow."

I nod. So this is probably the last time I'll ever see him. He'll be...gone. That's a weird feeling. "You excited?"

He shrug. "Yes and no. It's gonna be hard leavin...you know—"

I nod. AJ's really changed. Sure he look the same but he seem so different. So much more responsible and caring. So much more... manly. It really hurts, seein him.

I laugh nervously. "It's weird, I don't know what to say—"

AJ smile. "Yeah, but it's kinda nice, talkin to you—"

"Yeah—"

"So what you doing now? You still with my brother?"

"Nah—" I feel stupid. He probably think I was tryin to get back at him. Well maybe I was, but not no more. "I been workin—"

"Where at?"

"I'm a receptionist at Alpha Hair salon."

"That's good. I been workin too—"

Then Ruthie come up to stand next to him and take his hand. I just look at her. She look back but don't say nothin.

I fight off an urge to choke up and cry and look at AJ. "Well it was good seein you. Good luck in Florida."

AJ smile. "It was good seein you, too. Take care of yourself, okay?"

They walk away holdin hands and I watch, feelin hurt but feelin good at the same time. I did it. I talked to AJ without breakin down. Ruthie was wrong, I do have my dignity! Cuz I can get over him, I can! No matter how much it hurts!

"Hey Erika," Michella say. I guess she saw everything.

I swallow and turn to her. "Hey—"

"So when's he leavin?"

"Tomorrow."

"That's good. You can get him outta your system."

I nod, not saying nothin. I'm already almost there.

I sit on a couch by myself and close my eyes, thinkin about AJ and Ruthie but mostly about myself. I think about all the shit Ruthie said to me and it's weird to think I used to think so low of myself. But now, if she said it again, it wouldn't be true because I wasn't gonna believe that about myself no more. I don't need a guy to lean on, I don't need the girls to lean on. I can stand on my own. And for the first time in a long time, I feel proud of myself.

# AJ

Me and Ruthie left Michella's party early, around nine or
so. "So what do you want to do now?" asked Ruthie.

I thought for a second. "This is kinda weird, but—"

"But what?"

"I wanna go to Evergreen."

She looked confused for a second, then she nodded.
"Okay—"

I didn't say nothing as she drove to the cemetary. I had
to say goodbye to my mom. Cuz in some strange way I
thought she was responsible for bringing me and Ruthie
together.

Ruthie drove to my mother's gravesight and sat in the car
while I went to my mother's grave. The sun had almost set
but there was still enough light for me to read her headstone.
I sat down next to it, running my fingers over the engraving.
For a second I just sat there, no thoughts coming to my head
at all. But I shut my eyes and lay on my back, and everything

I wanted to say came to me.

I guess it's been a while, I thought. But I'm leavin, you know? Going to Florida State. I guess I'm the first one in our family who's going to college. That's kinda neat, huh. And Anthony, he'll be the second. He'll probably be a doctor or lawyer or some bigshot businessman. Ruthie's folks are gonna take care of him. That's real good of them, ain't it? Takin in another kid like that. I feel good though, cuz I feel like I'm gonna make it, and so will Anthony. I don't know if I'm gonna make the pros or not but even if I don't, I know everything's gonna work out for me. Maybe after college I'll go look for Ruthie and marry her or somethin. She's really great Ma, you'd like her. And I gotta leave her tomorrow. That's gonna be rough. She's been my life these past few months! I've never felt like this for a girl before! I know I've changed a lot and I know it's cuz of her. But she says I'm just growin up. Oh well. It's too bad you ain't here to see me. I know you'd be proud of me.

I opened my eyes and stood up and headed toward Ruthie's car. But I stopped and looked back and grinned. I went back to the car, where Ruthie was waiting for me.

"Was it good talking to her?"

I nodded.

Ruthie stared at the dashboard.

I grabbed her hand. "Hey...whassup?"

Ruthie sniffled and wiped her eyes quickly.

"What's wrong?" I asked, pulling her to me.

She put her head on my shoulder and sniffled again. "I just can't believe that tomorrow—" She wiped her eyes.

I sighed, feeling sad myself. "Yeah, I know—"

"I just can't imagine being without you—"

I kissed the top of her head. "What we gonna do?"

She shook her head. "I don't know. Call, write, see what happens. That's all we can do, really—"

I cupped her face in my hands and wiped away her tears. Then I kissed her, feeling even sadder. What was I gonna do without her?

She drove us to my house and we went straight to my room. I shut the door behind us and we sat on my bed. I put my arms around her. I could tell she was trying not to cry because her muscles was all tense. "Hey, don't be sad—" I said and kissed her. "We got tonight together, don't we?"

She nodded quickly. "I need to call my mom, tell her I'm staying over here—" She got up and went to the phone. I just sat there, staring into space. It was too much to believe that after tonight me and Ruthie might not be together no more. Cuz who knows what'll happen next year? I shook my head, not wanting to think about it. But I couldn't help it.

Ruthie came to sit next to me after she got off the phone and put her arms around me. And we just sat there like that for a while, holding each other like we'd never let go, not saying nothing.

After a while, Ruthie said, "Maybe we should get some sleep. You have to get up early tomorrow—"

"Don't worry about me," I said. "All I wanna think about right now is you. Let's make this last night special, okay?"

She smiled a pretty smile.

"That means no talkin about leavin or nothin."

"Okay!"

I kissed her and we hurried to get under the covers. I kissed her again, closing my eyes and trying to think of only her. This was our last night together and I was gonna make it special for both of us.

She smiled at me. "I remember the first night we spent together, when you came over to my house really late—"

I chuckled. "Yeah. That was nice, wasn't it."

She nodded. "I'll never forget it. It just seems like we didn't get enough time together."

278

"No, we didn't—" I said. "I wish we could've figured each other out sooner!"

She laughed again. "If someone told me in January I'd end up feeling the way I do toward you now, I'd have never believed it."

"Me neither," I said and kissed her, tightening my arms around her. "I love you—"

"I love you too—"

We stayed like that all night, with our arms around each other.

Ruthie was asleep when I woke up the next morning. I just lay there for a second, watching her sleep. She looked sweet that way. I didn't want to disturb her so I got up carefully and went to take a shower and get dressed.

She was awake when I came back to my room, sitting up in bed and smiling at me. "Hi—"

I went over to kiss her. "Hi."

"You're going to eat breakfast with Anthony this morning, right."

I nodded. "I'll come by your house around eleven, okay?"

She pulled on her clothes and stood up. "Then I'll just head home. See you later."

She kissed me and left.

I sat on my bed staring at all the trunks me and Ruthie packed last week, piled up by the door. I was leaving. I would be out of here at three this afternoon. Man, that was weird to think about.

I went to the living room and saw Dad sitting on the sofa. Dad stood up. "AJ! So today's the day!"

I nodded.

Dad pulled me to him in a big bear hug. "Well if I don't see you again today, take care of yourself!"

"I will. I'm on my way to see Anthony right now."

"All right. You can use my car, I'll be here all day. And

279

tell him to come by and see me sometime!''

I nodded. "Thanks!"

I got in Dad's Subaru and drove over to Ruthie's. Anthony came running out of the car amd jumped into the front seat. "Hey bro!" he said and grinned.

I patted his head. "How's it going, Anthony?"

"Good!" But then he looked sad. "You have to go today?"

I nodded.

Anthony burst into tears. "I don't want you to go!"

"Oh Anthony—" I hugged him real hard. For a second I wanted to cry, too.

"Take me with you! I wanna go with you!"

"Hey—" I tried to grin. "I thought you wanted to stay with Ruthie's folks!"

Anthony sobbed hysterically. "I wanna stay with you!"

I patted his head. "I have to go to college, kid."

"Why?"

"You know why! I have to try to make the pros! And I have to get a degree so I can get a good job!" I hugged him again. "I'll be back to visit you! I'll see you at Christmas!"

Anthony kept sobbing.

"C'mon, kid, let's go eat breakfast, okay? Don't cry! I'll call you and write you letters!"

Anthony looked at me with big wet eyes. "You will?"

I grinned. "'Course I will! Every day!"

Anthony grinned too and wiped his face. "Let's eat!"

We went to Village Inn for breakfast and Anthony was laughing and yapping away like I wasn't going nowhere. I guess it's kinda good little kids got such short attention spans. It made it hurt a little less to see him happy.

After breakfast, I took him home to see Dad and finished getting my stuff ready. Franco was sitting on the couch when I came in. He looked up at me and stood up. "So today's the day you clear outta here.''

I nodded, not knowing what to say.

Franco nodded slowly. ''That's real good you know. I hope you really make something of yourself.''

''I will.''

He grinned. ''Well you probably wanna get over to Ruthie and her folks now. I guess I'll be seein ya.''

I nodded.

He hugged me close for a second, then let go, still grinning. I grinned back. Yeah, he was screwed up, but he was still my brother.

''Go on, get outta here!'' he said.

I laughed. ''Help me load up my stuff!''

He grinned and we went to lug all my trunks to the car. Then me and Anthony got in and I turned to him once more. ''See ya—'' He waved back.

I headed over to Ruthie's. As I drove away I looked back at the house one more time. This was it. It was over. I wasn't gonna be seeing that house again for a long time. Then I turned to face forward and drove over to Ruthie's, feeling good. Yeah, I got my life figured out just as it was time to move on, but I wasn't scared of starting all over again. It'll be interesting to see what I do with myself this time.

# RUTHIE

It was so hard watching AJ leave. I tried not to cry, especially with my parents and Anthony and Derek at the airport with us. Poor Anthony was in tears. AJ sat with Anthony in his lap, speaking softly to him. I sat next to him with my head on his shoulder, not wanting to leave his touch. Mom and Dad and Derek sat opposite us and we all waited, not saying much.

But when AJ's flight was called the tears flowed down my cheeks as if they had a mind of their own. AJ kissed Anthony goodbye, thanked my parents one more time, then turned to me and took my hands. "Don't cry—" he told me softly. I clung to him, trying to curb my tears, but I couldn't.

He just smiled and kissed me softly. "I love you."

"I love you, too."

He kissed me one more time, looking like he was about to cry, too. But he turned away quickly and boarded his plane.

I went home and cried in my room all weekend. Andrea and Christian came over to sit with me, giving me Kleenexes and hugs.

"Thanks you guys—" I sniffled as I lay in my bed in tears.

They both smiled gently and Christian patted my arm. "That's what we're here for."

Andrea held me. "Poor Ruthie. I know it's hard—"

I couldn't answer.

AJ called twice, Saturday evening to let us know he'd arrived safely and Sunday to say hi.

I kept myself busy to avoid wallowing in pity, working and saving money for college. But I couldn't help feeling my life was somehow empty without AJ.

The biggest surprise of the summer was running into Erika at the grocery store a week before I was to leave. I was in the frozen food aisle doing some shopping for my mother when I saw her. When her eyes caught mine she stopped, and for a few moments we eyed each other suspiciously. I swallowed nervously, not knowing what to say. Her face wore an almost pleasant expression and she looked more beautiful than I ever remembered her to look. I didn't doubt that somewhere inside her was that mean streak she'd shown in high school, but I could see that she'd changed. It showed in her eyes.

I took a deep breath. "So how've you been, Erika?"

She shrugged. "How's AJ?"

"Fine. He says the practices are really hard but he thinks he's going to like it a lot—"

She nodded slowly, still looking at me suspiciously.

I sighed. "I guess I should get this off my chest—"

Now her nostrils flared. "What?"

"Some of the things I said to you...I shouldn't have said."

She rolled her eyes. "Oh?"

283

"I didn't have to be that cruel," I said softly. "I'm not asking you to forgive me. I just wanted to say it—"

Her eyes narrowed. "It must be so easy, being you!"

"Why do you say that?"

She laughed harshly. "To be able to screw people up and then say your sorry to ease your own damn conscience!"

I swallowed, ashamed. She was right. It was very hypocritical of me to say anything now, because that one day I'd meant everything I said and there was no use denying it. "You're right. That was shitty of me to say anything about it."

She laughed again. "You must be so proud of yourself, showin me up like that—"

I shrugged. "I don't feel any animosity toward you now. But I'd be lying if I said I liked you before."

She smiled wryly. "You sure is honest, ain't you!"

I shrugged.

"I'll bet you thought I was a real bitch cuz of how I acted, but I'll bet you never had to prove yourself to nobody, either!"

"Yes, I have," I said softly.

She rolled her eyes. "Get outta here!"

"People would see the way I talk and dress and think I'm just a wannabe. A sellout. I was never "black" enough, whatever that meant. So I was suspicious of everybody. I thought all black people saw me like that so I tried to avoid them. To avoid rejection, you know?"

"And what changed you?"

I shrugged. "Not one thing, really. I had only been looking on the surface of people. And there were still people who thought I was a sellout, but they didn't matter, anyway. When I really opened my eyes and looked at people, I saw I was just as suspicious and judgemental of other black people as they were of me. When I let my guard down, I saw not

284

everyone was out to put me down.''

She shrugged.

''I can see how you'd have to prove yourself, being mixed—''

''I ain't black enough for the black folk or light enough for the white folk,'' Erika said. ''When I was little all the darker girls'd be comin up to me startin up shit with me cuz I'm light.''

''And so you fought back—''

''I had to if I didn't want to get the shit kicked outta me.''

I nodded slowly. ''It's almost too bad we didn't get to know each other . . . before—''

''What's it matter now? And AJ, well, you was probably better for him than I was.''

I could see in her eyes how much she really cared for AJ and I wanted to take back everything I'd said to her.

''After he started gettin close to you he changed. He acted so much classier. So much more like a man—''

''He's done a lot for me, too—''

''I'm sure he did. So . . . what's up with you two now?''

''What can be? We're going to be three thousand miles apart.''

''So you two ain't together no more?''

''I can't predict the future. We'll see when we come home for Christmas.''

She nodded.

''Do you miss him?'' I asked softly.

''Yeah, I miss being with him. And it's hard seein him with you. But I can do without him.''

I nodded uncomfortably. ''Well, I guess I should be going. I never really knew you before, well, knew anything about you, really. I'm glad we could talk like this.''

She nodded.

''I doubt we'll ever be friends, but I mean it when I say

good luck to you.''

She nodded and smiled a little. ''Good luck to you, too.''

For a brief moment our eyes met and I realized how much we had in common. Not just the love of a boy, but our situations. Would I have acted any differently had I been in her place? I don't know.

But what I do know is that I'm ready to move on with my life. Back in January I'd felt I was ready for college but I wasn't, not then. I had too many questions and too few answers then. But I'm ready now. I don't have many more answers than I had then, but I have learned more about myself in these few months than I ever have in my life. And the most important lesson I've learned is that it's okay to have unanswered questions, to have vulnerability and innocence, for it is all a part of being young. And now I can look to the future with anticipation and not fear, feeling much more like a woman and much less like a child.

**THE END**

## ABOUT THE AUTHOR

Lorri Hewett began writing this novel as a senior in high school because, "...there wasn't anything out there about the experiences of black young adults."

Raised in Littleton, Colorado, she is a sophomore currently attending Emory University in Atlanta, Georgia. She is a voracious reader of African-American literature. And, as a member of the Emory Dance Company, her hobbies include modern dance, jazz, and ballet.

Says Lorri, "I am very interested in international affairs—maybe one day I'll do something with it."

# PSEUDO COOL

## By Joseph E. Green

Five seniors at a prestigious California university discover what's important is not always who you are but sometimes who you appear to be. They are scraping through their last few months by the skin of their teeth. Each has a secret: one sells herself to pay her expensive tuition; one drinks heavily and sleeps with white girls in an attempt to forget his color; another is gay and living in the closet; another is a poor girl adopted into a high society family; and two believe they were responsible for a friend's death. They all look forward to graduation, thinking that soon all their problems will be solved.

**HOLLOWAY HOUSE PUBLISHING CO.**
8060 Melrose Ave., Los Angeles, CA 90046